MICKEY FINN

21st Century Noir
Volume 2

Michael Bracken, Editor

MICKEY FINN

21st Century Noir
Volume 2

DOWN&OUT
BOOKS

Down & Out Books
3959 Van Dyke Road, Suite 265
Lutz, FL 33558
DownAndOutBooks.com

The characters and events in this book are fictitious. Any similarity to real persons, living or dead, is coincidental and not intended by the author.

Cover design by Zach McCain

ISBN: 1-64396-242-6
ISBN-13: 978-1-64396-242-9

For Temple
My Love, My Muse, My Everything

TABLE OF CONTENTS

Introduction   1
Michael Bracken

Washed Up   3
Nils Gilbertson

Final Fall   19
Stacy Woodson

Next Up   31
Sam Wiebe

Rules for Mistakes   45
S.M. Fedor

Winner Takes All   63
James A. Hearn

They May Be Gods   81
Stephen D. Rogers

KLDI   93
Josh Pachter

The Bridge   105
Janice Law

A Faster Way to Get There   115
Joseph S. Walker

Talk About Weird   131
Albert Tucher

Skin and Bones   149
John Bosworth

Job113   165
Robert Petyo

The Killer's Daughter-in-Law   177
Scott Bradfield

All Over But the Shouting   191
Rick Ollerman

Motel at the End of the World: 207
Tuesday Afternoon
Trey R. Barker

The Rundown   223
Gabe Morran

The Law of Lucy's Luck   237
J.D. Graves

Salvation   257
Michael Bracken

Confessions on a Train from Kyiv   273
Hugh Lessig

About the Editor   285

About the Contributors   287

INTRODUCTION

Noir: The story of a character's journey from a dark place to an even darker place.

Not everyone agrees with this definition. For some, noir is about cynicism and moral ambiguity. For others it's more about setting, mood, or a particular style of writing.

In selecting the nineteen stories in this volume, I tried to keep all of these definitions in mind. What drew me to these particular stories, though, was the fate of the characters. As I read each submission, I wondered how their lives could get any worse than they are when the stories begin. These writers surprised me, often taking me on dark journeys to unexpected destinations. Some are sad, some are tragic, and a rare few offer a glimmer of hope.

As in the first edition of *Mickey Finn*, I restricted the stories to the 21st century, challenging contributors to write modern noir stories that don't rely heavily on the technological restrictions of the past.

I hope you agree with me that each journey—dark as it may be—is worth the trip.

—Michael Bracken
Hewitt, Texas

WASHED UP

Nils Gilbertson

I didn't care to admit it, but the past couple years I more or less lived at The Shack. The name fit like a cork. A block off the beach, it was a dilapidated building that—I assume through a series of bribes—the city found fit for patronage. On the outside was a neglected buzzing sign that advertised entrance to "The hack" or "T Shack." Inside, fluorescent crimson engulfed the patrons. The glow emanated from several large neon mermaids swimming in squiggly blue neon lines that dominated the wall space. The color choice didn't make the bursting blood vessels on our faces and spider veins crawling across our parched skin any less noticeable.

Most hostile to newcomers was the stench that soured the murky hole. Our noses were long accustomed to it, but the unfortunate souls who stumbled in for the first time were bombarded with an unholy miasma of stale beer, cigarette smoke, dip spit, and the whiskey-laced sweat that leaked from our pores. It was so damn bad that the smell had to call in the other senses for backup. Before drowning the acrid tang with booze, the place tasted like you were being gagged with sweat-crusted gym shorts.

The clientele more or less fit the decor. The joke went that whatever muck washed up on shore coagulated and found its way to The Shack for a drink. There was Smiley Joe, who—

3

predictably—never smiled. He spent his days at the bar, grunting orders and emptying tins of Copenhagen like they were Big League Chew. Tattoos—most of which were skull-related—blanketed his ropey arms. It was more common for Smiley Joe to knock a row of teeth out than to string together a coherent sentence. We all have our strengths.

Brenda Jean could usually be found stumbling about the jukebox, hurling merciless insults at us regulars, and threatening any newcomers who dared to meet her gaze. Her sharp tongue never got her in any trouble. She'd been in that place longer than the rest of us could remember. Hell, rumor had it that she was born there and never left. We respected her and left her alone to guzzle gin and tonics and chain-smoke Camels.

Stump was our bartender. He was as wide as he was tall. He wore a black T-shirt a couple sizes too small, the sleeves doing their best not to rip at the seams. Stump didn't take much shit. His bald head and stern gaze warned us there was a line; if we didn't cross it, he'd leave us alone, unjudged, to consume our poison. If we did, we'd be banished. This—to us—was an iron-fisted punishment. We had nowhere else to go.

I was Mark the Narc. The nickname didn't sprout from a past career in law enforcement, or any other sort of narc-ery. Instead, it had to do with my wearing a collared shirt and shaving now and again. At first glance, I didn't fit in. In the beginning I had come in once a month or so to bask in the unseemly freedom of it all. Being there reminded me that at any moment I could toss my life aside and spend it there, drunk and miserable, instead.

So I did. A couple years back my rent went up, my career prospects went down, and my kids stopped coming around to visit. That's when I became an esteemed regular. We were our own, self-loathing, alcohol-soaked community—always reminding one another that, no matter how bad things got, the pit of misery perched on the next bar stool made your own story look like a Disney flick.

A new face in The Shack was rare. In a strange way, we were

the most exclusive social club in town. When a wayward group of casual drinkers joined us, they were rarely seen again. So, when a newbie came around, it was an event.

When Coach first walked in, we had him pegged for a one-timer. He was a large, oddly shaped man. His stomach bulged but his lanky limbs made him look like they'd mixed up the pieces when putting him together. He was about fifty, by my guess. Despite the heat, he wore frayed work pants and a sweatshirt from Apollo Cove CC, the local community college. A ball cap hid his patchy, balding head, and a light brown mustache anchored his thin, crusted lips. But drawing the gawks of a bar full of insensitive drunks was his right hand. It was mangled and missing the pinky and ring fingers. Like someone had hacked it to bits and he never bothered going to a doctor.

Coach took a seat at the bar, smiled, and asked Stump for a beer. As we stared at his hand, he turned and said, "I would shake, but..." as his voice trailed off, he raised it up for all to see and shrugged.

None of us said anything.

Brenda Jean, breathing gin, wobbled toward him.

"Hey Mister, this here's Stump," she barked, introducing the new patron to our bartender. "And if you ask me, one *stump* is more than enough 'round here." She looked down at his hand.

Then silence. She held her gaze, steely-eyed. He stared right back.

"C'mon, Brenda, no need for that," I said.

"Shut it, Narc."

She stood there, swaying, dragging on a cigarette. She looked like a smokestack in a hurricane.

He took a deep breath and a long gulp of beer, downing about half of it. Then he said, "Maybe tomorrow night you'll have something a little more clever prepared." He chased his sarcasm with a grin that reddened his cheeks, beer clinging to his mustache.

Brenda grunted, and Stump and I grinned.

"What's your name, guy?" I asked.
"Call me Coach."

It didn't take long for Coach to solidify himself as a regular. We learned he'd been a celebrated head coach of the basketball team at Apollo Cove. He was famous for grooming young players before sending them off to celebrated four-year schools. He explained that back in 2008, due to his player development skills, he accepted an NBA gig as an assistant. His dream of being a professional coach was in his sights.

When people tell stories of near-death experiences, it spoils the ending to know they survived to tell the tale. In a similar vein, when drunks at The Shack tell stories of their triumphs, knowing that the liquor-soaked protagonist will soon come crashing down spoils the tale. For most of us the fall is mild: low to lower. But Coach's dreams had been within spitting distance.

He told us how it started with getting a painkiller connection to help out his players. Soon, painkillers turned into about every drug you can imagine, and he started recruiting players with the promise of narcotics. Then, the drugs stopped going to the players and started filling Coach's veins. In his final season before starting his job in the pros, they found him in the bathroom, full of crystal, slicing his hand up so the bugs could get out.

Coach lost everything and was on the streets for a while. Eventually he got clean—save for booze. The athletic director, an old friend, got him a janitor's job at Apollo Cove. He'd held down the gig for the last five years.

Coach more than joined us; he became our spiritual guide. He handled tragedy with such grace and vigor, with such unrelenting love of life. Whether he spoke of his coaching successes or his drug-fueled homelessness, his demeanor never changed. Both were part of the same story, and thus inseparable. There was no difference between ups and downs, good and bad, happiness and sadness. To him, there was only that which is, and that which is not.

It was my birthday—the one day of the year when there was a sliver of hope my kids would show. Yet, the sliver was so thin that my disappointment was nearly guaranteed. I almost wished the hope in me would flicker and die and take the disappointment along with it. When my kids didn't make the trip, I had one of those once-in-a-while days when the notion of suicide transformed from a comforting last resort—a hypothetical—to a decision as material as what I would eat for breakfast.

A few fellas at the bar were arguing over which predator would win a fight to the death. Bear versus tiger was instigating physical confrontation between Smiley Joe and a few others. I was stuck in the crosshairs. Stump poured me a double— probably double and a half—and I slipped away to a booth in the back corner that offered solitude. Brenda Jean was fiddling with the jukebox in the corner. Music is a time machine, and "I Remember You" by Skid Row was sending me back to a time that made me want to chase my bourbon with battery acid.

About ten minutes later Coach joined me. He brought over a pint of amber ale and a basket of tater tots, nudging them forward as an offering. Oozing grease, they glistened pale yellow in the neon, like dime-store diamonds. I glanced at his hand. His palm—what was left of it—was like mudcrack. He asked, "Tough day, huh?"

"Aren't they all?"

"Some more than others," he said. I glanced up at him. His pockmarked cheeks sagged, and his lips looked like he'd fallen face-first into a heap of gravel. I cringed as he smiled, expecting them to tear and bleed. As he leaned in, his wide eyes asked what had me down.

"You have kids, Coach?"

He shook his head. "I always considered the players my kids. But no, never my own."

"I do. Sure as hell, I barely notice these days, though."

"Are they grown?"

"College. They used to visit once in a while. I thought they might today. But..." I shrugged and took a harsh gulp of whiskey instead of finishing the thought. I expected a train of questions to follow. Questions I knew would be well intentioned, but poorly timed. My mind was too tired to reflect and explain. He sensed this.

"Hey, Narc, I ever tell you about the time I was up to my eyelids in Vics and didn't shit for a week?" He saw the shock on my face and let out a hearty bellow. "Then, in the middle of an interview for a pro gig, I felt it. Backed up like L.A. traffic on Thanksgiving weekend for *seven* damn days, now demanding freedom."

He stole a grin from me. "So, what happened?" I asked.

"For a while I held it in. Y'know, when you clench your whole body until your stomach gurgles loud enough for everyone in the room to hear? But then I thought, given my drug consumption, I didn't have the luxury of being picky about when to shit. It didn't come often, and when it did, it did. So I excused myself, came back half an hour later—five pounds lighter—and made a joke about how they weren't the only ones in the room full of shit." His gelatinous jowls jiggled as he chuckled. Then he took a slurp of beer, wiped his mouth with the back of his hand and said, "Anyway, it worked out for a while until—well, you know the rest of the story."

We talked through closing time. He didn't ask about me or my life or my kids; yet he left ample opportunity for me to speak my piece if I wanted to. He reminisced on his shortcomings and, with much laughter, reveled in his downfall. There wasn't a whiff of *look what I've been through* in his tone. Instead, his vulgar anecdotes roared, *look how human we are!*

In the midst of the stories of his doped-up adventures, I cut in. "So you gave it all up—the drugs, I mean—for good?"

He paused, as if he were offended. His face mellowed. "Yes,

yes I did."

"But you still drink?"

"I do."

"Why? Usually, people either go cold turkey across the board or keep using."

He leaned on the table, his gravitation pulling me toward him. "When I drink," he said, "I believe in God."

So we drank and drank until I awoke in my bed, my mouth sandpaper. I couldn't recall how I got home. I figured Coach had carried me.

A couple of weeks later, Curly—the barback—ran in, babbling like he'd seen a ghost. Stump fixed him a drink and we circled around; Brenda Jean even turned down the jukebox and stumbled over. Curly told us the police had found Coach in an alley a few blocks away, stabbed, his guts staining the pavement.

A moment of quiet—broken only by a few mutters that Curly was full of shit—descended after Smiley Joe slammed down his glass and lifted the frail barback into the air by the front of his collar, his legs kicking like he was hanging from a noose.

"You fuckin' with us? If you are, I'll break this here beer mug and feed you the pieces."

Curly wailed and Stump and I grabbed Smiley Joe's thick, damp arms and pulled him back. I turned to Curly. "You sure about this? How close were you?"

"I—I'm not sure how close. I'm pretty sure it was him, though."

"Bullshit!" Brenda Jean said. "It's dark as hell out there in those alleys. This little worm is lookin' for attention."

"Fine," I said. "Then someone else has to go out there and get a closer look, maybe ask the cops what happened."

More mumbles. More slurps and more glasses returning to tables. A few of the fellas went back to the pool table. It was a stupid proposal; Shack regulars avoided cops like they did AA sponsors. I wasn't too keen on going out there either—not without knowing which cops were on the beat.

"Hey Curly," I said, "what'd the two cops look like?"

"Look like?"

"Yeah, look like."

He thought for a moment, like I was quizzing him. "Both about forty, one chubby, one lean. Both losing their hair."

I finished my drink and said, "I'll go, so long as none of you steal my stool while I'm gone." Nods and grunts assured me no such indiscretion would occur. As I headed toward the door a few others bowed their heads, like I was a valorous soldier headed into enemy territory.

The air was warm and soggy and the salty ocean mist on my face was refreshing. The waves crashed against the shore, reminding me of their power even as they hid in the darkness. I saw police tape ahead. I tried to get a glimpse without getting too close. Aging art deco buildings—pastels fading—shielded the streetlights and shadows blanketed the alley. I had to get closer. I approached the tape.

A couple of cops were waiting for the detective to arrive.

"Hi, officers," I said. "What's all the commotion?"

They turned. "Who wants to know?" asked the lean one, stepping toward me.

I shrugged. "I want to make sure it's not a friend of mine."

"Your friends turn up dead in alleys much?"

I peeked around him and saw a dark stain next to a large body. "Not so far, no."

The fat officer walked up beside him. "Don't worry 'bout it. His pockets say he's a dealer. Probably got gutted for his stash. Good riddance."

The first officer shot him a *shut your damn mouth* scowl.

"Got it. Thanks for the hard work, officers." They nodded and turned away. I looked up at the nearest streetlight. White mist surrounded the glowing yellow bulb like a giant, faded dandelion. I took a few steps to the right so that a sliver of light snuck by the corner of the building and illuminated the large corpse. I strained my eyes. In the puddle of blood lay a mangled hand.

One of the good things about being a drunk is that you don't have to break your routine when tragedy strikes. Not much changed around the bar in the following days. A few of us made half-assed tributes. The only real change was that we huddled around the TV in the corner of the bar—one of those black hundred-pounders with the huge back jutting out of it—and cringed through the local evening news, waiting for an update on the case. Each night, either the man with the hairpiece or the woman with her face glued on said, "Still no arrests for the murder that took place late Tuesday evening downtown near Ocean and Main. However, police suspect that the motive was drug-related." Loud and clear: good riddance. At least the cop on the scene had been honest enough to say it.

Another good thing about being a drunk is that if you want to get something done, all you have to do is drink, talk about doing it, drink more, and forget about it. Smiley Joe occupied a few late nights concocting schemes for revenge, each one as elaborate as it was grisly.

"If I catch the sunnuvabitch who done it, oh boy," he said, spewing beer and tobacco-laced saliva at the few of us willing to listen, "he'll wish his momma woulda sliced him from her belly and left him in the trash." He threw back a shot of Jim Beam and slammed the glass down, rattling his Copenhagen tin on the bar. He had a lip in—long cut, based on the dribble on his chin—but I couldn't tell where the dip spit was going. "I'll open him up and strangle him dead with his own guts." He nearly fell off his stool, mimicking his theoretical vengeance.

A week after Coach was killed, you'd think the whole lot of us had forgotten about him—about the spirit he infused into our otherwise feckless existence. After a few Bloodies on an early

Tuesday afternoon, I shook off the petulant voice in my head that kept demanding a few more, splashed my face with water, tucked in my shirt, and headed to the police station. A steak knife couldn't have cut through the sultry afternoon air. The oppressive heat reverted my thoughts to the icy condensation on the chilled beer mugs back at The Shack. I salivated but kept going. By the time I got to the station I looked like I'd floated over with the *Balseros* on a pool noodle.

The station felt like any other underwhelming office building around town. I approached the front desk. The bald officer behind the glass panel was chomping on gum and typing with his index fingers, staring at the keyboard like the letters had suddenly been rearranged. I stood there for a minute until I realized greetings weren't in his repertoire.

"Hey," I said, knocking on the glass.

"Huh? Oh." He looked up. "Sorry, pal, I'm not usually on the desk. You need something?"

"Yeah. I'm here to see Paula. Paula Asher."

He craned his neck like the answer was on the ceiling, showing off the ingrown hairs burrowing under his rough-shaven chin. "Nope," he said, shaking his head. "No Paula Asher in this department." He went back to poking at his keyboard.

I knocked again. "C'mon, she's assistant chief, or something."

"Oh," he said, nodding. "You mean Paula *Campbell*. Yeah, she's our deputy chief. Real tough cookie. You a friend?"

"Ex-husband."

His neck tensed. "Been there. As long as there won't be any trouble, I'll show you to her."

"No trouble," I said. "It's been a while. Hence the *Campbell*."

When I walked in, I didn't know what to say, so I stood in the doorway like an idiot. She looked up and squinted at me like she might be hallucinating. "Mark? What are you doing here?"

"Hi, Paula. May I?" I gestured toward the chair.

"Sure, come in." The initial bewilderment in her tone and on her face mellowed to run-of-the-mill surprise as she realized I was paying a visit—not being wrestled into the drunk tank. I sat down and looked at her. A touch of makeup muted the distinguished lines of her face. We sat in silence for a moment. She was from a different life. If not for our shared children, I might as well have been selling magazine subscriptions. The ache of a bruised heart would have brought color back into my world. But the dull haze that shadowed my every step wasn't chased away by a storm from the past. The songs Brenda Jean played on the jukebox shook me more than her presence.

"Can I get you a towel?" she asked, probably concerned for her chair.

"No, I won't be long. I'm sorry to barge in like this." I wiped my forehead with my shirtsleeve. "I'm only here for information." I meant it.

"If you'd called we could've gotten coffee. Now it feels so official." She grinned a little.

"So, Campbell, huh?"

The grin vanished quicker than it had appeared. "Jesus, Mark. Yes, Campbell, going on two years now. For shit's sake, you met him at Sophie's graduation."

I nodded. "He seemed like a good one. Were you married then?"

"Engaged."

"Sure."

Then a pause. Her face told me to ask whatever question I wanted because we both knew I wouldn't be back. When I didn't say a word she said, "While we're on the subject, when's the last time you called the kids? Or visited? They're only a couple hours away. Not that I'm encouraging you to operate a motor vehicle."

I exhaled, amused. "Can't argue with that. I've been meaning to call, but I thought they'd be down for my birthday."

"They're nineteen and twenty-one. *You* call *them*."

"Right. But sometimes I think it might be too late. And each day I don't, the harder it gets the next. Eventually it's easier not to." The words escaped from my mouth like runaway hostages. She didn't say a thing. Too damned honest to disagree. "Anyway," I went on, "that's not why I came. I'm here because a good friend of mine was murdered, and I'd like to know the status of the investigation."

She shook her head. "I can't do that."

"*Please*, Paula. Even if it's public record stuff. I'm sure it's news to me."

She turned back to her computer. "What's his name?"

I realized I didn't know it. "Coach. Well, that's what we called him. He didn't exactly share his name."

Her pupils took a lap. "I don't have time to keep tabs on your barfly buddies."

"He was stabbed in the alley down by Ocean and Main last week. I did some poking about and the cops said he was killed for his stash. But that's impossible because Coach has been clean ever since his days with the basketball team at Apollo Cove CC, you know, when the team was real good."

She stared at me, mentally sifting through the nonsense for the helpful bits. Then she typed and clicked for a few minutes. "Yeah, Jim Lewinski," she read from her screen. "Multiple felony drug charges, been in and out of prison for almost a decade. Under investigation for dealing but we only ever got him on possession. As far as I can tell, never coached any basketball."

"No—"

"And another thing," she said, now talking like a cop, rather than an ex-wife, although there was a narrow distinction between the two, "don't go asking questions at murder scenes. That's a good way to get your face on the suspect board."

I shrugged. "Good thing the two morons you had on the beat were, well, morons."

"Mhmm."

"Besides, you got it all wrong. Ten years back Coach was on the verge of getting an NBA gig. He got derailed because of drugs. Then he got clean, and now works as a janitor back at

Apollo Cove." As I rattled off all I could remember about Coach's story—so glorious when he had regaled us back in The Shack—her faced turned from annoyed to confused to concerned. My mind grasped for words that would make her understand, but, as I explained, I couldn't even convince myself. Her head was shaking, and I doubt she even noticed.

Then, I remembered the night of my birthday.

I stood up. "Fine. I get it. The fix is in on him. Your department doesn't want to scare the public with a killer on the loose, so you say the murdered ex-addict was a dealer. Murdered for his drugs. That's real great. To protect and serve, and all that shit."

She smiled through gritted teeth. "I've got to give it to you, Mark, I've never seen anyone so enamored of being miserable. Take care of yourself. And call the kids." She turned back to her computer and I left.

Next, I swung by Apollo Cove. I said I was there about a friend who worked as a janitor and asked for the principal, or dean, or whatever the hell they called it. Reception pointed me to the head of custodial services. I figured it'd do.

I walked into a glorified broom closet of an office. The man at the desk had a wiry frame and high cheekbones like cliffs above a hollow face. He wore a blue work shirt with the school's logo. It was fresh, like he hadn't scrubbed a toilet in a decade. He looked up at me. "You lost?"

"No." I sat down. "You're in charge of the janitorial staff, right? My name's Mark Asher. I'm looking for some information on a friend of mine. Jim…" I couldn't remember his last name.

He leaned forward on his desk and studied me, nodding like he already knew my life story. "Sure. I'm Henry. You shouldn't be coming around here. Hell, I never want to see a man gutted in the streets, but Jim was a real pain in my ass."

My ignorance must've been as obvious as a third eye, so he went on. "We hired Jim—Coach, as he went by—a few years back through some program for ex-cons to get straight. Sounds like some nice Kumbaya shit until you have to deal with them. I liked him at first. You expect the guy with a possession charge to be some punk kid, but he was older and talked like he'd been around. Almost wise."

I nodded.

"Anyhow, last week I come in late to pick up some files, and I see a bathroom light on. I walk in and he's snorting powder off the counter. Looked like he was having a taste. He was fillin' baggies. He ran out and I called the cops and told them what I saw. Next I hear he turned up dead."

I felt like I got punched in the stomach from the inside. "And, he never coached basketball here?"

He had a good, raspy laugh. "Don't let the nickname fool you, I've been here almost thirty years and he never did a damn thing besides scrub floors and spin a story or two over his lunch hour." He paused and stopped laughing. His pallid skin looked like it was too tight in some places and too loose in others. "Sounds like he spun a pretty good one for you."

I walked along the beach back to The Shack. The early evening sky was a dim gray, and a storm was gathering a few miles out. The storm clouds had smothered the sun but it was still hotter than hell in July. I walked fast, my heavy breathing and aching muscles a distraction from the lies Coach had fed us. My calves burned like my shinbones were matchsticks. As the alcohol from the afternoon drinks filtered from my bloodstream to my bladder, lucidity returned, and I accepted that Coach had been full of shit. A drug dealer. An addict. A liar. Our hero.

Being wronged by someone other than myself was novel. The pain lightened me and almost brought a smile. My anger wasn't dirty and spiteful. It wasn't accompanied by the hangover of regret that followed my own binges of self-sabotage. Without the sour of regret, pain went down easy. And justice would wash away any aftertaste that lingered. I'd tarnish his memory to the few people who had a damn decent thing to say about him. The storm out at sea rumbled, warning of its imminence.

When I arrived at The Shack, the regulars were huddled in a corner by the jukebox. I walked over, ready to spill it all. Then I saw Stump hanging a plaque on the wall. I tapped Smiley Joe on the shoulder, and he said, "Hey, Narc. We got started without ya."

Stump straightened the frame and took a step back. It said: *In memory of Coach.* "I didn't know his real name," Stump explained. "And I couldn't think of anything else to say."

"*We* know what it means," Smiley Joe said. "He was a goddamn champ, and we won't forget him." He put his hand on my shoulder, looked at me, and nodded.

"How 'bout Coach's favorite song," said Brenda Jean. "She Talks to Angels" by The Black Crowes. I smiled. Different song than the last ten times Brenda Jean made the same announcement.

"Now get your pathetic asses to the bar. Round on me for Coach," Stump said.

A drunken stampede followed.

"Where you been, Narc?" he asked once he was back behind the bar. He slid me a shot. "We were worried you'd miss it. I know you and Coach hit it off."

"Oh, nowhere. I don't live here, y'know. I'm not Brenda Jean."

"Watch it!" she said, the contents of her glass sloshing over the edges.

"To Coach!" Smiley Joe announced, reaching for the ceiling with his bourbon. For a moment, the anemic room twitched with life. I raised my glass and downed my drink. A muffled voice in me said I'd tell them tomorrow. I knew the voice would soon be a whisper, and before long, would be silent.

FINAL FALL
Stacy Woodson

I sat with my teammates in the back of a white paneled van—a standard issue government vehicle with wide faux-leather seats, a broken radio, and a diesel engine that whined. Diz was behind the wheel, Shrek and Gonzo on a bench seat behind me. Our parachutes, reserves, and other military gear were stacked in the back. Pine trees rooted in red-colored soil slipped past us through the window.

I drummed my fingers against my ballistic helmet. The camouflage material that covered the polyethylene was frayed at the edges, worn from years of airborne operations. The helmet was strong enough to stop a moving bullet, supposedly. I was grateful that despite my combat deployments, I never had tested its ballistic properties. But I had worn a helmet like this for ninety-nine parachute jumps, and it had protected my head from splitting like a watermelon.

I used to be petrified of jumping—the unnatural act of stepping out the door of a plane while in flight. But we received parachute pay if we jumped. The $150 was a pittance, and as lousy as it seemed, when you were a young enlisted soldier who made little money and had a family to feed, you did what you could to keep food on the table. Even if it meant falling out of a perfectly good airplane.

A lot had changed, however, since I had first started jumping. I was a non-commissioned officer now and had overcome my fear—even going beyond what the army required and competing in military-sponsored parachute competitions. It was to one of these competitions that we were headed today.

I tossed my helmet aside and pulled the Leap Fest invitation from my backpack. Each year, the best static-line parachute teams around the country were invited to Rhode Island to compete for the championship title. And after years of trying, our team had finally qualified. I ran my finger along the contest committee's smooth gold seal and thought about what a thrill it had been to receive it. But the joy was gone now, replaced by anger, an anger that had started in North Carolina and continued to grow during the ten-hour drive up the East Coast.

Our van slowed and turned onto Ministerial Road, the whining engine muted by the *thwap, thwap, thwap* of a Chinook helicopter overhead. We continued along another section of highway. More pine trees and a sign stuck in the ground: *Leap Fest Invitational. Drop Zone 2 miles.*

"Welcome to the Centurion Club, Jack Man." Shrek slapped my back, his baritone voice rippling through the van.

I forced myself to turn and face him. He leaned against one of the windows and grinned—a toothpaste-ad smile—the kind of smile that made women swoon.

The thought made my stomach clench.

Gonzo tugged out one of his earbuds and peered at me over his muscle magazine. "Jump one hundred, today?"

I nodded.

"Sweet." Gonzo grinned. He and Shrek glanced at each other, some silent exchange I didn't understand, and I didn't care enough to ask what it meant.

"Let's focus on the competition today," I said. "Not my jump log."

Shrek turned his phone toward me, a skydiving app open on the screen. "Says skies are clear, winds are good. Unless the aircraft breaks, this is your day, my friend."

My day. I stifled a laugh. It *should* be my day. The one-hundredth jump is a milestone few paratroopers reach, and I was about to be indoctrinated into an elite group, a brotherhood that spanned back to World War II. My picture would be in the Fort Bragg newspaper, and my name would be added to a book that would go on long after I left the military. I should be excited. I should be reciting tales about mid-air entanglements, collapsed chutes, and deployed reserves. And how, despite it all, I defied death and lived to see this day. Instead, I have only one thing on my mind. The same question I had when we loaded the van at Fort Bragg:

Which one of you is sleeping with my wife?

My mouth opened, and I nearly said it. But Shrek's face was in his phone, and Gonzo was focused on his magazine—an issue that promised rock hard abs in just eight weeks. His large biceps twitched as he shook out the July issue while his mammoth hands curled tight around the pages.

He glanced up at me. "You alright, man?"

An image of Gonzo touching Melanie flashed in my mind—his wide palms dragging along her waist and down over her hips.

I fought the urge to leap over the seat and swing.

"I'm fine," I lied.

I'd known Gonzo since Basic Training. We'd survived Air-borne School together. Fought side-by-side in Iraq. Sure, we didn't talk like we used to, but still, he wouldn't betray me.

Not Gonzo.

I tried to reassure myself. But the truth was I didn't know anymore.

I faced forward again, glanced out the window, desperate for some kind of distraction. But there were only more god-awful trees, and my mind continued to swirl.

I'd always dreamed about sharing this day with Melanie. My one-hundredth jump was more than a milestone. It symbolized fifteen years of military service, the countless deployments that came with it, and through it all, the strength and endurance of our marriage.

At least, until a day ago.

I sighed, gave up on the scenery, reached into my cargo pocket, and pulled out my knife. I turned it over in my hand. The black stonewashed titanium handle was faded, the same as the blade folded inside.

During airborne operations, we all carried one. We jumped static-line parachutes. A thick cord made of nylon webbing connected from the top of our parachute deployment bag and hooked onto an anchor line cable inside the aircraft. When we jumped, the static line went taut, the deployment bag pulled free and released the parachute. If the parachute malfunctioned, we could be suspended in the air—towed behind the aircraft by our static line—and someone would need to cut us free. Then, we'd pull the ripcord on our reserve parachute and hope for the best.

I turned the knife over again and then flicked open the blade. It locked into place. I disengaged the lock, closed it, repeated the movement.

Open.

Close.

Open.

I tried to focus on each step—the snap of my wrist, the click of the lock, the feel of the smooth metal between my fingers— anything to bring my blood pressure down. But memories of Melanie crept back into my head, including her whispered phone calls the night before I left North Carolina:

Do you think Jack knows?

Do you think we should tell him?

What if he finds out before you and the team get to Rhode Island?

You and the team—my mind still tripped on the words.

"We're here," Diz called from the driver's seat. The van scraped into a parking lot. He pulled up next to a row of other white panel vans and killed the engine.

This was it. Time to focus. No room for distractions, not on the drop zone. Not when a misstep had life-changing consequences.

I returned the knife to my pocket, took a deep breath, and slid the door open.

We clamored out, a sea of arms and legs and groans. And, somehow, I managed to slip into my normal stretching routine. I leaned against the hood, bent my knee, grabbed my foot, and pulled my heel to my butt. The cartilage under my kneecap popped. I winced, moved to the other leg, repeated the process, and then started with my neck.

More pops.

More cracks.

More groans.

The familiarity of the movements was comforting and for a moment, things felt normal again.

I finished stretching and finally looked up. In front of me was a building: white brick, red roof, and a sign that said *West Kingston Elementary School*. Confused, I glanced at Diz.

He took a drag off his cigarette and then thumbed toward a slab of sidewalk that disappeared behind the school. "Drop zone is around back," he said, the words coming out between puffs of smoke.

I sighed. I knew that. I'd looked at the map before we left Fort Bragg. But after I overheard Melanie's gut-wrenching phone call, everything else had seemed to blur.

I continued to eye Diz while he continued to smoke.

Was he the one sleeping with Melanie?

I considered the possibility. But haunting images, like the ones with Gonzo and Melanie, didn't surface with Diz. He was short and wiry, his teeth yellow from smoking, and I just couldn't see Melanie with him.

Diz crushed out his cigarette.

I cuffed the sleeves on my Army Combat Uniform, took a deep breath, and pushed back my shoulders. My focus needed to be on our competition—not on my cheating wife or my disloyal teammate or my jump log. I knew how to compartmentalize my life. I did it every time I deployed. Today should be no different. "All right gents," I said with more enthusiasm than I felt. "Let's do this."

We opened the back doors of the van, grabbed our gear, and made our way around the building. On the backside, white tents punctuated a field with spectators and more soldiers in camouflage uniforms. There were food trucks boasting gourmet seafood baskets and frozen lemonade. Red and white yard signs pointed the way to a platform where pre-jump training would be conducted. We found the platform, dropped our gear, and waited for the event to begin.

"Welcome to the Rhode Island National Guard Leap Fest Parachute Competition." A voice boomed over an invisible audio system. "We need all teams over at the platform. Your pre-jump brief is about to begin." The microphone clicked off and music filled the air, a nineties cover band that took me back to high school and making out with Melanie in my Camaro.

A group of soldiers in red hats and Jumpmaster T-shirts gathered in a gaggle in front of us. A female, whose blond hair was pulled back so tight it tugged at her eyes, hopped onto the platform. She waited for the song still blaring from the audio system to end before she began her brief. "Good morning folks. Again, welcome to Leap Fest. I'm Sergeant First Class Wallace."

Shrek elbowed me, eyed Wallace, and whistled.

"Before we begin," Wallace continued, ignoring him, "I want to review the rules of today's competition."

The guy to my right cracked his knuckles. The one to my left folded his arms and widened his stance. You could almost feel the testosterone surge through the crowd.

"Teams of four jumpers will exit a CH-47 Chinook helicopter," Wallace continued, "at fifteen-hundred feet above ground level using an MC-1C static line, steerable parachute." One of the other Jumpmasters joined her on the platform and held up a large poster-sized map of the drop zone. "You'll conduct two individual jumps, each with a proper parachute landing fall, and land, as close as possible, to one of these marked areas." Wallace pointed to four, red X's on the map. "What are your questions?"

Which one of my teammates is sleeping with my wife?

And just like that, my demons were back.

I stared at Shrek again, still ogling Wallace like a kid going through puberty. *God, he was a meathead.* Too much of a knuckle-dragger for Melanie. She had more pride than that.

Didn't she?

I waited for the images of Shrek and Melanie to start. Some suggestive pose that would confirm my fear. But there was nothing. Instead, all I kept seeing were images of her with Gonzo. His eyes were fixed on Wallace, who was still speaking. Melanie stood next to him, arms looped around his waist, her head against his chest.

My stomach tumbled and bile burned the back of my throat. I swallowed it back. When I blinked, Melanie disappeared, along with everything I thought was still right with the world.

Wallace finished her brief, and I was on autopilot now. I moved to a line of jumpers that was forming next to the platform and took my turn practicing my parachute landing fall. I winced when I hit the ground, my body like a bag of feed tossed from a moving truck. Pain from practice was common. During a jump, the landing was harder, but adrenaline usually masked the pain. Nothing, however, could mask the emotional pain that twisted my insides right now.

When we were done, it was time to don our parachutes. I helped Diz with his, and he helped me with mine. A Jumpmaster inspected our equipment. Our team would be the Chinook's fifth load of jumpers, and I found the orange cone with the sign that said *Lift Five*. We would remain here until our lift was called, and Wallace walked us to the aircraft.

I plopped onto the ground behind the cone and used my parachute, still on my back, as a cushion. A few jumpers sat like me. Some stood. Others were already jumping from the Chinook onto the drop zone. I pulled out my knife and flicked open the blade.

Open.

Close.

Open.

There was a rhythm to the blade that I found soothing. I took a deep breath, blew it out, sucked in another. My heart rate started to steady, and I was nearly relaxed.

Until I overheard a conversation between Diz and Gonzo.

"You're in love?" I heard Diz say, his voice filled with disbelief. "This is the same guy who made his way through the Carolina Panther Cheerleading squad? I don't believe it."

"This...this is different, man," Gonzo said. "I can't get enough of this girl."

I looked up at Gonzo, standing just feet away, and Melanie was back. She kissed his neck, her lips working their way up to his jaw. When she reached his face, she stopped, tilted her head back and stared at me. I gripped my knife so hard one of my knuckles popped.

Gonzo leaned closer to Diz. "I think this is the real thing."

Diz shook his head. "Bet it lasts a month. Tops."

"Not this time." Gonzo's voice softened. "There is something about her..."

I raised my knife and plunged it into the dirt. I started to stand to confront Gonzo, to tell him to keep his hands off my wife, but I stopped short.

A gut feeling isn't proof, I reminded myself.

What if I were wrong?

Was it worth jeopardizing the competition?

Was it worth jeopardizing a friendship?

Their voices faded, muted by the Chinook as it made its approach over the drop zone. Lift four, stick one exited the helicopter, and there were two good canopies.

I needed evidence, I decided, not some theory, and it would

be easy to get it when I returned to Fort Bragg. I'd simply go through Melanie's cell phone. Adultery was a crime under the Uniform Code of Military Justice. I'd gather the evidence I needed and pursue it.

It was a solid plan. It made me feel better—like somehow, I had the upper hand—and I was able to focus on the competition again.

"Lift Five," Wallace yelled. "Stand by."

I yanked my knife from the ground. Red soil clung to the blade. I wiped it against my pants and returned it to my pocket. Shrek walked over, grabbed my hand, and pulled me to my feet.

Even though the team and I were on the same lift, we were in separate sticks, and wouldn't exit the aircraft at the same time. Diz and I would jump first. Then, the Chinook would turn, make another pass over the drop zone, and Gonzo and Shrek would jump.

"Bet you a beer that I get closer to the marker than you do, Jack man," Diz said.

"You're on," I said. "Remember, I don't like cheap beer."

Diz shook his head. "We'll see who is buying the beer."

The Chinook was on the ground now. The wind from the rotators was whipping up a small cyclone of dirt around the tail ramp.

Wallace moved to the cone, and we fell in line. Somehow, I ended up behind Gonzo, and my eyes went to his parachute pack tray.

The yellow static line—snap hook on one end, parachute deployment bag on the other—connected to a series of stow bars held by rubber retaining bands. This simple construction kept the static line from tangling and allowed it to pull free with ease. It wasn't uncommon during the course of pre-jump activities for static lines to become loose, and a section of Gonzo's had worked its way free.

"Your static line is loose," I said, reflexively.

Gonzo glanced back. "Do we need to call a rigger?"

On the drop zone, normally there was at least one parachute rigger—a person trained to pack, maintain, and repair parachutes. But Gonzo's issue was easy to fix and something I was qualified to do.

I signaled to Wallace and pointed to Gonzo's static line. She nodded in understanding. "Meet you at the Chinook," I told her.

Wallace continued toward the pick-up zone. Gonzo and I stepped to the side and let the remaining jumpers continue along with her. We would find our stick positions once we were at the ramp.

I pulled one of Gonzo's retaining bands, looped it around the static line and reconnected it to the stow bar. I started to tell Gonzo he was set, that we were ready to continue to the Chinook. But he had his phone out, and I saw the screen over his shoulder.

I recognized that number.

Melanie's.

My chest went tight, air ripped from my lungs. Stunned, I couldn't breathe, couldn't think. All I wanted to do was grab his phone and read the message.

But Gonzo put the damned thing away.

He glanced over his shoulder. "Good to go?"

You son of a bitch.

It was one thing to *suspect* he was Melanie's lover, but it was another thing to *know.* I thought about the life I'd had with Melanie. High School. Our wedding. The deployments we'd survived, and our plans for the future that would never be realized. All, thanks to the man who stood in front of me.

And something inside me snapped.

I pulled out my knife, flicked open the blade. My eyes fell on his static line, now perfectly stowed. I tugged out a section and cut through it—the nylon resisting at first, but eventually giving way. I concealed the frayed piece under the retaining band.

Now you're good to go, you bastard.

"All set. I patted his shoulder. "Now, let's go jump out of a perfectly good airplane."

"More like fall," Gonzo muttered.

Little did he know…

A few minutes later we sat on troop seats inside the Chinook's cargo hold. The helicopter lifted into the air. The smell of jet fuel and dust swirled inside. Wallace stood and faced us. "Get ready."

Gonzo grinned. "This is it."

Wallace pointed to my side of the aircraft. "Port side personnel stand-up."

I stood.

Wallace continued with the starboard side and Diz stood. Then, she gave us the command to hook up. I disconnected my static line from the top carrying handle of my reserve parachute and hooked it onto the anchor line cable.

Wallace gave the final commands to check static lines, check equipment, and sound off for equipment check.

I gave her a thumbs-up. "All okay, Jumpmaster."

"Stand by," Wallace replied.

I inched toward the hinge of the ramp.

Wallace pointed to our release point—a panel visible on the ground and yelled, "Go."

I stepped off the ramp and pulled into a tight body position. I stared at my boots and counted to six waiting for my parachute to jerk free. I felt the tug and looked up. There was a twist in my risers. I reached behind my neck, grabbed the risers and bicycled my legs. My body whipped from side-to-side and then steadied under the parachute.

I grabbed my toggles and looked for the marked spots on the drop zone. I pulled down on the left toggle and steered toward the closest one. I crabbed the toggles back and forth until I was nearly over the "X," and then I landed like a lawn dart. I rolled, kicked my legs over, and forced a proper landing. I pushed to my feet and ran toward the marker, fighting the drag from my chute still attached to my riser assembly. I dove onto the marker.

A man with a clipboard appeared. "Jack Nelson?"

"That's me," I gasped, nearly too winded to speak.

He looked toward someone in the crowd and raised his hand in the air.

"Sergeant First Class Jack Nelson, congratulations on your one-hundredth parachute jump," the invisible voice boomed over the audio system.

What the...

Melanie appeared from one of the tents, beaming. She carried a large sheet cake with my name on it. More people still trickled from the tent—other members from my unit. They gathered behind her.

I stared, slack-jawed.

Her smile turned to a frown. "I know you don't like surprises. But Gonzo, well he insisted we shouldn't wait until you returned to North Carolina. I hope that's okay. It's just...he thinks the world of you." She glanced over her shoulder. "They all do, really."

A woman I didn't recognize joined Melanie. "Jack, honey. This is Rita, Gonzo's girlfriend." Melanie leaned closer to me and whispered. "I think he's serious about her."

My body turned cold.

Melanie continued to talk, but all I heard now was the *thwap, thwap, thwap* of the Chinook overhead. I looked up at the sky just as Gonzo jumped.

NEXT UP
Sam Wiebe

The bartender at the British Ex-Serviceman's Club lit a Silk Cut and kissed a plume of smoke toward the rush-hour traffic on Kingsway. The bruises and cuts on his face had been rubbed with ancient liniment. Petroleum and menthol melded with burning tobacco.

His name was Reddick. He'd been there forever. Someone had kicked the shit out of him.

"Karaoke night," he said. "Your guy came in near the end of the second set. You have to sign up during the break, so Marti knows which songs to get ready. Too late by the time he got here. He sits near the stage, puts his feet up on the table. A real shitkicker, your guy."

My guy: Colton Dance, twenty-three, from Steinbach, Manitoba. Recently discharged from the Twenty-sixth Artillery Reserves. Already two assaults to his name.

The way Reddick told it, Dance had cleared his throat and banged on the table till the second verse of "Lido Shuffle" died in some dental technician's mouth. He stood and took the stage. Marti was already cueing "One Hand in My Pocket," but held off as Dance glowered at her.

"Marti backs down, no wonder, since your guy's three times

the size of her. The music goes dead. The mic, too. But that doesn't matter 'cause your guy belts, and I mean *belts,* an old George Jones number, 'Tender Years.' And if I'm being honest, Dave? Kid has quite a set of pipes on him."

Reddick took me down a narrow walkway that led to the parking lot. Glass popped under our feet. He pointed at a bloody comma-shaped impression in the plaster.

"Benjy and me got him this far before he attacked. Bounced me into the wall a couple, three, four times. Broke Benjy's nose. Think he halfway wanted the fight."

"Did Dance say anything?" I asked.

"Just that you don't interrupt a man when he's singing from the heart. Told us it was rude."

"He used that word?"

Reddick smirked. Despite the damage to his face, part of him admired the man who'd hit him.

"Did he come in with anyone?" I asked. "A woman maybe?"

"A girl left around the same time he did. Asian, early twenties. She was standing by the door. That's why we tried negotiating your guy around back. Thinking on it now, she might have been with him."

"Any clue where they might be now?"

Reddick bounced his cigarette butt off the bloodstain on the building's side. "Haven't the foggiest. But that's what they pay you for, right?"

"Tender Years" was a weeper, recorded by George in his white-lightning-and-crewcut phase. I'd first heard it on an album left among my grandfather's things.

My adopted father would tell stories of his father growing up on the prairies. Some in admiration, some of the *"you-think-I'm-tough-on-you?"* variety. When a rookie officer arrived in town, my grandfather or one of the other locals would fight with him, beat him, for the "officer's own good." You had to learn your place in the community, learn at whose pleasure you served.

Stories like that are always told in nostalgic admiration. They never tell you whether the beatings worked. What I knew from fighting, from being on the job, was that violence carries a momentum all its own. A humiliated cop would take it out on someone else. Maybe someone weaker. Whatever Colton Dance had suffered, he seemed determined to spread it around.

The club was located in the heart of Little Saigon, a neighborhood of barred storefronts, Vietnamese cafés, and the slowly encroaching condos that were the blight and hallmark of the new Vancouver—the city in a housing crisis, eating up its lower-income neighborhoods to build micro-apartments nobody could afford.

Four weeks earlier, Dance had been discharged and had taken a bus west from Winnipeg. At some point in the trip, he'd met Jennifer Nguyen, a nineteen-year-old student at Langara College. The two had found somewhere to live together.

Jennifer had stopped attending classes and wasn't answering her phone. Her parents had hired me and Jeff Chen to find her. Maybe they figured an interracial investigative team would fare better at finding an interracial couple. Or perhaps they'd been captivated by the ads Jeff had taken out in the local papers, our names above a fedoraed silhouette. *Questions? We Find Answers. And People.*

Driving down Kingsway, I didn't feel close to finding either Dance or Nguyen. Colton Dance had no contacts on the west coast. He'd attacked a fellow reservist in Steinbach, hospitalizing the guy. Then he'd knocked down a couple at a rest stop near Edmonton. No driver's license, just an ID card and a restricted firearms permit.

Given the warrant out on him, the lack of a car or great sums of money, I figured Colton was living somewhere close to Little Saigon. I looked on Craigslist at sketchy apartment rentals advertised during the last month and found six that offered a spare bedroom or railway suite in the neighborhood.

I ran down four of the ads that afternoon. At two, no one answered the door. One had been rented to a student from Malawi, the other to a punk band, four members sharing three-hundred square feet of uninsulated basement.

The next morning, I tried the two no-answers, then the rest of the list. The fourth house was a raised Vancouver Special with a faux brick façade. The second suite entry was around the side and up some stairs. Diminishing returns: the two-bedroom suite had been subdivided again, the kitchen now a bedroom, from what I could see through the window: A faded quilt and pillow on the green vinyl tile, heater and phone charger plugged into the outlet on the stove. A bottle of silver nail polish sat on the lip of the sink.

I knocked and Jennifer Nguyen opened the door. Four-ten in socked feet, eyeshadow smeared at the corners of her eyes. A Hudson's Bay blanket repurposed as a Jennifer Lopez Versace dress, pubic thatch visible at the bottom of the plunge.

That was easy. I said, "Miss Nguyen? Your parents are looking for you. They're worried."

"And they sent you." Her tone made it sound like they'd've hired someone better if they really cared.

"Why don't we talk it over inside?"

"Nothing to talk about." She retreated from the door without closing it, which I took as an invitation.

The apartment was hot and smelled of sex and takeout food. I could hear water running in another room.

"They want me to go to business school," Jennifer said, sitting on the mattress, the blanket falling around her. "Be Miss Perfect and work in their dumbass restaurant. Don't care what I want. Nobody does, 'cept Colt."

"It's tough having parents," I said. "How about we phone them, so they stop worrying?"

I was dialing when I heard the voice, punching out the syllables of "I Saw the Light." Reddick was right. Give Colton Dance a bass fiddle and a trip eighty years into the past, and he'd've done all right on the stage of the Opry.

Jennifer Nguyen's father mumbled a peevish "Yeah?" on the other end of the phone. I thrust it toward his daughter as Colton Dance entered the room, dripping wet and naked, scrubbing an armpit with a hand towel.

"The hell're you?" he said, moving the towel to cover his crotch. His body was freckled, lobster-red from the shower with a deep farmer's tan on his arms.

"My name's Wakeland. Ms. Nguyen's parents—"

"He wants me to move back with them," Jennifer said.

"That's not entirely true," I said.

"It's not, huh?" Dance moved in toward me, the hand towel dropping to the floor.

"No one wants this to get ugly," I said.

"You sure about that?"

I could hear Mister Nguyen's voice on the phone, questioning.

"He was looking at me naked," Jennifer said.

I moved closer to the door. Dance closed the distance. "How 'bout I whup your ass?"

"Do it," Jennifer said. "Hurt 'em, Colt."

"Anything for my little darling," he said, grinning and grabbing for me.

I stooped, sidestepped, and snatched a fat handful of Prairie testicles. Colton gasped and winced. I twisted, then let him fall.

Stepping around him, I searched the floor where my phone had landed. As I did, the flesh beneath my right shoulder blade tore. I spun, saw Jennifer holding a meat fork. One prong was bent. I shoved her and made for the exit. Then I was off my feet, flying, colliding with something that gave reluctantly. I slid to the floor, half-buried in the remains of the wall, pieces of plaster caking my face and tongue.

Dance kicked me hard in the stomach. I heard the snap of a toe. He yawped and kicked again. I huddled down and took it.

Dishes and pots rained down upon me, along with a jug of oil. I felt it coat my sleeve. Coconut. Jennifer was laughing.

Dance picked me up like I was nothing and flung me through the screen door. That was it, I was done.

I was just sitting up when the police arrived. Nothing was broken, though my hip and thigh were fused into one hellacious bruise. It hurt like shit to walk. I turned down a trip to the hospital.

Dance and Nguyen had dressed and cleared out. A downstairs neighbor said her car keys were missing, along with her tan Accord. One officer took down the plate number while the other radioed in the BOLO.

My phone had survived the ruckus. I called the Nguyens but didn't get through. My second call was to my office.

"Any luck?" Jeff Chen asked. "Finding a redneck in Little Saigon shouldn't be hard. Even for you."

"Found them and then lost them," I said. "Could use some help, if you feel like getting out of the office."

Seventeen minutes later I was in the passenger seat of Jeff's Prelude as we drove toward the Nguyens' house. They lived on 13th, just off Oak. Blue flashing lights marked the location. My heart plummeted as Jeff slid to the curb.

The officer on perimeter duty reluctantly fetched his superior, a sergeant in Homicide named Rougeau. She lumbered toward us, greeting Jeff and me with a curt nod.

"Look like you been playing hockey with Claude Lemieux," she said, pointing at my face. The reference was lost on me. "Are they okay?" She looked toward the house, a two-story Craftsman, its porch light on. "We have two DBs," she said. "Male and female, both middle-aged and Asian. Male was beaten severely, broken fingers and nose. Both shot point-blank."

"Our clients," I said.

We filled her in on what we could. "Where did Dance get the gun?" Jeff asked.

"Mister Nguyen had a collection. We found his safe open, the rifles still there. Handgun case and, what you call it, trigger guard, on the floor, along with an empty cash box. Neighbor heard the shots and saw them leaving, maybe twenty-five minutes ago. Some sort of tan sedan."

I swore. A million alternate scenarios played out where I'd beaten Dance or talked him down. If I'd been faster, better, then the Nguyens wouldn't be waiting for the long trip in the silent ambulance.

"Either of you catch wind of them, you'll tell me," Rougeau said. "Right?"

I nodded I would.

"One more thing," the sergeant said. "The neighbor who saw them leaving said it was the girl who had the gun in her hand."

Back home at the office, Jeff poured us each a slug of Bulleit. My partner doesn't advocate drinking on the job, but sometimes exceptions have to be made. Jeff sat behind my desk, leaving me the client's chair.

"I don't want to hear it," he said.

"Hear what?"

"All the things you should've done different. You didn't shoot the Nguyens, so don't waste time acting like you did. What we got to do, Dave, is find them."

He was right. The unofficial channels, the places the police wouldn't think to look, had to be our focus.

It was a big city, especially taking in the Metro Vancouver area and its suburbs. But the border was below us, the coast to the west. There were only so many places Colton Dance and Jennifer Nguyen could run.

"Why shoot her parents?" Jeff said. "Why go from a few minor brawls to double homicide?"

"Define minor." My hip was starting to lock in place. I shifted on the chair, grimacing.

"You know what I mean. They're making each other worse. Escalating each other's behavior."

"Performing for each other," I said. "The look on her face before Dance jumped me—she was his audience."

"And he's hers for killing her parents?"

I made a gun of my finger and shot Jeff twice. "How much I love you. How far I'm willing to go."

We mulled over that in silence.

Around nine there was a knock on the outer door. We left the inner office and let in a thin, fiftyish man in a bespoke suit and a white Stetson.

"Charlie McCammon," he said, shaking hands. A thick Omega watch ornamented his wrist. "Which one of you is Dave Wakeland?" He smiled when I introduced myself. "'Spose I could've guessed, but these days I'd rather not presume. You West Coast folks get touchy, no offense. That wouldn't be sour mash I smell?"

Jeff found a third coffee mug, added bourbon and a dash of tap water. We settled back into our chairs. McCammon explained that he worked for Gord Parkington, former Premier of Saskatchewan, current president of the National Conservative Alliance.

"We've got ourselves a situation," McCammon said. "You've met Colton Dance. He's Mister Parkington's godson. Old family friend. Mister Parkington figures you might help us to rein the boy in."

I looked at Jeff. He smiled at our guest. "His godson," Jeff said.

"A very close family friend. Anything else you may have heard is conjecture."

"How'd you find out about us?" I asked.

"Friendly call to your police. I happened to be in town, so Mister Parkington asked could I pay you gents a visit."

"Can you give us any clue where Dance is heading?"

"Not specifically, but maybe as to his character, the type of fella he is."

"I have a pretty good idea," I said.

"'Fraid you don't, Mister Wakeland."

McCammon opened a fringed leather satchel and took out a manila folder, passed it over to me.

"Mister Parkington had a friend in the mental health business take a look-see at Colt. As a favor to the family, understand. He was a troublesome kid. Couple minor scrapes with his classmates."

I flipped through, caught snatches of jargonese. Hyperthymic, deficiency of attention, anti-authority and persecutory bent. "The bottom line?" I asked.

"I wouldn't say Colt is no good," McCammon said. "But at times he can be ornery."

"What about the singing?"

McCammon smiled. "He does have a voice on him, doesn't he? His mama loved the Carter Family, John and June, of course. His middle name is Kris with a K."

"Swell for him," I said. "Cornpone bullshit aside, what is your client going to do to help us find his son?"

"That's never been proved, Mister Wakeland."

"Nobody in this room gives a shit."

McCammon looked in his satchel and didn't find answers. He sighed.

"Colt told this doctor friend of Mister Parkington's about a fantasy he had. A recurring dream is what she calls it." He pointed at the report in my hand. "Page fourteen, I believe it's on."

I flipped and read it aloud for Jeff's benefit.

"I'm onstage at the Bluebird Café. That's in Nashville, the place Dolly got discovered. There's a big crowd, a real huge crowd. I start singing this song I wrote. You know "Waiting Around to Die" by Townes? It's that song, only it's better and it's me that wrote it. The crowd listens to me. Really listens.

They love my voice. But some of them don't like the song. Not that they don't like it, but they're afraid 'cause it's real and I'm real and so much of their business is fake-ass country, and they're scared of so much realness. Then I sing 'Are You Sure Hank Done It That Way' and one of them tries to shut me up and I shoot him and the crowd loves me and I shoot another guy, blow off his head so fast the rest of him is just standing there in his fancy suit, blood on the collar, and I go through the others, all the fakers, and the people are cheering, loving me, and we all get healed, the music, it heals us, least those of us who are real. We're all that matters. And the song."

For a moment none of us spoke. I topped up my mug, drank, felt the sting of the whiskey erupt in my chest.

"So Colton Dance is insane," Jeff said.

McCammon gave a philosophical shrug. "He gets a little out of sorts sometimes, yes."

Jennifer Nguyen's graduation photo adorned the next day's cover of the *Vancouver Sun,* along with a pencil sketch of Colton Dance. The sketch wore sunglasses, and the jaw was wrong. I wondered if that was Parkington's doing, or the best the newspaper could get hold of.

Jeff and I called in favors among social workers, hotel night managers, people working on the margins or in places the authorities might miss or not be welcome. I walked through the tent city in Oppenheimer Park. At night we checked the bars along Hastings.

October in the city might be the prettiest month, but it was also the beginning of the slide into the dead season, of cold rain and holidays that nobody felt anymore.

The twenty-eighth was a Saturday. Along Commercial Drive firecrackers filled the air with a gunpowder haze. Dogs whined from shuttered apartments. I walked through the fog to the Legion Hall, where the upstairs room was hosting karaoke night.

The place had years on it. From the staircase I could hear a mewling voice full of undeserved confidence tear through the Cardigans's, "Say That You Love Me." The crowd was young and costumed, all superheroes and lingerie. Pot and spray-on deodorant clouded the room.

The woman with the microphone had oranged her skin and was either going as Donald Trump or The Lorax. She made a big production of the final syllables, strafing the notes with scatter-shot falsetto. Rasputin had met a better end than that song.

A couple did "All I Wanna Do," followed by an ambitious older man in a Canucks jersey who sang "The River," the Joni Mitchell one, not the Springsteen version. I was jostling toward the exit when I heard, "Next up is Jenn. Give her a hand, folks."

Jennifer Nguyen was dressed in a camouflage jumper, a bandolier of plastic bullets slung across her shoulder. "This one's for my baby," she said.

At first, I couldn't hear the song above the gunshot. The drums were crushing and the melody recognizable. The crowd thrilled, frozen in place by confusion and fear, a jumble of masks and cellphones. Someone crashed to the floor. The second shot broke the spell, and they began screaming.

"Never ever gonna stop," Jennifer sang.

One of the double doors at the back of the room was locked, but people were still entering through the other, causing a bottleneck. I was near the stage. Amid the confusion I could see the glow of a laptop in the corner, a frightened woman holding it and nodding at Colton Dance as he took the stage. He was dressed to match Jennifer in olive drab fatigues, face streaked with green and brown greasepaint.

"My honey's gonna sing one," Jennifer said, trading the mic for the pistol and aiming it two-handed at the woman holding the laptop. "Don't you fucking go nowhere," she screamed at the crowd as she backed her way down off the stage.

People ran faster, tore against one another. A man lay face down, swaddled in a yellow cape like a slain soldier in a sci-fi film.

Colton began singing about driving the main road for the county. His combat boot stomped four on the floor. Jennifer looked up at him adoringly. Her left hand clapped silently against the grip of the pistol.

With the lights low, the commotion centered around the door at the back, and Jennifer Nguyen's attention split between her honey onstage and the woman cowering behind the laptop, I felt my odds were better than average. They sure as shit weren't going to get better.

I inched my way close, then wrapped my arms around her from behind, our hands overlapping on the gun. The flesh of my palm tore on the hammer. I bent the barrel upward till Jennifer howled in pain, her fingers loosening enough so I could wrest it from her. The singing stopped. I turned as Colton Dance launched himself off the stage, barreling toward me, his knee coming down on my chest. The gun slid away like a wayward puck in a hockey fight.

Dance beat on my chest like he was trying to cave it in. When I got an arm up, he used both of his to force it back. I struck at his throat, his eyes, but I had no leverage. Black atmosphere swilled around me.

The pressure shifted, began to relent. I let my head fall in the direction of the door. Four officers approached with weapons drawn, bawling commands, inaudible over the music bed.

Colton Dance stood up. He stared stupidly at the officers. In a Vancouver PD uniform, he wouldn't have looked much different from them. He stepped off me. Began running, at them, or at the door.

I heard the shots and saw him fall, but not before reaching the cops, bowling into them even as he sank. He was dead when he landed.

The officers sprawled, helped one another regain their feet. Relief and nervous laughter supplanted the music.

I pushed myself up tentatively. One of the officers holstered his gun and approached to give me a hand. Approached and then seized up, bucked, and fell, tipping forward so our shoulders knocked together.

Behind him, the others were already directing the muzzles of their weapons toward Jennifer Nguyen, who welcomed them with a smile.

RULES FOR MISTAKES
S.M. Fedor

My right hook landed, and Cokehead's yapping mouth crumpled, yielding like a juice box expelling the final drops of sugar-water to a thirsty child. I felt his jawbone shatter, a fractured twin to the orbital socket from the prior punch. My fist, a heavy brick of meat and bone, withdrew from the pothole I'd constructed on his face. My knuckles were broken open and glistening. Strands of mucus and blood united us, strung between my fist and his face, before gravity severed the bond and painted red the lapel of his bomber jacket.

The club partied around us.

Deep rolling bass thumped against my chest, vibrating my body with a mix of violent rhythms and massaging pleasures. A choir of electronic squelches buzzed in refrain, while a pseudo-angry, face-tatted, white boy screeched through the oversized speakers hanging above us.

Dancers did not break form as they continued their gyrations, swaying in glittering couture that cost more than I'd make in a year; the garments barely deflecting charges of indecent exposure. A few looky-loos peeked at the commotion I'd caused, but the mass were enthralled by their worship of sound, fermented liquids, and chemical compounds. Not that they would have given a shit about us if they had been sober. The white boy wasn't famous, and I was just hired help.

Cokey hugged my leg, seemingly desiring to hold onto anything solid. If he could still see through his swollen eyes, I imagined his world must look like a kaleidoscopic nightmare.

A dense fog of smoke engulfed us, chaotic swirls of cigarette and vape haze fighting for marketplace domination. The tendrils flashed red, blue, purple, under pulsing disco lights, until the walls of smoke were pierced by green lasers sweeping across the room and forming pot-leaf-shaped patterns against the back wall.

The flashing strobe lights locked Cokey's face in a time-stasis, freezing his waterfall of tears and blood into an impressionistic still-life. I thankfully couldn't hear his moans over the noise the kids danced to. No musicianship, no emotional depth in the songs these days. Dead inside music, perfect for this hollow insta-generation. The Cure, now there was a band.

"Boys don't cry," I said, picking Cokehead off the reflective dancefloor by his torn shirt collar. His head swung like a pendulum. I dragged him over to the booth we'd been sitting in a moment prior.

Ms. Wilder perched at the edge of the curved vinyl seat. Her suggestive blood-red dress screamed paradoxical signals—danger, desire. Anger boiled behind her eyes, trying to find a gap in the black-lined borders in which to escape. Before her on the table, beside a battery of half-drunk vodkas, lay seven small glass vials filled with white nose-candy.

I flipped the front flap of Cokey's jacket and revealed the silken liner pocket within. Snatching the vials off the table, I dropped them into his pocket opening—slowly, one at a time, so he'd know that I wasn't ripping him off. When the vials were secured, I politely patted his jacket against his chest and smoothed him out.

His body swayed, his legs failing. Nice guy that I was, I caught him by his shoulder before he hit the floor. I held him upright and tossed one of his limp arms around my neck to keep him standing. "Not yet amigo. Soon," I told him, watching his consciousness drowning in the kiddie pool of his mind.

I replayed the last few minutes in my head, reliving the footage like a second-run dollar-cinema projection, its bulb half-burned out. I recalled Cokey leaning over Ms. Wilder, leering down her dress as he whispered something in her ear. She'd nodded an affirmative, but not before a mischievous glance in my direction. The vials had made their debut in the scene. I did the math. I did the math again, as it was never my forte.

I held out my open hand before Veronica.

"Ms. Wilder, I do believe there is one vial unaccounted for," I said. Though it's doubtful she could hear my words over the music, the venom in her eyes said she understood my meaning and intention.

With a dramatic flourish, the kind that had once made her top-billed, Hollywood's *IT* girl, she danced her red manicured nails along the frontier of her plum silk and lace bra, reaching her fingers inside her cleavage, and producing the missing eighth vial. She slammed it into my palm. Her petite hand, a vampiric pearl white that had never seen sunlight, looked like a dollop of cream against the rough sandpaper lines of my brown mitt. The vial leaked warmth into my skin, radiating heat infused by her pressed flesh.

I beamed at her in gratitude, happy to not have a drawn-out night fighting over her denial of possessing the vial. She turned away, acting like a scolded child, arms folded against her chest. Her focus drifted to a woman clad in head-to-toe black latex who was grinding against two male dancers wearing gold-foil shorts and glitter body oil.

I rejoined the stray vial with its brethren in Cokey's pocket. Grabbing his limp arm, I puppeteered it, making it dance back and forth in a wave of goodbye to Veronica. She snorted but was quick to recover her simmering stone facade. True professional actress, that girl.

Cokey and I synchronize-walked to the anteroom of the club as if in a three-legged race. Sal, the doorman, a living, breathing advertisement for better living through steroids, laughed as we approached. "Having fun tonight, Angel?"

His pecs danced to the rhythm of the hip-hop beat, his black T-shirt stretched taut to reveal every nuance of the performance.

"You think it's possible for you to buy a loose-fitting shirt for me sometime, Sal?"

He laughed again, and I'm pretty sure his left pectoral waggled as if to wink at me. Sal unhooked the velvet security rope and then pushed open the barricaded black steel doors. They opened with a clank, birthing us onto the L.A. streets. I breathed in the fresh morning smog.

I ducked my body from under the arm of Cokeman and he kissed the sidewalk with a crash as his support pillar disappeared. The predawn morning momentarily transformed into high noon, ablaze in camera flashes. The army of paparazzi lowered their phones and slung curses in my direction, angry I was wasting their time with this sacrificial offering. I shrugged a fake apology at the parasites, *be happy with what I give you.* I returned to the noisy, black cavern, Sal resealing me within the pleasure tomb of the rich and famous.

I was pleasantly surprised to find Veronica still sitting at the table—black cigarette burning in one hand, vodka careening against the walls of the glass in the other. She glared at me as I rejoined her.

"You're a fucking asshole, you do know that right, Angel?" she screamed over a song that may have been different than the previous one, but if so, I couldn't tell how.

"You know the rules Ms. Wilder, no hands *on* you, no chems *in* you."

"Ha, right. *Rules.* Like it makes a difference," she answered and then emptied the glass of vodka down her throat as if that proved her point. "That was a son of a producer, you know. Coulda been my next big break you just destroyed. I should tell Monty you're cock-blocking my career."

"It's Hollywood, Ms. Wilder. Everyone is a producer's son.

Even the orphaned ones raised by the maid. Monty pays me to keep you from mistakes."

Her face went rigid, eyebrows arched with disgust. I'd said harsher truths to her before, I didn't understand the extreme reaction, but then I noticed she was studying my shoulder. I followed her gaze. *Dammit.*

Cokey, the wayward son of producers, had left a bloody handprint on the one club-appropriate shirt I owned. I brushed at the stain, but the blood had soaked deep within the soul of the fibers. Great, now I'd have to buy a new one. That would wipe out the night's paycheck.

"Monty might pay you to keep me out of trouble, but who are you gonna pay to fix your mistakes, Angel? He can't be paying you enough to cover your own issues," she laughed, slamming another vodka tonic and joining the latex woman on the dance floor.

I watched the trouble swirl like the eddies of smoke. Mistakes loved to dance.

I weaved my way through the crowds of shoppers, tourists, and would-be stars at The Grove. In my hand was a newly purchased club shirt, folded neatly within an organic-biodegradable-homeopathic bag. I could not wait to escape the crowd and get home. My mood fouled after being forced to spend three hundred and seventy dollars on a shirt. I'd never purchased such items before taking on Ms. Wilder as a client. I was a five-dollar-white-T-and-bag-of-tube-socks guy. My store of choice was Marguerite, the *viejita* in a straw sunhat, hustling on the corner of the 405 off-ramp.

My walk through the mall took me past kiosk row, small stands with made-for-TV wares that interrupted foot-traffic flow. A small Japanese woman emerged from behind her stall and lunged in front of my path. In her hand, she held a necklace of dubious gold material. "Bring home your girlfriend a beautiful gift. Almost as beautiful as her," she smiled quizzically, dancing the jewelry to catch the sunlight and glint.

"Sorry, no girlfriend for me," I answered and tried to move past her.

"Big man like you, no girlfriend?" her eyes narrowed, studying me. She disappeared the necklace with the skill of a Vegas magician, her fingers misdirecting me to a row of bracelets. She selected a silver one with a small clover charm on it. "Perhaps, for your *special friend* then?"

I chortled, my hands up in playful defense, "No special friend, either." As I watched the silver clover dance in the wind, my mind reconsidered. "How much?"

"Yatta! For you, only twenty dollars. You make friend very happy."

"I'll give you ten, I just spent the rest of my money on a shirt to hang out with my *special friend*," I answered, holding up the bag as evidence.

"Big date night for big guy, very nice. Okay, for you I do ten, but you no tell anyone I so cheap, right?"

"Cross my heart," I said as I pressed the ten into her waiting palm. She vanished the money as smoothly as she had the necklace before, and I walked away with the bracelet in my bag.

I doubted Veronica would appreciate the gesture, but maybe, if I was lucky, a token of peace could soften our hardening work relationship. Our mutual antagonism was bound to explode, to go wrong sooner than later if not addressed. My father had been hard-nosed with me when I'd found myself in trouble growing up in Mexico City. He'd beat me, whipped me good. I rebelled harder. I wasn't Veronica's father, but the dynamics were eerily familiar. Something had to change or she'd recklessly spiral further out of control. I didn't want to see that happen to her.

I explored the expanse of the parking lot, dotted with luxury rides. My car was easy to spot next to the rows of shining Mercedes—the old girl's age and rust made for an ideal tracking beacon.

I swung open the worn, brown steel-frame door; it greeted me with grunts and squeals. A voice called out from behind me, "Angel? Angel Herrera? Hey, that's you, right?"

I turned and instantly regretted not jumping into my car and driving away. Coming toward me was a 'roided-up gym rat, decked out in Adidas fashion-striped workout pants, a tight Tapout graphic shirt, and a hat that exclaimed the man wearing it had No Fear. The red Mustang he'd parked was covered in matching decals and stickers. His body reflected the burning afternoon sun, skin doused in product and lotions. He was the embodiment of date rape in human form.

"Uh, yeah, what's up, man?" I replied tentatively, my hands still set on my car's frame.

"Holy shit, man. I used to watch all your fights when I was a kid, back in the day. I thought you were a beast. You should have been a legend, dog." His eyes sparkled with an obsession that left me uncomfortable.

"Well, you know, that's the way the circuit goes sometimes. You work hard, try your best, take your shot. Didn't work out for me, but thanks bro," I replied, moving to get into the car.

The glow in his eyes died, turned hard. His mouth curled into a smirk. His arm snapped out, grabbed onto my wrist before I could shut the car door behind me. "Nah, man, I'm sure it worked out for you fine. Everyone knows you're a pussy who took a dive. Played the Vegas scene hard I heard. Pissed off a lot of mob boys I bet," he took in my beater, flicked a bit of rust off the side with his foot. "You drivin' this shit pile to hide the shady fortunes?"

I stared at his ruddy face, dripping with sweat and the glow of bronzer. "You don't know what you're talking about. I suggest you remove your hands right now and back away."

"Sure thing, Tough Guy, hate for you to have to fake an injury again," he laughed and released his grip. I pulled the door shut; he kicked the side of it as I did so.

My hands tensed, but I placed them on the steering wheel,

fighting off my worst instincts. Through the rearview mirror, I watched him laughing as I drove away.

Once I was out of view, I swerved to the shoulder of the road, cars behind me honking in protest. I punched the steering console over and over, imagining his smug face. The console twisted and bulged with each blow until it cracked. The rage expelled, I swung back onto the road and raced to my apartment—an over-priced shirt, an apology bracelet that would likely be trashed, and some fresh damage to an already damaged ride being my purchases for the day.

My apartment was a single room on the third floor of a whitewashed adobe walk-up. I opened the plywood door and was simultaneously in my bedroom and kitchen. There was no bathroom—that was at the end of the hallway, shared by three other rooms. In L.A. real estate, the place was a steal for six-fifty a month.

I crawled over the twin-sized mattress and greeted Herb, Chuck, and Jesús, my trio of jade plants. They rested on a small ledge abutting a narrow slot window whose design had been imported from a prison. Through the window, the boys and I gazed upon Gabriela, the palm tree. "Her fronds are looking spectacular today, eh boys?" I said to them, winking at Jesús.

The air tasted of salt. If I strained, arched my head just right, peered down the alleys and past rooftops and satellite dishes, I could see a sliver of a corner that shined. Oceanview property as it was listed in the rental advertisement.

I rolled to the other side of the bed, kitchen side, which consisted of a small counter with a hotplate and one cupboard for storage. I grabbed the empty glass I'd left next to the hot plate and took it down the hall to the communal bathroom. After a quick piss, I washed my hands and filled the glass with tap water. Returning to my room, I watered the boys and trimmed their leaves with small pruning scissors. "Gotta have your leaves done nice if you're gonna have a chance with Gabi," I cooed.

I opened the bag I'd brought home from the mall, held the shirt up, examining it again. It was a hideous thing, loud and gaudy. Black synthetic fabric slashed with blue material that seemed to glow. Four large letters in silver ran across the chest—*RCIO*. The lettering had no meaning to me, but apparently to those in the know, it made the shirt five-times more valuable and opened exclusive doors. I hung the shirt off an exposed pipe that jutted from the bubbled ceiling, disgusted with myself for the purchase, with the need for it.

That left the bracelet. I toyed with it, sliding its links between my fingers, watching the silver dance with the light. I wasn't sure why I'd bought it. Veronica only wore stuff that came from a *proper* store. She'd probably make some snide joke about her skin turning green and toss it into the rubbish.

I pinched the clover charm between my thumb and forefinger, examined its shape, the small imperfections that to me made it unique. I realized then why I had purchased it, and I wondered what that meant—this was something that Sophia might have once worn.

Sophia, the woman I'd sacrificed my career for, that I'd destroyed myself for. The woman who'd taken everything I'd ever had and even now that she was gone from my life, her ghost still haunted me. The tendrils of memory she'd left embedded in my mind ever corrupting.

The gym rat douche at the mall had been right, in a way. I had taken a dive. I had played the gamblers. But it wasn't for my benefit, it had been for hers. She'd come to me crying, a tale of woe in her story. Through streaming tears, she'd told me the money would help save her little brother back in Mexico. I'd known that life, how could I deny her, *mi amor?*

I learned she, too, could have been a fantastic movie actress.

The day after the fight, I had only one visitor—Gus, my manager. His eyes told me he knew what I'd done before his admonishment confirmed it. I was blacklisted from the fight

53

circuits. Sophia was gone, her pharmacy perfumes and kiosk jewelry in the wind, along with the money.

My cellphone buzzed. I glanced at the screen, Monty, Veronica's agent and manager.

"Hey'a Angel, I need you on the clock tonight," he greeted me in his rushed auctioneer voice. Monty always spoke at a rapid pace, as if there were a thousand more important things he should be doing, but he was gracing you with a moment of his time.

"She's going to the club again?" I asked, wary of another night of the same.

"What? Oh, no, no. Dinner, schmoozing with Albert Brackett. He put in a special request to meet her, Angel, this is important. If she's ever to get back on top, Brackett can make it happen. Make sure she does not fuck it up. Right, my friend? Bring her sober and charming and beautiful. She can be half those things on her own when she wants, you just make sure she shows up with the others. I'll have Madeline text you his address. Get her there, tits and teeth, my boy."

The phone line went dead. A moment later, the phone buzzed with a text message from Monty's assistant, Madeline Murphy. The message was brief, an address in the Hollywood Hills.

I entered my code to the gate of Veronica Wilder's villa and drove the long driveway to the actual house. The place was a mockery of architecture, built around endless, seamless windows. These modern see-through monstrosities always made me think the people inside were lying to themselves, fronting that they had nothing to hide—obscuring truth via false transparency.

I parked my car in the rear corner of the garage, the light to my stall turned off. Ms. Wilder had made a point of shaming me for the vehicle the few times she'd spied it. I inspected the Rolls Phantom I'd be driving that night. A beauty of craftsmanship and lines, but it still just transported a person from *A* to *B*.

I let myself into the house and called out, "Hello, Ms. Wilder?

I'm here to take you to your meeting."

There was no reply.

I wandered through the opulent rooms, looking for her. Awards and trophies were prominently displayed on the shelves. Studio-lit pictures of Veronica and posters of her movies lined the walls. There was a rapid decline in the quality and frequency of the films as I traveled forward along the historical timeline. I spotted nothing hanging for the current year.

Hollywood was cruel to actresses, a town run unofficially by pedos. Actresses who'd crossed the threshold of thirty, especially if their troubles were regularly published in the tabloids, might as well pack up and move back to Oklahoma. We were both ghosts.

Sounds of a bottle pouring caught my attention and I followed its music. I stopped near a half-open doorway and peered in.

Veronica Wilder stood nude in front of a full-length mirror, her hair wrapped in a plush towel. Her body shimmered, fresh from the shower. A rivulet of water navigated the curve of her shoulder. In one hand she held a glass of vodka, sipping from it as she turned, thrusting her hips at the mirror, re-discovering her best angles. Her other hand, splayed, crawled across her breasts, down her abdomen, pushing against any bit of flesh that disappointed her.

Veronica's face expressed a sadness, a desperation I'd never seen in her before. A look that reflected a lifetime of self-doubt, a fragility I'd not previously recognized in the boisterous party-girl. She bit her lip, sucked her teeth. Whispered to herself, "You got this, girl."

I was seeing Veronica Wilder, rather than the persona, the actress, for the first time.

I stepped back from the doorway, realizing this was a private moment. The movement was a mistake, and her eyes in the mirror were drawn to me with predatory instincts. As the vulnerability in her face vanished, the self-assured mask retook.

"Oh hello, Angel. Do you like what you see? Like watching me?" asked her reflection. Her voice was a low murmur, a seductive call that beckoned even as it dripped with poison.

"I'm sorry, Ms. Wilder, I was just coming to pick you up, to take you to your meeting that is," I stammered, looking to the ground, at the wall, anywhere but her nudity.

"Is this why you're so protective of me at the clubs, Angel? Is it because you love this body, Angel? Always forced to watch me move, perform, while you're in the shadows?" she asked, her fingers dancing down her skin. Her hand faltered as if having discovered a flaw. She frowned, guzzled her vodka. "You do love me, don't you, Angel?" Her voice quivered.

She finished the last drops of vodka and rested the empty glass on the marble side table. She unwrapped the towel from her head, dropped it to the floor, and shook her hair free. "Are you gonna pound me like you used to those boys in the ring? Because you love me? Because you want to taste fame again?"

My throat dried. Sweat ran down my cheek, "Ms. Wilder, Veronica, I do care for you. But not like that, not like this."

I shut the door and retreated through the house. A scream chased me, a guttural roar. As I entered the garage, I could hear glass shattering against her bedroom walls.

I sat, waiting, in the driver's seat of the Phantom. An hour later, Veronica emerged, dressed in a low-cut black cocktail dress, hair and makeup done, a smile on her face that reeked of alcohol and lies.

"Driver, I believe you have the address," she said as she entered the back of the car.

I turned to face her, "Veronica—" I started, but the look in her eyes stopped me. There was a darkness, a pain that said she would not hear my words. "Yes, Ms. Wilder, I have the address," I replied.

"Good, then take me there. I'm about to be someone again," she said and rolled up the privacy window between us, boxing me out.

* * *

Albert Brackett's mansion was to Ms. Wilder's villa what her villa was to my apartment. I could not fathom how a man could need a home like this for only himself. If I lived here, there would be fifty distant cousins staying with me. What else was the point of all that space?

I knew very little about the man, other than he had produced a string of movies that were both box office hits and critical darlings. Monty was correct—if there was a man who could resurrect Ms. Wilder's career, it was Albert Brackett. I silently prayed that she was sober enough and calm enough to impress him.

When she got out of the car, Veronica tried to slam the door, but it was impossible for the door of a Phantom to actually slam, so it whispered at me harshly. I watched her enter the mansion doors and then I circled my way back down to the end of the driveway. When she was finished, she would call me to pick her up. Until then, I would wait in the car.

I was about two hours into Roberto Bolaño's 2666, investigating the unsolved murders within the town of Santa Teresa, when the electronic locks on the Phantom triggered and Veronica threw herself into the backseat. I turned in surprise, glancing at the phone to make sure I hadn't missed her call somehow, but the screen was blank.

I gasped when I saw her.

Her face was strewn with tears, purple-black eyeliner streaked down her cheeks. Her dress was disheveled and crooked, her left breast not fully covered. Wet blood coated her hands.

"*Dios!* Ms. Wilder, Veronica, are you okay? What happened?"

"Just drive, Angel," she said, voice quiet, barely a whisper.

"Ms. Wilder?"

"I said to fucking drive, Angel!" she screamed, spittle flying from her lips.

I shifted the car into drive and began to pull away, the gravel crunching under the rolling tires. I scrutinized her in the rear-view mirror, watched as her chest heaved up and down, gulping air and anxiety in equal doses. I stomped on the brakes, unable to go farther.

She looked at me, head down, eyes raised beneath the tangled hair. "Please, Angel, drive."

"I'm sorry, Veronica, I can't." I got out of the car, and before she could say another word, I set the locks, sealing her within.

I walked the lengthy driveway to the entrance of the mansion, threw open its door, and stepped into the belly of the beast.

I was overwhelmed, blinded by the amount of white that greeted me. White marble floors, nearly translucent walls, every-thing an absolute brilliant shade—an absence of color that felt sinister, a falsified purity. The place was immaculate, except for the fresh blood splatters.

I followed the red trail and it led me to an ostentatious living room bespeckled in white-gold trim. In the center of the room lay an extravagant white leather couch, soiled in blood. Before it sat a mirrored coffee-table, vodka and cocaine reflected in its surface.

A moan called out from behind the couch. I stepped around the cushions and met legendary film producer Albert Brackett. He lay naked, twisting on the white carpet. A pair of pearl-handled scissors jutted out of his lower left abdomen. Based on the smell, they'd likely punctured his colon.

When he saw me approach, his eyes went wild, before calming. "Oh, thank god, I thought you were that crazy bitch. Please, call the hospital."

I knelt down next to him and studied the small twisted body. Liver spots and plump veins crisscrossed his skin, ducking beneath fields of rough silver hairs that grew like weeds. Beneath the aromas of blood, shit, and fear, his body smelled of talcum lotion and nursing homes.

"What happened, Mister Brackett?" I asked him, my voice steady, calm.

"That crazy bitch stabbed me, are you stupid? Call the goddamn ambulance."

I pressed my hand against the wound, the blood staining my

hands as it had Veronica's. Brackett grunted, yowled as I pressed hard.

"Why are you naked Mister Brackett? Why is your table covered in coke?"

"What?" he gasped. "It was a party, man. She wanted to party."

"And then you forced yourself upon her?"

"No, I swear I didn't. She begged me to make her a star again. She wanted a role. She knew the rules."

"Rules. Yeah. Yes, I've talked to her about rules. About boundaries and mistakes. I'm supposed to keep her from mistakes," I answered.

"She fucking stabbed me, asshole," he screamed through clenched teeth.

"That's exactly the problem," I said and grabbed the pearl handles of the scissors. I pushed the twin blades farther into his elderly body, twisting them, rotating clockwise and then counter. I forced open their jaws and snipped them closed again, chewing, slicing, cutting organs until Albert Brackett had no story left to tell. No mistakes for him to speak of.

I drove Veronica home in silence. In her garage, we looked at each other's bloody bodies, ruined clothes, and embraced. I squeezed her tight, a hug I think we both knew meant farewell.

Before she went inside her villa, I reached into my pocket and pulled out the silver charm bracelet. I clipped it around her wrist. She examined the clover and mouthed *thank you*.

I got into my rusted car and left the homes of the rich and famous behind. Curved, winding roads became potholed streets built on a grid, mansions morphed into multi-unit flats.

The sun had set, but the air was still hot, heavy, the salty air adding a layer of sweat to the atmosphere. Four blocks from my apartment, the night was lit by dancing red and blue lights, as if I were heading to the club.

* * *

It was movie night in San Quentin. My fellow inmates and I jostled amongst the bolted aluminum benches for the best spot to see the tiny TV screen.

Static burst over the loudspeakers and a slow melody of piano and orchestra strings began to play. On screen a title card announced the film *The Lost Generation*, starring the reborn Hollywood *IT* girl, Veronica Wilder.

Veronica's career had skyrocketed after the events three years prior. She'd become a feminist icon, a woman who'd fought back against a system that had tried to abuse her, drug her, rape her. Victim turned heroine. Her story had won over the hearts and minds of America, confirmed their belief systems about the morality of Hollyweird.

My name had been briefly mentioned at the start of the event's news cycle—the bodyguard who was sentenced for murder. The foreign man with a violent past who'd sought vengeance for failing at his duty to protect the ingénue from the craven perverts. Her new PR team worked quickly to excise me from future versions of the story, and the tale became wholly Ms. Wilder's. I did not fault her for that. It's what I wanted for my friend.

Veronica Wilder, or rather Shelly Fields, her character in the film, ran across the screen in an evening dress, a partially opaque slip, taut stomach showing through.

From the far-left corner of the room, an inmate catcalled the screen, "I hope we see her titties, eh boys? Look at her." His voice rang out to laughter.

I lurched from the bench, stalking in the direction of the voice, fists already tightening. I identified the source, a wiry inmate who looked like he was up the river on drug charges. He discovered my hands could still punch as if built from bricks. It took several minutes and five guards to pull me off what was left of the Crackhead's face. I spit a piece of his flesh onto the concrete floor.

I had rules when it came to Ms. Wilder, and people would best respect them, even if it cost me a few more years.

WINNER TAKES ALL
James A. Hearn

Floyd Kent emptied his pockets of two dollars and fifty-seven cents—his change from a black coffee and a breakfast burrito at Sonic, minus his customary tip for Josie, the curvy carhop. He added the sum to the pile of money on the kitchen table of his motel room, his home since selling his ramshackle house for cash.

A sigh escaped Floyd's lips, blowing out from behind a thick gray moustache that would've made Sam Elliot envious. All the money he had in the world, fifty thousand two dollars and fifty-seven cents, and it was barely enough for the buy-in to Doc Brannigan's no-limit Texas hold 'em game tonight.

"No risk, no reward," said Floyd to himself. If he beat the God-damned bastards who ran Longview, he'd walk away with three hundred thousand dollars and a chance for a new life. A life without crawling into attics on arthritic knees in the Texas summers, hauling HVAC units into what felt like hell's asshole.

The very thought called for a cold beer. Floyd retrieved a can from the mini-fridge and returned to the table. As he re-counted the money, dreams drifted behind his bright brown eyes.

Maybe he'd buy a one-way ticket to Tahiti or Costa Rica and live in a seaside cabana. He'd live simply, not drinking or whoring too much. In these recurrent fantasies, he'd find a nice, middle-aged ex-pat like himself. Someone like Josie, with her rain-or-shine smile.

Or better yet, a local woman who didn't speak English. Talk was overrated. Floyd's ex-wife, Liz, had proven that years ago, when their marriage collapsed under the weight of her words.

But would three-hundred grand be enough? At fifty-five, might he expect another twenty good years? Floyd shrugged. Five years or twenty, it'd be fun to find out.

So, Tahiti or Costa Rica?

Floyd fished a poker chip from his pocket. The battered chip from a now-defunct New Orleans casino was a token from an earlier life. The chip danced across his knuckles, slipping easily between the fingers of his calloused hands. On one side was a Mardi Gras mask, on the other, a jazz band.

Floyd flipped it into the air. The chip spun, end over end, and clattered onto the table. Jazz band.

Costa Rica.

But what if you lose? The questioning voice belonged to his long-dead father, a Methodist minister who, despite not sparing the rod, had raised a wastrel and reprobate. His own words.

The old man had died alone, suffering with cancer Floyd never even knew he had. Floyd had always imagined himself returning home to play the part of the prodigal son, a gift for the old man before he passed. Place a ring on my finger, Dad. Kill the fatted calf. I love you and I always have.

But there came a day when Floyd found himself standing alone by a fresh grave, with nothing but his father's medical bills and the old man's dog-eared, leather-bound King James Bible as a legacy.

Floyd patted the book beneath his jacket, right above his heart. The Bible's solidity was both a comfort and a weight, a punishment like the dead albatross around the sailor's neck in that crazy poem he'd read in high school.

What if you lose, son?

"They're amateurs," said Floyd. "I can beat them without

even looking at my cards, just by playing position and watching their bets." And if he was unlucky, if the cards went against him, his backup plan would kick in.

Floyd pulled a deck of cards from his pocket and began shuffling. Back and forth they went, slipping against one another with the *swish-swish* sound he loved. He checked the top card: jack of spades. He shuffled, dealt hands to five imaginary opponents, and checked the top card again: jack of spades. He still had the touch, after all these years.

None of his opponents tonight had ever heard of Floyd "Stacks" Kent, former New Orleans card sharp. For all they knew, he was plain Floyd Alexander Kent, divorced HVAC repairman who'd recently come into some money. Good ol' Aunt Matilda, God rest her soul, had remembered him in her will and left him a tidy sum. Or so the story went.

As Floyd shuffled the cards again, his shabby motel room became the Black Pearl Casino in New Orleans, and he became Stacks, a cocky, small-time gambler who picked tourists and locals clean. Somewhere along the Mississippi River, he'd fallen in love with a greedy cocktail waitress named Lola, who shared her bed but not her heart. Happiness could be bought, and cheaply.

Then a pit boss who was sweet on Lola falsely accused Stacks of cheating, had him roughed up, and thrown out of the Black Pearl. In one night, he'd lost his bankroll and Lola. But the worst part was being put on the communal list of known cheats. To his dismay, he couldn't even scare up a game in the backwoods casinos of Mississippi, much less Atlantic City or Vegas.

Deprived of his livelihood at twenty-five, with no education or money, Stacks became Floyd again. He ended up in Longview, Texas, when his car broke down on the way to a Dallas job fair. Through the mists of a blown head gasket, Floyd had spied a *Help Wanted* sign in a shop window. He'd walked in, and Billy Condon of Condon HVAC had hired him on the spot.

That was thirty years ago.

Floyd dealt two cards to five opponents, face up, so he could play the hands. He put out chips for the small and big blinds, the two positions on the dealer's left who were forced to bet.

"Doc," said Floyd to the imaginary opponent on the big blind's left, "you're under the gun, and you have pocket sevens. You call, not because you're smart, but because you're a wuss."

Harold "Doc" Brannigan, the host of tonight's game, was a retired psychiatrist. Liz Kent had been Doc's patient once upon a happy marriage, and though Floyd couldn't prove it, he thought his ex's string of extra-marital affairs had started with Doc. The good doctor's advice to Liz had been to "find herself." Apparently, that was code for her to feel good about divorcing Floyd. A string of wrecked marriages and a few suicides could be traced back to Brannigan's couch.

"Judge Rudy," said Floyd to the next opponent, "you have something between jack and squat, an off-suit two and a seven. You're an idiot, but even you know to fold that like origami."

The judge was a self-important man who probably slept in his black robes. Before winning his first of many elections as a county judge, Rudy Gonzalez had chased ambulances and closed down bars as a down-and-out attorney. Now, he made his money by tossing out environmental lawsuits brought against Big Oil.

Play nice, Floyd. Maybe she'll come back. That had been Rudy's disastrous advice to Floyd during the divorce. In the fifty-fifty split, Liz got the gold mine and Floyd got the shaft, as the song went, and he found himself living in his truck, a brand-new Ford F-150 he'd managed to keep.

Next, Floyd looked at the pair of kings he'd dealt. "Chuck Wagon Tanner, you fat slob. You're sitting on pocket cowboys. You're sly, but you're greedy." Floyd moved a large stack of chips into the pot.

Soon after Floyd's divorce, the portly banker, Charles "Chuck Wagon" Tanner, had sent his goons to repossess Floyd's F-150. It had been the first and only late payment, a loss that hurt worse than the divorce.

It's just business, Floyd. No hard feelings. As if "business" excused squeezing hard-pressed people down on their luck, raising interest rates, or foreclosing on generational family farms. In the lean times, men like Tanner grew fatter.

Floyd looked at his own cards: the jack and ten of diamonds. A suited connector, and a reasonably strong hand. He put in chips to see the flop, then proceeded to the small and big blinds.

The final two opponents were his boss, Billy Condon, and Billy's shiftless son-in-law, Jack Crenshaw. Jack had taken the cushy desk job that Billy had always said would be Floyd's when he turned fifty-five: a reward for his years of service. To add insult to injury, Jack relished giving Floyd the attic jobs, or sending his helpers to the wrong locations and blaming Floyd for the delays.

"Billy, you've the queen of clubs and the six of diamonds. You could defend the small blind, but Chuck Wagon's over-bet has you scared. You fold."

Next, Floyd addressed the big blind, the player forced to bet the most before even seeing his two cards. "Jack, it figures you'd have pocket aces. You've never worked a day in your miserable life, so why not have the best cards? You raise."

Floyd folded Doc's pair of sevens and called with the rest of the hands. It was time to deal the first of the community cards, the flop.

"Gentlemen, we have an interesting flop: nine of diamonds, eight of clubs, and the king of spades. Chuck Wagon is looking nice with three kings. I've a possible straight with eight-nine-ten-jack. No help for Jack's pair of aces."

Floyd went through another round of betting, then dealt another community card.

"Two of clubs. No help to anyone."

Jack put in a token bet, and everyone else called.

"It's time for the river," said Floyd. He dealt the fifth community card, a seven of hearts that completed his straight.

Floyd finished the hand, meeting every raise from his opponents, and raked the pot toward himself. He dealt more hands to pass the time, playing them as his opponents would—for Floyd knew their foibles better than their own wives, in ways beyond just living in the same small town for decades.

It began five years ago, during a particularly scorching summer, when Floyd was sent on an urgent call to fix the A/C in Doc's lake house.

"You gotta go tonight, Floyd," Billy had said one Thursday evening.

"What's the rush, boss?" Floyd had argued. "It's a long drive to Lake O' the Pines."

"You think I give a damn? Fix it before tomorrow night. I can't concentrate on the game if I'm sweaty."

"What game?"

"Never mind, Floyd. Just do it."

So Floyd made the drive, found the key under the mat as he'd been told, and ventured into the sweltering attic. After fixing a sticky capacitor and sweating buckets, Floyd went looking for a cold beer.

On the way to the kitchen, a flash of something emerald caught his eye. There, in the living room, was a green felt tabletop, smooth as the surface of a cool lake.

A poker table!

Floyd couldn't believe it. So *this* was where his boss and his boss's cronies had their annual high-stakes game. It was no problem to return the next morning and set up a WiFi camera in the attic. The camera, mounted in a ceiling vent, caught every lifted eyebrow, sigh, and twitch, as the men folded, checked, called, raised, bluffed, or bet everything by going all-in.

Floyd watched for five years as greedy amateurs played poker, all the time racking his brains for a way to break into the game. He needed a stake, and he needed a story. After saving every penny and selling everything, he had the stake. The story of rich, childless Aunt Matilda gave him cover by removing the reek of desperation. He was supposedly a man of means now, though still not quite an equal.

"All in," said Floyd, as he called an imaginary bet from Judge Rudy. "Sorry, Judge. My flush beats your three of a kind. Lady luck is with me tonight."

And if luck goes against you, son?

"That's what backup plans are for, Dad," said Floyd. He pulled his Ruger GP100 out of his jacket and laid it next to the cards, money, and chips. The gun was a six-shot .357 Magnum revolver with double/single action, and the sights were filed for close quarters.

But it wouldn't come to killing, Floyd was sure. If he lost, duct tape and handcuffs would do the trick as he made his getaway.

Floyd flipped open the Ruger's cylinder, spun it in his deft fingers to check the loads, and snapped it home. He returned the gun to the jacket's right interior pocket, opposite the family Bible.

The drive from Longview to Doc's lake house took Floyd through the piney woods of Texas, down narrow two-lane country roads and through one-stoplight towns. His phone's signal played out south of Warlock, as if the towering trees could not abide technology.

Floyd found the house on a remote bluff overlooking the Lake O' the Pines, just as he remembered it. Six vehicles were parked outside, five of them easily worth ten times his Tacoma. The sixth was a battered Kia Soul with balding tires and a dozen bumper stickers.

Floyd parked beside it, grabbed his satchel of money, and exited his truck. One bumper sticker showed Wonder Woman delivering a right cross to an orange-faced politician, and two others blared *Insured by Smith & Wesson* and *Real Girls Play With Guns*.

Floyd was still chuckling over the stickers when a familiar

face answered the lake house's doorbell.

"Josie?" said Floyd.

The carhop gave a small cry of surprise. "I know your order, but not your name. You're breakfast burrito and black coffee, right?"

"That's me," said Floyd with a grin. "Name's Floyd Kent."

"Josie Weathers."

"Hey, Josie," called a baritone voice. It sounded like Chuck Wagon Tanner. "Another beer over here. And some more sandwiches, huh?"

"Just a second, Mister Tanner," said Josie as she rolled her blue eyes. She turned to Floyd and his satchel. "If you have a delivery, just leave it on the step."

Josie was about to close the door, but Floyd put a hand on her arm. Despite the heat of the day, goosebumps prickled beneath his hand. She looked at him from beneath long eyelashes, the corners of her lips curving into a grin. Her red mouth reminded him of Lola.

"You don't understand," said Floyd. "I'm here to play." He hefted his satchel, as if she could see the money inside.

Josie's smile faded. "You shouldn't play with these jerks, Floyd," she whispered. "Take your money and run."

"If it isn't Floyd Kent, nouveau riche," said Doc Brannigan as he elbowed his way past Josie. He was ten years older than Floyd, with a wrinkled but still handsome face, and twin shocks of gray at his temples. "Come in, I'll give you the tour."

The lake house's living room had a commanding view of the lake below the bluffs and was dominated by a green felt poker table and a gun safe. Western décor was scattered throughout, with paintings of half-nude cowgirls riding horses or señoritas bathing in streams.

After showing Floyd around, Doc added Floyd's fifty thousand dollars to the gun safe. The safe's door closed with a heavy clang, and the image of three-hundred grand lingered in Floyd's mind. Beside him, Josie was holding her breath, her gaze boring into the safe.

"May I take your jacket?" asked Doc.

Lost in his reverie, Floyd almost said yes. His backup plan—the Ruger .357 Magnum—was secreted in an interior pocket, opposite the family Bible.

"This is my lucky jacket," said Floyd.

"Hot as blazes, but suit yourself," said Doc.

"Hiya, Floyd." Billy Condon stepped up and shoved a beer into Floyd's hands. Jack Crenshaw was standing behind Billy—he always seemed to be lurking in his father-in-law's shadow. While Billy's face was fleshy and pale, Jack's was lean and brown, like a pork chop that had been left on the grill too long.

"Hiya, Floyd," repeated Billy with breath that reeked of alcohol. He wrapped an arm around Floyd's neck and walked him to the poker table. "Fellas! This is my oldest and best employee. How long have you worked for Condon HVAC? Twenty-five years?"

"Thirty."

Billy whistled. "Damnation. Well, you're no worse for wear. Look at how things worked out for you. Your Aunt Martha leaving you all that money. Now you're on Easy Street, eh?"

Floyd corrected the lie. "Aunt Matilda."

"Matilda." Billy raised a beer to her and drained it.

"Are we gonna play some cards, or gab like a bunch of old ladies?" asked Jack.

"I'm with the young buck," said Judge Rudy. He wore a black silk shirt with gold buttons, stretched too tightly over a paunchy stomach. With his jeans and snakeskin boots, he looked like an extra from *Urban Cowboy* who'd outgrown his old costume.

"Let's play!" said Chuck Wagon. The robust, balding banker had already secured a spot at the table, complete with a beer and plate stacked with sandwiches.

Josie stood beside him, her face as red as the queen of diamonds. Floyd didn't need to see the fat hand resting on her posterior to know it was there.

Doc Brannigan held up his hands for quiet. "Gents, I'll keep this short. This is no limit Texas hold 'em, winner-takes-all. The buy-in is fifty thousand, for a grand total of three-hundred thousand. The small blind starts at five hundred, the big blind at one thousand, and the minimum raise is twice the big blind. For table etiquette, no subject is taboo here, as long as you don't reveal your hole cards."

Floyd swallowed hard. He was finally here! He glanced at the vent above the poker table. He'd removed the WiFi camera in the attic the previous weekend, as a precaution, using the key under the mat. It wouldn't do to have the police find the device, if worse came to worst.

"If you lose early, I'm looking at you, Judge," continued Doc, "you can watch satellite TV, go fishin', or find something else to occupy your time." He gave a lecherous wink at Josie. "This weekend's soiree is catered by Josie's Fine Foods, by the way. Now, turn off your cell phones and hand them to the little lady. It's time to play the game of kings."

It wasn't the Judge who exited early, but Chuck Wagon. The banker had been slamming beers as fast as Josie could bring them, and he was rip-roaring drunk by the tenth hand. His over-betting through the pre-flop, flop (a rainbow of two, six, ten), and turn (three) had scared off all opponents, save for Floyd and Jack.

Floyd had started the hand with an ace and six. In the face of Chuck Wagon's wild bets, he'd briefly considered folding. After all, Floyd was ahead in the chips, and it was early in the game. But the banker's betting pattern told Floyd one thing: the man had started with a nice pocket pair, possibly even pocket rockets: two aces. The uninteresting flop of middling cards, from which no one might form a straight or flush, had not deterred Chuck Wagon, who kept on betting through the turn and river.

"Raise," said Floyd. He met Chuck Wagon's raise of five thousand with an additional fifteen thousand. Jack, the last remaining player, cursed and folded. It was now just Floyd and Chuck Wagon.

"You're one cool customer," said Doc to Floyd. "You deal cards like Liberace tickling the ivories."

Jack scowled. "Who the hell's Liberace?"

"He was a pansy who played the piano," said the Judge. "Call his bluff, Charles."

Josie appeared with a fresh beer for the banker. She leaned into the fat man, who was beginning to sweat. "You ain't scared, are you?" she whispered in his ear.

"Scared?" sneered Chuck Wagon. "Of this nobody? I'll do better than call. All in." He pushed out his chips with a look of confidence only the supremely drunk can achieve.

Floyd feigned hesitation and appeared to study the five community cards. From the corner of his eye, he watched Chuck Wagon's Adam's apple bob through his thick neck. His three sixes would be enough.

"Call," said Floyd, pushing out his chips to match the all-in bet. "Now, show me your pocket pair. Is it aces or kings? Queens?"

The banker was silent.

"Or was it jacks, for such a jackass?" Floyd scoffed.

Josie smiled at Floyd, picked up some empty beer bottles, and headed for the kitchen.

"Floyd, this is a friendly game," said Billy. "You're my guest, remember?"

"Show your cards first," said Chuck Wagon. "Then I'll show mine."

Doc shook his head. "Floyd paid for the privilege of seeing your cards. You must show yours first, by rule."

Chuck Wagon turned over his pair of jacks. "Two pair," he said weakly. "Jacks and sixes."

"Three sixes," said Floyd as he turned over his own cards.

"Nice hand," said the Judge.

Floyd nodded and organized his chips. He was now far and away the chip leader, with roughly twice as many chips as the next man. That opened him up to new tactics. He could bully smaller stacks with large bets and more or less control the pace of the game.

The banker stood up from the table and stretched. "I tip my cap to you, Mister Kent."

"Go fishing," said Doc. "There are rods and tackle down by the dock."

"There's something else I'd like to reel in." Chuck Wagon made a lascivious show of adjusting his belt, then ambled toward the kitchen after Josie.

Floyd was about to go after him but was reluctant to leave his chips unattended. An old habit from his days as Stacks. He sat back down. Josie was a grown woman and looked like she could handle herself if the banker got fresh.

Billy shuffled the cards and dealt another hand. From the kitchen came a clanging sound, as if someone had dropped a metal pan. None of the players said a word.

Chuck Wagon stumbled back in, rubbing a red welt on his head. "She's playing hard to get. But I'll wear her down." He flopped on a sofa and was quickly snoring. Josie emerged a minute after with a tray of hors d'oeuvres, her mouth set in a hard line.

Acrid cigar smoke hung thickly in the air as the remaining gamblers traded chips, told bawdy stories, ate from Josie's platters, and drank. While the others boozed, Floyd paced himself with Scotch and soda that was mostly soda. Jack Crenshaw alone refused any alcohol.

The younger man played with a ferocious intensity that Floyd recognized as the hallmark of a gambling addict. He hung on every card, every raise, and every victory, as if his life depended on it. Floyd guessed Jack was playing with Billy's money and resented it.

Night fell. Judge Rudy was the next man out, followed by Doc. The Judge had fallen, trying to fill a gut-shot straight on the river to Jack's full house, while Doc's pocket rockets were blown up on the launch pad by Billy's three sevens. The Judge, Doc, and Chuck Wagon watched TV and told ribald jokes while Floyd, Billy, and Jack continued to play. Josie ran herself ragged trying to serve both groups.

Shortly after two o'clock, Billy Condon lost all his chips trying to go all-in with a king-high flush to Floyd's ace-high flush. When the last card fell, Billy called out to the other losers, "I'm out, fellas. It's just Jack and Floyd."

As the others came back to their seats to watch the heads-up match, Josie was heading outside.

"Going somewhere?" said Doc. "You've been engaged for the entire weekend, young lady. Leave now and you won't be paid."

"I'm not leaving," said Josie, eyes averted. "I'm, uh, going to the car for supplies. Be back in a jiffy."

Floyd detected the tremble in her voice, though no one else seemed to notice. Was it any wonder? The poor girl was probably sick to death of these men.

"Your deal," said Jack as he handed Floyd the cards.

Josie forgotten, Floyd took the cards and began shuffling them. He used a standard shuffle, as he had all night, giving no hint of the skills learned in his former life. So far, he'd played every hand according to Hoyle, never dealing from the bottom of the deck or even peeking at someone's hole cards. There was no need to cheat with these amateurs.

Floyd had a comfortable lead in chips, $205,000 to Jack's $95,000. Even so, it could be a long night. He dealt the cards as Josie returned to resume her duties as hostess.

Floyd and Jack's respective stacks changed very little as the two men swapped the dealer button, and neither man seemed capable of winning more than two hands in a row.

Chuck Wagon fell asleep on the table, his mouth drooling on the green felt until Doc slid a napkin underneath his chin. The Judge went to the couch to watch a replay of an Astros game, while Billy and Doc placed wagers on the gamblers. Billy took Jack, even though his son-in-law was behind in chips.

At five o'clock, Doc requested a break for a breakfast of steak and eggs. This roused Chuck Wagon from his stupor and brought the other gamblers back to the table.

The hardy breakfast seemed to revive the men. Floyd cleaned his plate, gulped black coffee, and organized his stacks of chips. Once again, Jack ate nothing and drank nothing. He seemed to be fueled purely by the adrenaline of the game.

When play resumed, the chip count stood at one hundred and ninety thousand for Floyd to one hundred and ten thousand for Jack. Jack, playing in the small blind, had the button and dealt the cards.

As Floyd waited for his cards, he felt the Ruger and the Bible in his jacket weighing him down like anchors. He straightened his spine with an audible crack.

"Sounded like a gunshot," laughed Billy. "Old age is a pain in the ass."

"Beats the alternative," said Doc.

Floyd ignored the banter. He tipped up the corners of his cards: the ace of diamonds and the ten of clubs. Not bad at all, especially for heads-up play. He glanced at Jack. The younger man's eyes were wide, his lips parted. He had good cards.

"Fifteen thousand," said Jack.

Floyd fought the urge to raise. He was tired, and Jack looked like he could go on forever. Floyd took a breath and called.

Jack burned a card and dealt the flop: ace of clubs, seven of hearts, four of spades. Floyd's eyes sparked as his ace became two aces. It was time to put some pressure on Jack.

"Twenty thousand," said Floyd.

Jack stared a long time at the ace of clubs on the board.

Floyd put him on a pocket pair, possibly queens or something lesser. Then Jack called.

The turn card came up a ten of hearts. Jack's nervous habit of folding a stack of poker chips into itself became a rat-a-tat-tat of machinegun fire. He liked that card. Floyd narrowed his opponent's hole cards to pocket tens—that would give Jack three tens and would beat his own two pairs of aces and tens.

Floyd checked, and Jack wasted no time in betting thirty thousand, which stirred excitement among the onlookers. Josie was moving closer, peering with interest at the growing pile of chips in the middle of the table.

"Call," said Floyd.

Jack burned a card and dealt the river: the ace of spades.

"The death card," said Judge Rudy. He crossed himself with a nervous laugh.

"Shut up," said Chuck Wagon. "It's just a card."

"Gents," said Doc, assuming the role of an announcer, "we have a pair of aces on the board, with no chance for a flush or straight draw."

"There might be two pairs out there," offered the Judge.

"That doesn't beat three of a kind," said Billy, "if someone is sitting on an ace."

"None of that beats a full house," said Josie. Every head turned to her. Jack's eyes were daggers. "Well, it's true, isn't it?"

No one bothered to answer the rhetorical question.

"Well?" said Jack as Floyd examined the board. The man was eager to bet or perhaps go all-in.

Floyd didn't answer. He had *the nuts*—the best possible hand given the cards that had been played. Full house, aces over tens. But what to do?

Floyd decided to slow-play with a token bet of fifteen thousand. Jack, sensing weakness, would raise or go all-in. If the latter, it was all over.

Jack peeked at his cards one last time. Suddenly, the chips in his hand were still, the machinegun silent. "All in," he said, trying—and failing—to put a quaver into his voice.

Floyd smiled devilishly. He was sure of it now: Jack had started the hand with pocket tens and was salivating over the board with his own full house, tens over aces.

"Call," said Floyd.

Jack turned over his pocket tens. "Full house!" he whooped triumphantly. "Tens over aces." He reached for the chips in the middle of the table.

Quick as lightning, Floyd's hand seized Jack's right wrist in an iron grip. "You haven't seen my cards yet."

Jack's eyes blazed with fury. "You'd better let go, old man. Otherwise, you'll be picking up your teeth with broken fingers."

"And if you don't let go of the chips," said Floyd, "you'll be picking up your fingers with broken teeth."

Doc, Judge Rudy, and Chuck Wagon roared with laughter.

"Jack, take your hand off the chips," said Billy. "Do it now." His son-in-law reluctantly obeyed, and Floyd released him. "Floyd, show your cards."

"Gladly." Floyd turned over his ace and ten. "Full house. Aces over tens. That beats tens over aces, Jackie-boy."

Floyd raked in his winnings and wondered if there were a more beautiful sound than chips rattling against one another. He saw the sandy beaches of Costa Rica, a hammock strung between palm trees, and a girl bringing him a drink with a little umbrella.

Jack's mouth was open, a zero frozen between his lips. He kept looking at his cards, as if willing them to be something they weren't.

"Winner, winner, chicken dinner!" cried Doc. He went to the gun safe, dialed in the combination, and took out a satchel of money. It hit the table in front of Floyd with a loud thud, while all but Jack clapped.

Floyd smiled with genuine happiness for the first time all night. No, for the first time in years. He'd done it. He'd won!

"Boys, that was one helluva game!" said Billy.

The congratulations were interrupted by the unmistakable sound of a gun's hammer cocking. The men turned to see Josie holding a silvered Smith & Wesson revolver, her eyes glinting with avarice.

"I'll take my payment now," said Josie. "I'd say it's been a pleasure serving y'all, but I'd be lying."

No one moved for a few seconds. Then Chuck Wagon stood up, his hands spread expansively. "Little lady, you should put up that gun before you hurt yourself." He took a step toward Josie.

"She's not bluffing," warned Floyd. He was easing his hand toward his Ruger. If this idiot didn't spook her into gunplay, he could clear the holster for one clean shot. Perhaps wing her, rather than kill her.

Chuck Wagon wasn't listening. He lurched toward Josie, one meaty hand reaching for her wrist. She calmly shot him right between the eyes, and the banker crashed to the floor.

Judge Rudy bent over his fallen friend. "He's dead!" he said, as if the exit wound at the back of the banker's skull left any doubt. Doc was thunderstruck, eyes wide. Billy was moaning like a demented ghost, while Jack was a coiled snake unsure where to strike.

Though his heart raced, Floyd felt calm. His hands were rock-steady, ready to deal out death.

"Everyone, hands on the table!" said Josie.

The men obeyed.

"Hell's bells," muttered Josie. "This was supposed to be a simple robbery. I have your cell phones—thank you very much for that—and I already slashed your tires. With some rope, I'd be in Mexico before anyone was the wiser. But now, I have five witnesses to murder. Sorry, boys." She raised the gun.

Doc found his voice. "Josie," he began, "perhaps we can come to an accommodation?"

Dr. Harold Brannigan never finished the thought. Four shots rang out and four bodies hit the floor, leaving Floyd the last man alive. He'd kept his hands on the table, but had positioned his right to where it could reach the Ruger inside his jacket. The woman was a crack shot, but if he could keep her talking, he might have a chance.

"Josie," he said, "you know me. I'm not like these other men." *These men who didn't deserve to be gunned down in cold blood, whatever their sins,* Floyd thought.

"Oh? That money you came with tells me different."

"I came here with fifty grand, sure, but only after I sold everything except my truck. What say we split the pot?" He actually managed a grin.

Josie looked him over from head to toe, as if considering the proposition. "I like you, Floyd. I really do. But I can't take any chances." Her gun came up.

Bluff called.

Floyd simultaneously jumped to his left and pulled the Ruger from his jacket. His aim went wide of Josie's face, while her return shots impacted to the left of his sternum. Floyd's gun slipped from his hand, and stars exploded in his vision when his head thudded against the floor.

Floyd lay still, chest on fire, listening for shots that never came. Moments later, he heard a car racing away from the lake house. Slowly, he opened his eyes and found himself staring at the ceiling vent above the poker table. Idly, he wondered how hot it was in that musty attic.

With a groan, he pulled the old Bible from beneath his jacket. The slugs from Josie's gun had stopped just short of penetrating the back cover, and his ribs were sore as hell. As he laughed, the book of books slid from his fingers and landed beside the Ruger.

"Told you I'd win, Dad," coughed Floyd. He rose on wobbly legs and placed a hand on the poker table for balance, head bowed. Finally, he picked up the Ruger and headed for the door, leaving five dead men sprawled around a bloody poker table.

The Bible had saved his life, but he wouldn't be needing it on the road he was traveling.

THEY MAY BE GODS
Stephen D. Rogers

Can you keep a secret?

Something people don't always realize when they come to Cape Cod is that the locals do more than serve them. Even more than resent them. We watch.

When you unload your vehicle into the cottage you've rented for the week. When you lug your chair, bag, and cooler down to the beach. When you sit in the restaurant cracking open a lobster. We're always watching.

Part of it is you're an outsider. You're not a threat, exactly. You're simply exotic.

You wander in and out of stores wearing "Cape Cod" as if an article of clothing might fool somebody into thinking you belong here, and we watch, not because we're afraid you'll slip a shark tooth into your pocket but because you might be someone famous, someone important.

You come here because you're on vacation. We're stuck here because we can't afford to move somewhere else, somewhere it's easier to make a living year-round.

I say this as a finish carpenter, recognizing I'm luckier than most, knock on wood. When new building slows, I'm kept busy with renovations, and the rich who own the summer homes never tire of making cosmetic changes. I don't directly depend on the flow of tourists like so many of my neighbors and friends.

My sister follows the weather forecasts with the obsession of a farmer, the stoicism of someone who makes a living at sea. Two days of rain means she's eating out of cans.

We watch. We search for signs of approval. We hunt for proof that we should keep the faith. After all, to hear you talk, we don't know how fortunate we are. We're "living the dream."

The first time I saw Saffron, she was a wide-brimmed hat floating above the passenger seat of a convertible, one bare arm conducting the sky, the color of her nails visible from across the street. Mailbox checked, junk retrieved, I went back inside, parting a curtain to see the car she had abandoned on the cobblestone drive.

The second time I saw her, she was standing on my porch in a sundress, hatless, her long golden hair unrestrained. She met my gaze. "We're renting the cottage across from you."

"I watched you move in." Did she emphasize the plural so I would understand she wasn't available?

My second sighting—our first conversation—and already she held me in her thrall. She could have asked—demanded—anything.

"Could you tell me a good place for clams?"

"Broiled or fried?"

Her eyes reflected the color of the ocean, just before dawn.

"When on Cape Cod..."

"You want the fried clam plate at Cappy's, and don't pass on the tartar sauce. Also, despite the pile of onion rings and French fries that come with the plate, you want to save room for the slaw."

"Maybe you should join us."

"I'm not sure that's such a good idea." I leaned against the doorframe. "My doctor has started using hand puppets to demonstrate the friendliness of different fresh vegetables."

A smile lit her exquisite features. "I should be getting back."

"Your husband the jealous type?"

"No. He's a killer."

She turned away before I could read her expression, walked away before I could push off the doorframe to reach out and stop her.

The third time I saw her was at Cappy's, not seated at a table sampling the native fare with her husband but sitting at the bar alone with a glass of white wine, her perch on the stool showcasing just how high this particular sundress was slit.

I put my hand on the empty stool next to her. "Taken?"

"Not yet."

Climbing up, I nodded to Peter behind the bar.

He took a fluted glass from the shelf and poured me a draft.

She chuckled. "Did you get a kickback for sending me here?"

"I won't know the answer to that until I hear how much he charges me for the beer."

Peter placed a coaster in front of me and the glass on top of that. "Thirty dollars."

"I guess I'll start a tab."

"You mean add to it." He walked away.

Saffron raised her wine. "To your thirty-dollar domestic."

I raised my beer. "To kickbacks." I sipped. "He usually charges me fifty dollars, an attempt to keep me from coming in and ordering the clam plate. My doctor's his brother."

"I thought medical professionals weren't supposed to talk about their patients."

"Here on the Cape, everybody knows everything."

She dragged a fingertip around the rim of her glass. "You don't know anything about me—a stranger come to town."

"You could be a goddess."

"A demon."

"A demon goddess. That's why I'm here asking questions, trying to determine if you're safe."

She spun to face me. "How do I know that you're safe? Tell me, what do you do when you're not asking questions?"

"I guide people like you to the hidden treasures."

"People like me?"

I shrugged. "It's not an insult."

"Is it a compliment?"

"It can be." Even though she was married, I still couldn't keep myself from flirting, assuming I was, assuming I still knew how.

I'd tired of bedding summer people a long time ago. A long time before that, the locals had tired of me. Flirting? It had been a long time.

She lifted her glass. "And when you're not a walking billboard?"

"I'm a finish carpenter."

"You work with your hands."

"And tools. Driving nails is a lot easier with a hammer. Easier on…" I touched the long side of my hand. "Whatever you call this."

"Where your second thumb would be if you had one?"

"That's a long name."

"Probably why I'm not in the business of naming things."

"And what is your business?"

Saffron took my question as a sign she should finally take a sip of wine, and she lingered so long on that action that Peter had time to appear before us.

"You two need a bet settled?"

I frowned. "What makes you say that?"

"I noticed you pointing at the side of your hand."

"Ah. The lady thinks it's called 'Where the second thumb would be if you had one.'"

"And you?"

"I'm going with 'Frank.'"

"Well, in karate, we use that surface to make a knife-hand strike."

"But what do you call it?"

"The surface we use to make a knife-hand strike."

Throwing an eye roll at Peter, who laughed as he moved down the bar, I leaned toward Saffron. "Just so you know, I preferred your name. Just as wordy, but less violent."

"You dislike violence?"

"Depends on what I'm fighting over. If I were fighting over you, violence would be appropriate. Fighting over what to call the side of my hand, not so much."

She spun her stool to face forward. "You don't want to fight over me."

"Why not?"

"You'd lose."

"That's right. Your husband's a killer." I tapped my chest. "I know how to use a trim puller."

"You should finish that beer and leave before my husband shoves that trim puller up your ass."

It wasn't so much that I disapproved of her language as I was shocked by the coarseness. Until she swore, I'd felt that our conversation had tip-toed between subjects, had skated effortlessly over a thin veneer of ice that only hinted at the dangerous waters below.

With a simple "ass," she had turned me into one.

I left the rest of my beer untouched.

The fourth time I saw Saffron, I ducked into a store to avoid being seen and watched through the plate-glass window as she and her husband strolled down the opposite side of Main Street, their faces animated, their manner relaxed.

He didn't strike me as a killer, not wearing shorts and sandals, a shirt decorated with colorful birds. I saw nothing in his posture, his gestures, that suggested he was haunted by the dark deeds he'd committed.

But then what did I know?

The couple stopped to read a mounted menu at the gate in

front of Joie de Mer. They swayed in unison. Stopped. Leaned into each other.

I had the impression that, if asked, they would deny acting like giddy teenagers drunk with the thrill of claiming their love in public. And then they would glance at each other and giggle.

Taking his measure, I grunted. Rubbed my mouth with the back of my hand. No, he didn't look so tough.

Carpentry was physical work. It was prying things apart, banging things together, and cutting through nails. It meant holding sixteen ounces of metal above your head for extended periods of time.

This tourist out there with his dopey smile? I bet I could take him in a fair fight. As to whether killers fought fair...

Apparently deciding against Joie de Mer, the couple sauntered on, taking in the day, her head thrown back in laughter, throat exposed.

I entertained the idea of jumping out into the street, knocking him down, and dragging her back in here. Thoughts that weren't mine but placed in my head by her.

Saffron would probably approve of my acting like an animal, a woman who chose to be with a killer, no better than an animal himself.

"Is there something I can help you find?"

I blinked several times before turning to face the young clerk, bracketed by displays of baby clothes. The whole store: pink, blue, and frilly white.

"No, sorry. I'm good."

The fifth time I saw Saffron was through two windows—my living room and her bedroom—while her husband backed out of the cobblestone drive and drove away between us.

The sixth time I saw Saffron was at her front door after she answered the bell.

She smiled. "If it isn't my inquisitor."

"And local guide."

"That goes without saying." Saffron smirked. "And where would you like to take me today?"

Even staring into her eyes, I didn't know how to interpret what she said. Was she friendly, flirting, or suggesting I actually take this relationship to the next level? Was she implying I should remove her killer-husband from the picture so I could have her all to myself?

If I was going to be honest with myself, I was fine with any of those possibilities so long as I could spend more time in her presence.

Demon goddess indeed.

Behind me, the sound of tires on cobblestone.

Whenever I'm down on my knees, I recall being at jobsites with my father while he installed hardwood flooring. That was his specialty. He was known the length of the Cape for being able to lay perfect floor in antique homes, rooms that weren't square, weren't even level.

The only problem was he hated the work.

The whole time I was with him, he complained bitterly about the New Yorkers who came in and bought these properties so they could vacation here two weeks a year.

Stomping the flooring he worked so hard to install without noticing the craft. Grinding in beach sand. Throwing down rugs that held the damp.

He had to prove he was better than them, that he was above their desire for high gloss, and so we lived with worn linoleum and wall-to-wall carpeting.

Dad sitting in his recliner, beer in hand, screaming at the television, jeering the Yankees and the rest of those New Yorkers who thought they were better than everybody else.

No son of his was going to be down on his knees, groveling at their feet. No, he wanted me to do something else, something he never managed to identify, and so without any other direction I fell into place beside him, tongue in groove.

He never found peace with that. Never accepted that he might feel honored I'd followed in his footsteps instead of disappointed.

I laid the board flush, pressed the butt against the perpendicular wall, and drove home two finishing nails every sixteen inches.

The seventh time I saw Saffron, I couldn't really see her at all. She was a silhouette rising out of the ocean, a shadow emerging from the sun still cresting the horizon.

A mermaid. A siren. A creature who graced us with the understanding that life could be more than mere existence, that magic was just past the end of our fingertips.

Sometimes I walked the shoreline in the morning to clear my head. Today it wasn't working.

I stood by her belongings and waited, the only thing not moving in a landscape defined by wind, waves, and the gulls that shrieked warnings as they knifed through the sky.

Striding toward me, Saffron used both hands to twist her long hair, darkened by the water, made salty if only I dared pull the strands through my teeth.

Saffron stopped in front of me, all but naked, her skin glowing.

I ignored the towel on the ground between us, glancing back and forth between her face to the beads of rainbow that nestled along her collarbones.

"How was your swim?"

"Cleansing. How was your walk?"

"This early in the morning, it's October-quiet."

"Did you follow me here?"

"No, although I'm glad to have found you. I wanted to apologize for my awkwardness around your husband."

"Then feel free to do so."

"I apologize."

"None needed." She leaned down to pick up her towel, exposing the knot at her back.

With a single sweeping motion, I could easily pluck her free.

Saffron straightened, patting her face dry. "He's not my husband."

"Excuse me?"

"The man I came here with. He's not my husband."

I shifted my footing in the sand. "It's none of my business."

She patted her shoulders before wrapping the towel around her waist. "It changes things, though, doesn't it?"

"I don't—"

Saffron cut around me and marched as though certain I would be pulled along in her wake.

I hurried to catch up, and once I reached her side, I struggled to match her pace across the uneven ground. "I hope you didn't think I was hitting on you."

"Should I?"

"You're a married woman."

"And my husband's a killer. If he knew I came here with someone, he'd see us both dead."

"Don't expect me to tell him."

Saffron stopped and waited for me to face her before she touched my arm. "Can you keep a secret?"

"I've been known to do so."

"The man I came here with, he wants more than I can give. My husband isn't the type to grant a divorce."

"And if he were?"

Saffron shook her head. "The man I came here with is nothing more than a fling. He didn't understand that. He wouldn't accept the way things are."

"Some people are never satisfied."

"What about you?" Her eyes searching. "Could you be satisfied?"

"With what?"

"The remainder of the rental? An afternoon? Right now?"

"I'm not sure—"

"You know exactly what I'm saying."

"You already have a husband and a lover."

Again, she cut around me and marched.

This time I waited a beat, watching that towel.

Could I be satisfied, bedding a goddess?

I already knew, whatever happened, that she'd haunt me. Walking the shoreline, I'd see her in the clouds. Cutting a board, I'd see her in the grain.

I rushed to draw alongside her. "Look, it's not that I don't appreciate the idea, but what you have seems complicated enough already. I like to keep things simple."

"You're someone who works with his hands, right?"

"Exactly. A finish carpenter...I'm not saying I don't run up against challenges...it's all problem-solving...but the work itself is straightforward."

"And what does a finish carpenter do exactly?"

We were off the beach and walking along the public access, the space between the brambles thin enough that we brushed against each other, and I could feel the heat coming off her.

"Finish carpentry includes everything from flooring to ceilings, from framing windows to hanging doors. Wainscoting, which most people—"

"Do you build cabinets?"

"Definitely. Both—"

She led me across the yard of her rental, up the stairs, and through the door.

"Good." Saffron drew me into her arms, against her lips, a taste of salt and sea.

It had been a long time.

She stepped backward, bringing me with her across the room, down a narrow hall, backing until she knocked up against a closed door.

Having brought me that far, she finally broke contact, giving us both a chance to gasp for air.

She exhaled. "Remember what you said."

"About what?"

"Keeping secrets."

"Your husband will never hear about this from me."

Saffron smiled. "You don't even know what this is yet."

She reached back and turned the knob, pushed the door open and pulled me inside.

I followed her into the bedroom, telling myself that I wasn't about to do anything wrong, that she'd long since passed on her vows.

She stretched her long arm and pointed.

I turned to see the bed covered with blood, her lover unmoving, covers rolled up along the edges of the bed to keep the blood from spilling onto the floor.

"It was him or both of us. If I let him tell my husband, we'd both be dead."

"We need to call the police."

"No, we don't." Saffron took my hands in hers, moving sideways to turn me away from the sight of the dead man on the bed. "This is our secret."

"You can say it was self-defense. He tricked you. He attacked you." She'd described her swim as cleansing.

"I can burn the bedding by myself. What I need from you is finish carpentry."

"What?" Even though we'd stopped moving, my head continued to spin.

"If you can build a cabinet, you can build a coffin. You're from here. You know where it's safe, somewhere nobody will be watching."

"Safe?"

"For the burial, of course. You're my local guide."

That was me, the perfect tool: living the dream.

KLDI

Josh Pachter

"...K-L-D-I," a woman's voice blared from the speakers mounted at the ends of the rain gutter that stretched from side to side of the one-story adobe-brick building, "your oldies station in the heart of the Brazos Valley, where we got the top pop and the rock that *socks* it to ya..."

Locking his K5 Blazer's door with the doohickey that'd come with the car, Helmut Erhard stood in the dusty parking lot and looked around. There was nothing much to look *at*, just brown fields as far as the eye could see in every direction, except for the squat radio-station building, the two other vehicles parked in front of it, and the tall transmitter tower that loomed behind it, pointing at the cloudless blue sky like an upraised middle finger.

Dotting the map within a thirty-mile radius of town, there were half a dozen similar enterprises: KVMJ played Top 40 and was licensed right there in Hearne, KVLX in nearby Franklin was Christian Contemporary, KAMU was the NPR affiliate down in College Station, KVMK in Wheelock called itself "Aggieland's Country Alternative" and boasted a playlist featuring "One-Hundred Percent Red Dirt."

If you wanted "the rock that *socks* it to ya," though, you tuned your dial to KLDI, 89.5 FM, which occupied this one ramshackle structure out in the middle of nowhere, halfway between the Hearne Municipal Airport and the Brazos River.

"It's ten-seventeen on a gorgeous Thursday morning," the voice from the speakers blared, "and time to reach all the way back to 1970 for one of my favorite one-hit wonders, 'Spirit in the Sky' on L-D-I, your home for all the oldies!"

Sneaking up beneath the patter was the driving beat of the song's intro, and the DJ timed it out perfectly, flipping off her mic right as Norman Greenbaum began to sing: "When I die, and they lay me to rest / Gonna go to the place that's the best…"

The song was one of Erhard's favorites, too. His daddy had somehow managed to score an advance copy of the 45, and he'd found it in his stocking on Christmas morning, 1969, a month before its official U.S. release. Just last week, he'd heard it on the TV, background music for a Budweiser commercial. Erhard shook his head at the irony of a fifty-year-old song about Jesus licensed to sell beer to millennials and, humming along with the lyrics, he swung open the front door and stepped inside.

He expected to find a receptionist, an ad salesman, *someone*, but the lobby was deserted. "Anybody home?" he called, and a male voice hollered back, "Hang on one sec! I'll be right there."

Erhard took a seat on a ratty couch that looked as if Guglielmo Marconi himself might have bought it new, and, two minutes later, as the song was coming to an end, a harried barefoot thirtysomething in board shorts and an untucked pink Oxford shirt came out from behind a door marked "Station Manager." Brown hair curled over the tops of his ears, and he wore the first soul patch Erhard had seen since their fifteen minutes of popularity amongst white men who weren't jazz musicians had withered and died a decade back.

"Freddy Czapanskiy," the guy said, grabbing Erhard's hand and pumping it. "It's pronounced *zuh-PAN-skee*, but don't worry about the spelling, it's close to impossible. You're Helmut? Sorry to keep you waiting, man. I had the owner on the phone, and that's a call I gotta take, you know what I mean?"

"Okay with me," Erhard said. "You're paying for my time."

"Understood," the station manager nodded.

"Reaching all the way back to the Fabulous Fifties for this next number," the DJ said, her volume less annoying indoors from a wall-mounted speaker a third the size of the outside pair, "here's the legendary Buddy Holly and his Crickets from 1958 with their smash hit, 'That'll Be the Day.'"

The song began, and Freddy Czapanskiy made a "come with me" motion with his index finger. "Let's have a seat," he said, "and we can talk."

He stepped back into his office, settled behind a desk almost invisible beneath piles of papers and file folders and CD jewel cases, and waved a hand at a metal folding chair propped against a wall covered with posters for concerts the station had sponsored at the Wolf Pen Creek Amphitheater in College Station and Sefcik Hall in Seaton. Erhard unfolded the chair and perched on it. It was unstable, and he worried it might not be strong enough to support his weight.

"Okay," Czapanskiy said, "so here's the deal." He nodded out toward the lobby. "That's Katie on the air now. Her real name's Mandy Garcia, but she's as Anglo as you and me. Garcia was her married name, she kept it after she and Gerry got divorced. Gerry Garcia, can you believe it? No relation, I promise you."

Fishing his notebook from his pocket, Erhard flipped it open, scribbled the date and time at the top of the page and then wrote the DJ's name. "On the air, though, she's Katie? Katie what?"

"Just between you and me," Czapanskiy said, "I thought she made a pretty sick choice, but she insisted."

Over the lobby speaker, they heard the woman's voice announce, "This is Katie Genovese on K-L-D-I, bringing you stacks of wax from the backs of our racks!"

* * *

"Spare me your righteous indignation," Mandy Garcia said, spooning sugar into her coffee. "In 1939, *at the same time* Adolf Hitler was invading Poland and World War II was getting underway, Charlie Chaplin was shooting *The Great Dictator* and playing a character called Adenoid Hynkel." She paused to blow steam from her cup, then went on. "If you don't have a problem with *that*, then explain why me calling myself Katie Genovese fifty *years* after Kitty Genovese got herself stabbed to death in New York while Lord knows how many of her neighbors watched it happen and not a one of 'em called the cops bums you out."

Helmut Erhard thought the speech sounded rehearsed. But KLDI had hired him to protect this woman from a possible attack, not to judge her career decisions or her twisted sense of humor.

"Point taken," he said, sipping his own coffee, which he took black, no sugar, just the way it came out of the bean. They were sitting in a booth at Penny's Diner on North Market. Mandy Garcia had been too busy spinning records and reading thirty-second advertising spots to discuss her situation while she was on the air, so he'd hung around the station until her shift ended at two p.m. and "Uncle Monty" Montgomery—whose real name was Jim Bob Jones—replaced her at the microphone, then led her up 485 and two blocks south on Market to Penny's.

"Ask me," she grumbled, "I don't need my body guarded. Those letters are pure bullshit." She was a reasonably attractive woman, thirty, maybe thirty-five years old, with long brown hair and spiky bangs framing a face not quite round enough to call pudgy. She wore a white V-neck T-shirt over faded jeans and a heart made out of what sure *looked* like real diamonds on a silver chain around her neck. A thin gold ring piercing the left nostril of her snub nose reminded Erhard of that girl on that sitcom with the other girl and the gay guy.

"Could *be* bullshit," he acknowledged. "But Freddy Cza-panskiy's taking 'em serious enough to call me in."

Her lips parted in the first smile he'd seen from her so far, revealing a mouthful of teeth so perfect he figured they had to be capped. "Oh, Freddy," she sighed. "I swear, that man thinks he's my big brother, not just my boss."

The smile faded as Erhard pulled the three anonymous notes from his jacket pocket and spread them out on the table between them.

eveRy breath YoU take, the first one said, the letters cut from newspapers and magazines and glued onto a folded piece of printer paper, like something out of an old kidnapping movie, *EVErY moVe yOU make, everY bONd you BreAk, eVERy steP you TAke, i'll bE waTchiNg yOu.* Erhard wasn't sure the Police exactly counted as an oldie, but he gave the wacko who'd crafted the note bonus points for effort.

ReaL cLaSSy, the second one said, not quoting a song lyric this time, *spiTTing on ThE MemoRy oF THat pOOr KitTY geNovEse—yOu'rE goNNa Get whAt's COminG tO yOu, KatiE.* The "Kit" in "KitTY" and the "Kat" in "KatiE" had been scissored from the red-and-white wrapper of a KitKat bar. The third note, all in capitals, was short and to the point: *I AM GOING TO KILL YOU, BITCH.*

Scowling, Mandy Garcia stacked the three sheets in a little pile and refolded them and handed them back.

"Seems like one of your listeners is a tad bit torqued off by your *nom de radio,*" Erhard said.

"Think so?" He could almost hear a *duh* at the end of the question. "Look, I'm real in your face on the air, that's my schtick. Anybody doesn't like it, they can tune to a different station. You'd have to be some kind of nuts to waste your time cut-and-pasting these stupid notes."

"Obviously," Erhard said, "but that's what Freddy's worried about. Anybody who listens to your show and is nuts enough to go to all this trouble just might be nuts enough to—"

"Really?" she cut him off. "You really think I'm in some kind of danger?"

"I don't know," he said, shaking his head. "What I *do* know is that's why I'm here, just in case."

Erhard eased his Glock 19 out of its shoulder holster, laid it on the passenger seat beside him, and resettled his camouflage ball cap on his head. The cap was one of his favorites, but he seriously doubted it would ever prevent anybody looking for him from spotting him. It was a ball cap, not Harry Potter's danged Cloak of Invisibility.

South San Marcos Street was residential, mostly one-story bungalows, and the San Marcos Apartments stuck out like a sore thumb: a three-story building in desperate need of refacing. The good news was that the only way in was the front door, so he didn't need to subcontract help to watch back or side entrances.

Freddy Czapanskiy was concerned for his star DJ's safety, but he was positive any attempt on her life would come after dark.

Erhard had tried to convince him that babysitting Mandy Garcia eight hours a day didn't make a lick of sense if she would be left on her own for the other sixteen, but Czapanskiy hadn't been authorized by the station owner to pay for 'round-the-clock surveillance.

A gamble? Sure, but it was a gamble the station was apparently willing to take.

That put Erhard on the job from ten p.m. to six a.m., when the Garcia woman reported to KLDI for her morning-drive-time shift. After he'd left her at Penny's, he'd mowed his poor excuse for a lawn and done two loads of laundry, grabbed an early dinner at Toodie's, then returned home for a three-hour power nap. He filled his Thermos and bought a box of Little Debbie's Nutty Buddies at the Te-Jo's, and at nine-fifty p.m. he pulled into the parking lot at 608 South San Marcos and settled in for a long night's watch.

Up to now, it had been an uneventful evening. Just after eleven, a young couple in a beat-up old F-150 had pulled into the lot and gone inside, their arms wrapped around each other's waists. The man had a key, and Erhard figured they lived in one of the other apartments and were back from a late dinner or karaoke night at the Pony Express. Otherwise, he hadn't seen a soul in—he checked his watch and saw it was a little shy of two a.m.—in the four hours he'd been sitting there. *Easy, easy money*, he hummed, not sure if Billy Joel really counted as an oldie, either. *I could get lucky, things could go right...*

Rock 'n' roll had been the soundtrack of Erhard's life. He was sixty-five years old—old enough to retire, if he could afford to, which he couldn't—and although he drew a blank on his buddy Tito Rodriguez's cell-phone number, he knew the lyrics to most likely a thousand songs, maybe more. The Beatles, the Stones, the Dead, Frankie Valli and the Four Seasons, what Katie Genovese had called the "one-hit wonders" like the Five Stairsteps and Hamilton, Joe, Frank, and Reynolds, playing that music inside his head had helped him through many a stakeout.

I can hear music, he hummed, dropping a quarter into his mental jukebox and punching up the Beach Boys, *I can hear music / The sounds of the city, baby, seem to disappear...*

Nodding along, he realized he was beginning to nod off. Maybe his age was starting to catch up with him. He reached across his weapon for his Thermos and poured himself a slug of coffee, still nice and hot and caffeinated. Not for the first time, he wondered why Glock had named a gun that held nineteen rounds the Model 17, when they also manufactured a Model 19, which was smaller and held fifteen in the mag and one in the chamber.

Gulping coffee, he put Linda Ronstadt on the turntable inside his mind. *Love is a rose, and you'd better not pick it / Only grows when it's on the vine...*

Possibly just a coincidence that *that* was the song that had come up next in tonight's rotation, but maybe his subconscious was trying to tell him something. Roses—yellow ones—were what had put him back in touch with Bonnie Barnes a year and

a half ago. He'd grown up down the street from Bonnie—
Bonnie Ulrich, then—and had always admired her, but she was
two years ahead of him in school, which had put her out of
reach. She'd eventually married Mitch Barnes, and Erhard
hadn't seen her in a coon's age when he walked into Daisies and
Daffodils, her flower shop on the corner of West Fourth and
South Magnolia, eighteen months back, to ask her about yellow
roses, having found one on poor Elsie Jordan's dead body out at
the Camp Hearne Historic Site.

Roses. That yellow rose had been the clue that had allowed
him to figure out it was Mitch who'd killed the girl. Mitch was
over at the Eastham Unit, now, serving a life sentence without
possibility of parole for capital murder. Bonnie had filed for
divorce—right around the same time as Mandy Garcia had cut
her husband loose, come to think of it—and Erhard had gotten
a call just the other day from Ursie Cantrell, the Hearne PD's
only female detective and the town's unofficial matchmaker,
informing him that the decree had been finalized and encouraging
him to get off his ass and make a move, now that the coast was
clear. Maybe he would. Maybe he *should*...

It's a little bit funny, this feeling inside, he was humming,
wondering if the "your" in "Your Song" might just turn out to
be Bonnie Barnes, after all, when he heard the gunshot.

Vaulting out of his Blazer, Glock in hand, Erhard raced across
the parking lot to the apartment-house door. Mandy Garcia had
given him her spare key, and he fumbled it into the lock and
bolted up the metal stairs to the third floor. He'd checked out
her apartment and cleared it before heading back down to take
up his watch, so he knew right where it was, at the far end of
the carpeted hallway.

All along the corridor, tousled heads were poking out of the
other units on the floor. "Get back inside," he shouted. "Lock
your doors. *You*"—he pointed at a middle-aged African-American

man—"call nine-one-one. Tell the dispatcher there's a shot fired at this address, apartment 3G, and an officer on the scene in a brown corduroy jacket and a ball cap needs backup *right now*."

The man had no idea Erhard was *not* in fact a cop, and "officer on the scene" might get the Hearne PD there thirty seconds faster than "private investigator on the scene"—and those thirty seconds might make all the difference in the world. The black guy's eyes went wide, and he shut himself into his apartment, where, unlike Kitty Genovese's neighbors, he would hopefully make the call.

Erhard found the door at the end of the hallway standing open, and he put his back flat against the wall beside it.

Ears straining to catch any sound from inside, he reached around the jamb and pushed the door wider with the barrel of his gun.

Years of experience—first as an MP stationed in Erlangen in what was then West Germany and later as a beat cop in Houston for twenty years before retiring from the force and coming home to Hearne to set up as a PI—had taught him how to enter a crime scene when you didn't know if there might still be an armed perp in residence.

Erhard took a deep breath and swung around and through the door, gun and Maglight clasped in both hands in a low-ready position. People thought the two-hand grip was just a TV thing, but he'd learned during his military training that it made for a more stable platform and was better for controlling recoil, while extending the arms gave you more accuracy.

He found the living room empty. He did a quick sweep with the light. His ears buzzed in the silence as he inched down the dark hallway he'd seen earlier to the bedroom door. His feet made no sound on the pile carpet. It was possible the gunshot they'd all heard had come from somewhere else, but that would be a hell of a coincidence. And why was Mandy Garcia's apartment door unlocked and open? She'd promised him she'd stay inside and wouldn't admit anyone but him.

Erhard reached the bedroom door. It stood slightly ajar. He had tritium inserts in the Glock's sights to help him aim in the dark, but there was a light on in the bedroom. He dropped the flash in his pocket. He peered through the crack and could just make out a form lying face down on the bed, not moving, surely Mandy Garcia, hopefully asleep and not shot. Standing over her was a man he'd never seen before—medium height, solid build, dark hair, wearing a pair of black jeans and a black T-shirt. His back was to the door, and he seemed lost in thought, unaware of Erhard's presence. He held a handgun—lookie that, a Glock 17—in his right hand, which hung limply at his side.

"Listen up, pardner," Erhard said softly, extending the gun. "I am pointing my weapon at your head. If you don't put up your hands and turn around *real* slow, I will take you down. Play it smart, okay? Don't make things worse than they already are."

Maybe ten seconds ticked by, and then the guy raised his hands and began to turn.

Ursie's going to have a long night taking this feller's statement, Erhard thought.

Then, moving so fast there wasn't time for Erhard to do anything about it, the man twisted his wrist and put the 17's barrel in his own mouth and pulled the trigger. There was a roar, and the guy dropped to the carpet, his head a mess of blood and bone and brain matter.

Erhard let out a breath he hadn't realized he was holding and went into action. There was no doubt the guy on the floor was dead, but Erhard's training took over and he scooped up the fallen Glock, just in case, and only then checked on Mandy Garcia. She was dead, too, God damn it, shot once through the back, probably sound asleep and never knew what hit her.

Reaching carefully with the tips of his thumb and index finger, he slid a thin leather wallet from the dead man's hip pocket and flipped it open. There was a driver's license visible behind a clear plastic window. The photo matched the brief glimpse of the face he'd seen before a bullet blew it apart. The name was Geraldo

Garcia, and the address was 608 South San Marcos, Apartment 2D, Hearne, Texas. This building, down one flight of stairs.

He and Freddy Czapanskiy and Mandy Garcia had been so sure from the anonymous notes that the threat was came from an outsider, none of them had even considered the possibility that it was Mandy's ex-husband Gerry who was out to get her. Maybe that had been the *point* of the notes, to divert suspicion. But why the *hell* hadn't Mandy told him Gerry was living right there in the same building? Probably still had a key to her apartment, and that's how he'd gotten in.

And why had Gerry sent the notes in the first place? Maybe he hadn't planned to kill himself. Maybe he'd thought he might be able to shoot his ex and get away with it. Maybe the notes were meant just to scare her at first, and then he'd changed his mind and decided to waste her, after all.

Really a waste of *time* to wonder about it, Erhard thought. There's never a good explanation for crazy. That's why they *call* it crazy in the first place.

Dialing the Hearne Police Department's number from the landline beside Mandy Garcia's bed, he prepared himself for a long night of questions, and for the self-recriminations he knew he'd have to wrestle with for a long time after all the questions had been asked and answered.

THE BRIDGE
Janice Law

They were in Sig's trailer, going over the final details, and even with everything that he usually found calming—the brigade flags, the stacked rifles, the boxes of ammo and dried rations, the generator, and the water purification unit—Davis found it hard to sit still. He was keyed up and nervous, and his heart was racing, even though he wasn't on anything. Not even weed, since he'd joined the Citizen Army.

But he didn't have the sense of certainty he normally had at meetings. Of course, this was an ops meeting and he was in, which was why he had tried to ask some questions, but Sig had cut him off every time with, "Need to know, Davis. Need to know."

"But my ass is going to be on the line," Davis said at last.

"All you got to do is drive the truck," Sig said. "That's all. Just drive the truck to where we tell you."

"At the time we tell you," said John.

"The precise time. That's important."

"Crucial," said John.

"I can do that," Davis said eagerly. "I can do that. To the minute. I can take care of the whole thing."

"Best not," said Sig. "Division of responsibility, remember?

Chain of command."

Though Davis craved responsibility and the accompanying glory, he loved the chain of command. The gradations and all the military lingo gave a structure to the jangling chaos of the world and kept him in the loop. "Right," he said.

Sig smiled. "All settled then." He took out a roll of bills and peeled off three fifties. "This should do you. Lou will have the truck ready. The Chevy outside is for you."

Davis had seen the wretched beater and protested, but Sig shook his head.

"You can't risk your own car. Lou will dispose of the Chevy once you're in the truck." Then his voice took on a different note, Sig's formal, this-is-important, this-is-a-command note. "Rendezvous at oh-nine hundred Tuesday; you leave now."

They all stood up. It was going forward. They were ready to roll out of the boonies and into history. Davis stuck out his hand. After the briefest hesitation, as if this were the real signal, the real moment of decision, Sig and John clasped hands with him and clapped him on the shoulder and handed him the keys to the Chevy. "We'll see you at the bridge," they said.

Davis nodded and shoved the door, which stuck, as always, in the cheap aluminum frame. He momentarily felt the implausibility of any great thing coming out of two trailers and a defunct miniature golf course, but Sig always said that World Historical Individuals can arise anywhere. And why not here? As likely here as anywhere, Davis thought. He avoided Sig's barking guard dog and got into the Chevy.

When he started the car, Davis was reassured. The body was trashed, but the engine sounded sweet. It will work. He knew it would, and he, Davis Trent, would be on TV and in the papers and on the net, though John and Sig insisted that they would all get away. *Important,* Sig had said. *Important to be away and anonymous. We want people to know that the Citizen Army is everywhere.*

And not just, Davis thought treacherously, in two trailers in

Woodville. But Sig and John, especially Sig, whose real name, Davis happened to know, was Bill Stockport, had lots of big ideas. He, Davis, had one little idea: *He was going to be famous.*

Yes, indeed. He switched on the radio. Rush Limbaugh was out of the loop as far as the Army was concerned, but Davis still liked the sound of El Rushbo's voice: calm, soothing, deliberate. With Sig, ideas always had a nervous, thrusting edge, as if the words had to struggle to get out, to get made real. Whereas Rush always sounded like he was telling you stuff that was gospel for sure and not to be debated.

Davis liked that, especially now when he was finally acting, when he was in on the ground floor and taking the first step to recover the country. Yes, it was a good feeling, and though Sig had warned him to drive carefully, Davis floored the gas and let that sweet motor out.

"Idiot," said John, who was still standing in the doorway. He could hear the roar of the Chevy accelerating on the state road. "You better be right about him."

"Davis will be all right. He wants to be famous, man."

"If he's caught, he'll be famous all right, and so will we."

"That's the beauty of the plan," Sig said. "He won't be caught, because he parks that truck, the timer goes, the bridge is hit, and there's nothing left of Davis to connect him to us. We eliminated the weakest link and once word gets out, we'll see quality recruits."

John nodded, though he, himself, would never have come up with anything so bold—or ruthless. He would just have washed Davis out of the Army and dealt with the consequences, but Sig said that they had to be like the IRA: once you joined, you joined for life. John doubted the advisability of that in his own case but usually quashed the thought. When this was over, they'd be anonymous but known. Known in the right circles, to people who counted. Then he'd see what his next step would be.

* * *

Davis drove west most of the afternoon, and the sun was blazing straight into his eyes by the time he reached Lou's farm, a hard-scrabble affair with a collapsing barn and rusting metal roofs. The truck was in a shed of half-rotted siding, but there was a good locked door on the front. Davis switched off the engine and touched the Glock in his ankle holster before tapping the horn. Lou appeared from behind the barn with two large dogs. Davis wished that the members of the Army were not so devoted to large and aggressive canines. He sat where he was and didn't open the car door.

Lou looked him over. The farmer was tall and broad-shouldered with a marked list to his left. He had a stiff knee, too, and despite his jet hair, Davis pegged him as fifty. Maybe more, for his heavily lined features had settled into a sour and disapproving expression. "You the driver?" he asked, like this was some big mistake.

"Sig said you'd have the truck ready." Davis made himself open the door and step out, even though the two wolf-like dogs immediately pressed up against him to get a closer sniff.

Lou gave a grunt to the dogs and unlocked the shed. Inside was a nondescript, green van with out-of-state plates that struck Davis as very big and real in an unexpected way. They exchanged keys, and Davis started the engine. When he heard a little stutter, it crossed his mind to point out a problem, but this was his one and only chance and he had to take it. He backed out smartly, scattering the dogs.

"She's heavily loaded," Lou warned.

Davis threw him a snappy salute. He was tempted to peel out of the driveway, until an awareness of the explosives just over his shoulder made him cautious. Though John, who knew about such things, had assured him everything was safe until detonated, Davis still felt uneasy. But because risk was necessary, he told himself. As Sig had said, no risk, no glory.

Just the same, he would have felt better with some company. Or even a working radio! Davis hadn't anticipated silence, and he regretted leaving his charger. He could have plugged in his phone and had some music or caught Alec Jones, his favorite of all the talk jocks. Now he couldn't risk running the battery down. Not when he was "under orders." He had to do this right, take no chances and follow instructions.

Although Davis was sure he could manage, his nerves were jangling by the time he pulled off the interstate some hours later. He wasn't used to so much time alone with his thoughts. When he could answer back and argue with some sports show or commentator, everything became clearer. And it was important to be thinking clearly today.

At a gas station, he bought a couple of energy drinks, a soda, and a hotdog from a rack rotating inside a heat unit. He was at the exit door when the girl stopped him. She was skinny and pale, with long, fair hair and a welt under a swollen right eye. Not exactly a looker but not bad, either. Davis sensed he wasn't seeing her under the best circumstances.

"I need a ride," she said.

Though the right answer was obvious, he hesitated just long enough to take a slug of his soda.

"I really do," she said. And in a lower voice added, "He wants to kill me."

Davis held the door for her and when they were outside, asked who.

"Guy I've been living with. I'm going to New York," she said. "Soon as I can get my bag."

"Where is it?"

She lifted her head. "Just up the road. He'll kill me for sure if I go alone. But if I have a ride..." She put a thin, pale hand on his arm. He could see the blue veins in her wrist and her bitten fingernails.

Davis felt his gut contract. "I got a delivery I gotta make. Long way to go. See, I'm only paid for on-time delivery."

"Half-a-mile. What's an extra half-mile? And you'll have company. Any trip goes faster with company."

An echo of his own thoughts! Davis turned and walked to the van without answering but she was right behind him and somehow it happened that he clicked the key twice and she opened the passenger door and climbed in. "Left out of the station," she said.

Of course, as Davis had expected, it was more than a half-mile. A state road, then a town road, then a dirt track with weeds that flapped against the sides of the van as if to bring him to his senses. The track stopped at a cottage with a swaybacked roof and missing clapboards. No dogs; that was the only positive.

"I'll turn the van. Go get your bag," he said.

Big maneuver between the lawn and the track before he got the van pointed back toward the interstate, the plan, the schedule. He turned off the engine to see her still standing to one side.

"I thought you wanted your bag," he said.

"He's got a rifle and he's drunk."

"Maybe he's passed out. He ain't deaf, is he?"

"You've got a gun," she said.

So she'd noticed, an observer, a problem? Normally, no question that Davis would have gotten the hell out of there. But he was ferrying enough explosives to blow a bridge on the Connecticut River, and he had a Glock strapped to his ankle. He was a member of the Army and a dangerous guy. What was the point of being scared? He got out of the car and took the pistol from the holster.

She led him up to the house and opened the door directly into a dark, shuttered room. Davis stepped around a clutter of boxes and beer cans, bulging black plastic bags, dirty hunting boots, old jackets. The place smelled of cigarettes and garbage, and since the only light was from the afternoon ballgame on TV, it took a moment before he saw the man slouched in a big padded recliner.

"I've come for my stuff," the girl said.

"Yeah? You and who else?" He reached down beside his chair for what Davis saw was a semi-automatic, and he felt himself step from what still could pass for normal life, normal life with the Citizen Army, anyway, to something else.

His heart was jumping. All his life Davis had had trouble coming up fast with the right words. Give him time and he could produce, but at that crucial moment, all he could find was, "Don't! I have a gun."

The man laughed. "Good for you." He was sure drunk, but he had that rifle up and the barrel wiggling around and sweeping left and right, and once he got one of his thick fingers on the trigger there would be lead scattering everywhere. He, Davis, had a job to do. He lifted the Glock with both hands the way he'd practiced and squeezed off a shot, then another.

The man's torso jumped and the semi sent a rattle of bullets into the ceiling and down the wall and how they weren't all ripped to shit Davis didn't know. The girl screamed and he did, too, but the man had been thrust back in the recliner with blood pouring from his neck, and when Davis and the girl finally shut up, it was clear to them both that he was dead.

It took Davis a minute to process this information. The girl was quicker off the mark. She disappeared and returned with a backpack and a tote bag. "What do we do with him?" she asked.

Davis took a breath and swallowed hard. Then he held up one hand and went to open the back of the van. He pretended that he didn't know what the sacks and barrels were about, even though now he was counting on them.

Back inside, he gestured for her to take the legs. Course, it was nothing like on TV, just like actually shooting someone was not at all like target practice. Shooting was terrifying, and the results were awkward and heavy and stinking enough to make you lose your lunch. Fortunately, she didn't ask what he was delivering or what he had in mind. If she had, just at that moment, Davis was afraid he might have shot her, too. That was an idea he didn't want to revisit.

They washed their hands and wiped their clothes and left the house unlocked. Though Davis started the van right up, he had to put his head down on the steering wheel for a moment. A deep breath, two, three, then he put the van in gear, and they drove away. Well after dark, they stopped at a motel within easy reach of the morning's target. He told himself that the girl was good cover, that having her along was somehow a plus instead of a massive screwup and totally bad ops.

In the morning, he knew it was a mistake. To take her along was impossible, but to drop her at one of the rest stops was potentially disastrous. She'd remember him for sure, and she was sharp; he'd realized that belatedly. She'd had a look at the barrels, and with all that was on TV lately, she might have figured out what they were and how he planned to dispose of Jackson. That was the man's name. He'd killed a man without knowing his name. He guessed that was an Army thing and it made Davis deeply uneasy.

Round about seven a.m., when they were caught in the morning rush hour traffic and Davis was having to concentrate like mad because the clock was ticking and the van had no pickup on the hills, she told him she wanted him to drop her off.

He shook his head. "It's complicated," he said. That's what people wrote on Facebook when they were in complex relationships and, boy, was it apt now.

"You gonna shoot me, too?"

He glanced away from the road, felt the van bear in toward the fast lane, and had to jerk the wheel to recover.

"You gonna put me in the back like Jackson?"

He denied it, though Sig's voice somewhere in the back of his mind said that eliminating her was the obvious solution. *Obvious solution* was one of Sig's phrases. Davis had once liked it a lot more.

"There's a rest stop in ten miles. There will be truckers. I'll get a lift."

Davis glanced at her again and thought she probably would. There was something chilly and able beneath the waif-like exterior that had impelled him to help her. "I'm under orders," he said, his voice little more than a mumble. "And you're a security risk.

Need to know," he added, although that sounded fantastical to him now.

"You think I'm calling the cops? With Jackson's blood all over the house? *Please officer, it wasn't my fault, this strange guy with a handgun walked in and shot him.* You see that flying?"

He didn't, if he was honest. "Jackson will be gone," he said. "Jackson's not the worry."

She was silent then but maybe anxiety was making Davis sharp, too, because, clear as if she'd spoken, he knew she planned to jump out of the van. She'd put her backpack on her knees and stuffed some things from the tote bag into her pockets. Lucky they were rolling along at fifty miles an hour with streams of traffic on both sides.

"I don't want to die," she said finally. They were close to the exit Davis needed, and he began hoping to miss the traffic lights.

"Nobody's going to die," he said, and now he thought maybe it would be best if they were stopped at a light. If she jumped out like a crazy person, dodged the traffic, and got the hell out of his life, John and Sig would never need to know, would they? They'd come out of the "control" shack and shake his hand and the Citizen Army would get in Sig's car and head out while behind them the sky turned black and red. They wouldn't need to know, so now instead of hoping to miss the lights, he began looking for one. "Nobody's going to die."

"Huh, I know what you've got in the back," she said. "I know the smell of fertilizer—any farm kid knows."

"Yeah, it's for this big commercial farm down the valley."

"Bullshit. You're setting off a bomb."

Davis gripped the wheel, his nerves fried, his teeth chattering. He couldn't speak for a minute and then he said the foolish thing, "Not me, it's not me. On a timer. I just have to get the van there, that's all. There by oh-nine hundred. Nine o'clock, not a minute later."

He was slowing for the side road that led to river access. "We're going to make it, we have five minutes," he said, as if

113

she might have been all worried about the success of the op.

"Idiot! We'll all be killed, you, me, everyone! No witnesses! No evidence!" Her voice rose to a scream. "Slow the hell down and let me out!"

Not true, Davis told himself. He trusted Sig and John. She was just one of the haters, but in spite of himself, he must have let up on the gas because her door swung open and she tumbled off the seat. He snatched at her shirt, caught her, lost her and lunged again, sending the van wobbling across the track.

He regained the wheel but now it was too late. The numbers were turning over on the dial above the clapped-out radio, and his door was open and he was flung toward the gravel. Davis had to stop her, he just had to, so he'd have an explanation for Sig and everything could still go forward. He hit the ground with a tremendous thump, rolled over twice on the sharp gravel and emptied the air from his lungs.

He tried to shout, to warn, to explain, but he had no breath. The girl was stumbling up the track on her feet, on her hands and knees, on her feet again. Davis had time to wonder what Sig would do about her before the van accelerated toward the control shack and burst with a great roar.

The van heaved itself into the air. Like a cow struggling to its feet, Davis thought, and the problem of what to do about the girl was replaced by terror. He would not see her reach the roadway, her eyebrows singed, and her face blackened. He would not see her waving to startled drivers, sirens wailing in the distance. He would not see the TV clips or the screaming headlines. Davis was going to have a moment of fame, but his very last thought was of a tremendous cow-like something that leaped into the air. Then one of the metal sides blew out from the truck, crushing him as the fireball engulfed the shed, Sig and John and Davis, himself, and every living scrap all the way down to the rocks along the river.

A FASTER WAY TO GET THERE
Joseph S. Walker

Haden Stoker was in his second season as a promising defensive lineman for the Kansas City Chiefs when the final play of his career made him the most talked about NFL player of his generation. The Chiefs were playing their fourth game of the season at home, against the Seahawks. Seattle quarterback Paul Osterman was in the middle of the field, down on one knee, following a completely routine pass play that had gained four yards. The players on both teams were milling around, working their way back into their lines, when Stoker walked up behind Osterman, knocked off his helmet, and latched a giant forearm across his throat in a vicious chokehold, at the same time using his other hand to claw at Osterman's eyes.

It took the other players a few seconds to realize what was happening, and a few more seconds to get to Stoker and pull him away. By that time Osterman was unconscious, his windpipe nearly crushed, one eyeball mangled. Paramedics saved his life, but he lost the eye and, thanks to the minutes his brain was without oxygen, his reflexes. He would never play football again.

Neither, obviously, would Haden Stoker.

A picture taken from the sidelines, showing him seeming to laugh with glee during the assault, was on the front page of every newspaper in the country the next morning. By nightfall he had been banned from the game for life, forbidden to set foot in a stadium—even if he bought a ticket. Weeks of stories followed, detailing Stoker's childhood of poverty and deprivation in Appalachia, his mother dead of a meth overdose, his father killed in prison. Stern editorials made him a household name, framing him as the embodiment of everything from the drug epidemic, to the collapse of rural America, to the viciousness of the modern game, to the abuses inherent in white privilege. Stoker himself never said a word. He gave no interviews, issued no statements, and in due course became what every American celebrity becomes: a vaguely remembered footnote.

Three years later Stoker was leaning back against the wall in a poorly trafficked corner of a casino in Tennessee, sitting on a folding chair on the verge of collapsing under his considerable bulk. His arms were folded across his chest and his eyes were hidden behind jet-black shades, despite the dim lighting in the room. The banner hanging from the table in front of him read *Meet Haden Stoker* in giant red letters. Underneath this, smaller lines in black offered autographs for twenty dollars, personalized photos for forty, and "Osterman reenactment photos" for one-hundred. Cash only, please. In the twenty minutes I'd been watching him from my perch at a slot machine thirty feet away, he'd had no takers. One woman, clearly drunk, had staggered up to the table, but the man with her had grabbed her arm, whispered urgently into her ear, and she had turned away with a look of revulsion. Stoker gave no indication that he'd noticed her at all.

"This is boring as fuck," Junebug said. "Let's just go talk to him. That's what Lester sent us to do."

I stuck a quarter in the machine and pushed a button. I'd been doing this once every few minutes in case any casino employees got curious about our presence. I knew it was a wasted effort, because Junebug, genetically incapable of standing still for more than ten seconds and wearing a yellow shirt I was afraid to look at directly, had surely been a focus of attention for the eyes in the sky since he'd walked through the door. My suggestion that he wait in the car had not been well-received.

"That is the largest human being I have ever seen in real life," I said, "and he is globally infamous for ripping a man's eye out while attempting to squeeze his head off his body and nearly succeeding. I'm not going to go interrupt his effort to make a few bucks."

"Christ, I hate the way you talk," Junebug said. "Just say you're scared of him."

"Okay," I said. "I'm scared of him."

Junebug snorted. "I'm gonna go hit the head."

"He's supposed to be done at three. That's only a few minutes off."

"Whatever. Try not to let him kill you before I get back." He turned and practically bounced off the machines on either side of the aisle as he walked away. There was a better-than-even chance that his sudden urge for the facilities was more chemical than biological. If security decided to search him, we would be in a hell of a mess.

While I had been talking to Junebug, Stoker had gotten himself some actual customers, three clean-cut men in their early twenties. They were holding drinks and wearing matching T-shirts with Greek letters on the back. I couldn't hear what they were saying, but the tallest one reached into his pocket and was counting out bills while his buddies laughed and punched his arms. He tossed a wad of cash on the table. Stoker took it and tucked it in his pocket. He put his sunglasses on the table, stepped out from behind it, and gestured.

The tall boy handed his drink and phone to his buddies and got down on one knee. Standing behind him, Stoker looked like Andre the Giant visiting Munchkinland. He leaned forward to put an arm across the boy's throat and one massive hand over his face, then looked at the boy with the phone and twisted his expression into a dead-eyed approximation of his hysteria in the real Osterman photo. None of the boys were laughing now. From this far away I could see the tension in the tall one's body. The boy with the phone took a couple of pictures quickly, and the tall one almost fell over in his haste to get up and out of the hold. He grabbed for his drink and walked away without looking back, his friends trailing behind him.

Stoker picked up a duffel bag from behind the table and put a stack of photos in it, then began folding the banner. It was a couple of minutes before three, but apparently, he wasn't running out the clock. Junebug was nowhere to be seen. I got up and crossed the floor.

"Mister Stoker," I said. "Can I have a minute?"

"Time's up," he said, not looking at me. "I'll be back next month, catch me then."

"I'm not here for an autograph. Do you remember Lester Trawley?"

Now he did look at me. I almost took a step back. "I don't talk to reporters."

I held up my hands. "I'm not a reporter. I work for Lester. He'd like you to come have a talk with him."

The big man put his sunglasses back on. "About what?"

I shrugged. "If my boss wants to talk to his long-lost cousin, who am I to ask questions?" I reached into a pocket and spread five one-hundred-dollar bills on the table. "He said this is yours, just for coming to hear him out."

I couldn't see his eyes, but the money was having an impact. "Last I heard, Lester was inside."

Junebug chose that moment to rejoin us. He seemed a little less jittery, though his pupils were pinpricks. "Hey, hey, Haden!" he said. "Is my man here filling you in?" His eyes flashed to the money on the table and I saw his mouth twist. He'd spent most of the drive trying to convince me that three hundred would do the job, and that he and I could split the other two. Stoker might have seen the look. He picked up the money and tucked it away.

"Lester's been out a little over a year," I said. "Prison overcrowding."

"Where is he?"

"He's at a place in northern Alabama. About an hour and a half. We can take you there and bring you back, or just lead you if you want to take your own car."

"Don't have a car," he said. He finished putting the banner in the duffel bag, zipped it up, and shoved it into Junebug's chest. "Carry my shit. I hope you didn't bring a fucking Prius."

We hadn't brought a fucking Prius. We had one of the big black SUVs Lester liked his people to drive, probably because that's what Tony Soprano drove. I opened the passenger door for Stoker, but he ignored me and got into the back seat, sliding to the middle of the bench as the shocks adjusted to him. I shrugged and walked around to the driver's side. Junebug took shotgun, putting Stoker's bag between his feet.

"Go through that McDonald's up there," Stoker said as I pulled out of the casino's big parking lot. His shoulders filled my rearview mirror. "Get me five Big Macs and two large Cokes."

Junebug twisted around in his seat as I got into the drive-through line. "I'm Junebug," he said. "I'm, like, Lester's number-one guy, so you'll be seeing a lot of me. This here is Doc. He mostly just drives, but he's good for errands."

Stoker had no comment on this. He was still wearing the shades, and his face showed about as much expression as the steering wheel.

Junebug ran a hand over his mouth. "You and me never met, I don't think, but I grew up around here, same as you. Remember when that casino used to be a mill? Back when we was kids you had to go to Vegas, you wanted to gamble."

I ordered Stoker's food and pulled ahead toward the window.

Junebug punched me in the shoulder. "Asshole, you think to ask if I wanted anything?"

"You had plenty of chance to say something. You can't count on me to think of these things, June. I mostly just drive."

"Asshole," he said.

I handed Stoker his food. He made no gesture toward paying. We got back out onto the main road. For a few blessed moments Junebug sat and sulked quietly to himself. I couldn't tell if it was because I hadn't gotten him any food or because Stoker was ignoring him. He kept sneaking peeks at the big man, who was working his way through the sandwiches at an impressive rate. As he finished each one, he rolled down a window and tossed the wrapper out. I managed to refrain from saying anything about littering.

After a few miles Junebug twisted around again. "Haden, man, I'm sure everybody asks you this, but I gotta know, dude. Why'd you do it? Did Osterman fuck your woman or something?"

Stoker opened the window, dropped out a wrapper, and closed it again.

"I've always told people that's the only thing makes sense, you know? I mean, that would explain why you looked so fucking happy when you were choking that dude out. I was watching that game, man, in a bar in—fuck—I wanna say Birmingham. I swear to Christ I stood up and cheered. Fucking hilarious. Damn, man, it is unreal to be in this car with you."

Stoker finished one of his drinks. He took the lid off and shook a few ice cubes into his mouth and threw the cup out the window.

Junebug looked at me, back at Stoker. "Hey, man, nobody will hear anything you got to say from Doc and me. Not even Lester. I dig you've got this whole mystique thing going on, but I got to know man, I swear. Why'd you do it?"

"I couldn't think of a reason not to," Stoker said. "Turn on some music."

"Absolutely," I said, reaching for the controls of the satellite radio. "Anything in particular?"

"Something loud," he said.

I found a station playing rap and cranked it. Junebug shouted something I couldn't catch, but I heard Stoker's reply.

"Louder," he said.

I obliged. Junebug opened his mouth to shout again, realized it was useless, and slumped back into his seat, shoving his hands into his pockets. I wouldn't have been surprised to see him kicking his heels against the floor.

We rode along like that for a little better than an hour, rap pounding, Junebug pouting, Stoker staring straight ahead, me just trying to eat up the miles. We crossed into Alabama and a little while after that I took an exit, the first of several turns we'd be making onto progressively smaller roads. Junebug reached for the radio and snapped it off. "Pull into this gas station," he said. "I need the crapper."

I parked at the edge of the lot. Junebug hopped out of the car before I'd fully stopped and half jogged toward the building. I opened my window and killed the engine. After the past hour the silence was like a physical presence. I let my head fall back against the seat and shut my eyes. A few minutes passed, the only sound an indistinct buzz of conversation from some women standing around their cars by the pumps.

"You actually a doctor?" Stoker said.

"No," I said. "I was in the doctoral program for literature at Alabama. Still am, I guess, technically."

Stoker shifted his weight, and the car rocked a little. "I haven't seen Lester since I was fifteen," he said. "But you don't seem like the kind of guy I'd expect to be around him."

I let that sit for a minute before I said anything. "I've got a brother," I said. I stopped and cleared my throat. "A brother. He owes a lot of money to your cousin."

"So let him work it off."

"He can't," I said. I didn't elaborate. I opened my eyes and watched Stoker in the mirror. He stretched his neck and rolled his shoulders.

"Don't know anybody would work that kind of debt for me," he said. "Haven't got a brother and my mother never had time for anything she couldn't snort. My daddy spent the first ten years of my life beating the shit out of me with anything he could lay a hand on. Then he went to jail after he killed a man in a bar for saying something he didn't like. I went to visit him once, when I was sixteen. My high school coach said I needed to make peace with him. Daddy thought that was the funniest thing he'd ever heard. You know the last thing he ever said to me, before somebody did the world a favor and shanked him?"

I didn't say anything.

"'See you when you get in here,'" he said.

Before I could reply to that, Junebug opened the passenger door and got in, carrying a bag of Doritos and a bottle of soda. "Let's go," he said. I started the engine and pulled out, leaving the radio off. Junebug tore open the bag and shoved a fistful of chips into his mouth. "I guess it was my turn to get you nothing, Doc." He wiped orange grease and crumbs across his chest.

"No worries, June," I said. "I could have said." I glanced in the mirror. Stoker's face was dead again, a blank stone wall.

Unless you'd been to Lester's country place before you'd have a lot of trouble finding it. The last several miles were on back country roads that sometimes washed out completely in the spring rains. Lester had houses in Birmingham and Chattanooga and, I think, other cities, but he liked the country place, where anybody trying to come get a look at him would stand out like they were lit in neon.

We pulled into the yard about half an hour after leaving the gas station. There was an old wooden barn with ghosts of red paint still visible in a few spots, and a ramshackle white farmhouse where Lester had the help sleep. He slept himself in a big, fancy RV parked alongside the barn. A new prefab shed, with a generator and satellite dishes, filled the space between the barn and the house. Various vehicles were scattered around, including three heavy-duty pickups parked in a row, each hitched to a trailer with a motorboat. I'd never seen the trucks or the boats before. A few men I knew and didn't like were on the porch of the house, drinking beer.

I parked close to the trucks and killed the engine. As we were all getting out of the SUV the door to the RV opened and Lester came out, pulling a shirt over a wiry torso dark with indecipherable ink. He came toward us, grinning and running one hand through his greasy mop of black hair.

"Haden by-God Stoker," he said. "You done growed some since I set eyes on you last, boy."

"Lester," Stoker said. It might have been a greeting, or simply an acknowledgement, or an identification. He didn't take off the glasses or hold out a hand.

"Yeah, we got him, Lester," Junebug said. He waved an arm at Stoker like he was showing off a car he'd just bought. "No trouble at all. We made good time. Haden had some burgers on the way down."

"That's true," I said, leaning against the SUV. "It was real damned exciting. I'm sorry you missed it."

Lester wasn't paying any attention to us. He stuck his hands in his back pockets and rocked back on his heels, surveying his cousin. Stoker had a-foot-and-a-half and probably two-hundred-pound advantage, but Lester looked at him like he was a prize bull he was thinking of bidding on. "Your daddy and mine surely did raise some hell back in the day," he said. "Put the fear of God into everybody south of Nashville for a lot of years, when they wasn't whupping on each other. You remember those days?"

"Yeah," Stoker said. "You wanted me, I'm here. What do you want?"

"I was real sorry to hear about it when your daddy passed," Lester said as though Stoker hadn't spoken.

"I wasn't. What do you want?"

"My daddy's still inside," Lester said. "Angola, you believe that shit? Don't ever get popped in Louisiana, you can help it. I don't get over to see him as often as I should, but he'll be real happy to hear about you and me getting our heads together."

Stoker walked over to the RV. He took hold of the mirror mounted by the driver's window and, with no apparent effort, snapped it off. He tossed it in the dirt at his cousin's feet. "Lester," he said, "if you don't tell me what the fuck you want right the fuck now, I'm going to break some more of your toys. I might start with your little toy soldiers."

The men on the porch were standing now. At least two of them had guns on their hips. Junebug whistled softly but, mercifully, for once, didn't say anything.

A storm flickered across Lester's face, but he tamed it. "Damn, Haden," he said. "I just figured you and me would ruminate on the old days some before we got down to business."

"Business," Stoker said. "I like that word. Talk more about that."

"Okay, Haden," Lester said. He turned and walked toward the prefab shed, waving a hand at the men on the porch to tell them to settle back down. "Come with me and I'll show you what's up. Doc, you come, too."

"How about me, Lester?" Junebug said.

Lester didn't break stride or look at him. "Naw, June. You already know what's happening. Go have a beer with the boys."

Stoker and I fell in step behind Lester. I'd never been invited into the shed before. I would have been just as happy not to go in there now. Lester usually called it his war room. The shades on the windows were always closed tight, and nobody ever used it when he wasn't around. He opened the door and went in. Stoker had to turn sideways and duck a little to follow him. I went in last. Lester told me to close the door behind me as he turned on the lights.

A couple of card tables and some folding chairs were the only things in the room. Lester sat down at a place with a laptop computer, hit a few keys, and a big TV mounted to the wall came alive, showing a map of the Gulf coast.

Lester leaned back and looked up at Stoker. "You and me weren't around yet in '92," he said. "But you must have heard the story about what our daddies did. They loved telling that one." He hit a couple more keys on the computer and the map on the TV suddenly showed weather information, including a big storm that had begun dominating the news in the last few days. "It's time for us to do an encore, cuz."

Stoker took off his glasses and stared at the screen. "You're fucking kidding me."

"Nope," Lester said. He was clearly delighted with himself. "Would I kid about a chance that comes along a couple of times a decade, maybe?"

I raised my hand. "I'm not versed in all the family lore," I said. "Somebody want to fill me in on 1992?"

"Hurricane Andrew," Stoker said. He was still staring at the map.

"Biggest ever to make landfall in the States, until Katrina," Lester said. "Hit Miami like a goddamn nuke. Wiped out thousands of houses. And our daddies were ready for it. They got a truck and a boat and slapped Red Cross logos on them and spent a week and a half absolutely fucking pillaging."

"I think the term you want is looting," I said.

"Call it what you want," said Lester. "Man, you'd be amazed what people leave behind in a time like that. They found safes still full of cash and jewelry. They started out grabbing TVs and computers, but there was so much to take that they stopped picking up bulky crap like that. Focused on shit they could hide easy. Bearer bonds. Watches. Guns, man. Hell, they found a couple of actual gold bars in one house. Biggest score of their lives."

"It's bullshit," Stoker said. "Two idiot rednecks making up stories."

"No way," Lester said. "My daddy showed me some of the shit he hung onto for a rainy day. It happened." He got up and pointed at the map. "And right now, right this minute, Hurricane Daryl is coming in, and it makes Andrew look like a summer breeze. It turned last night. Was supposed to hit somewhere in Texas, but now it's heading straight for a bullseye on Mobile. Landfall tomorrow morning."

"Mobile isn't Miami," I said. "Not nearly as much wealth."

"It ain't a fucking slum," Lester said. "There's plenty of rich people in Mobile, and let me tell you something about rich Southerners, Doc. They don't never trust banks completely. They always keep something liquid nearby, just in case all those boys up in New York get ideas."

"So you picked up those boats out there," Stoker said.

Lester nodded, pleased he was getting through. "I got three boats, we send three teams, we oughta do three times as well," he said. "I've got Red Cross and FEMA decals for the trucks and the boats. You leave tonight, wait out the main part of the storm somewhere around Auburn, then you'll probably beat most of the real disaster teams there. I figure you two plus Junebug and maybe one other man as one of the teams."

"What about you?" I asked.

"I'll be staying here," Lester said. "Coordinating."

"That sounds like something you might could use some help with," I said. "Can I nominate myself for the coordination team?"

"Doc," Lester said. "We're done talking about this. You're gonna do any fucking thing I tell you to do."

"I told you I won't kill anybody," I said.

"I don't need you to. I got people for that."

"So get people for this."

"I got people for this," he said. "I got Junebug, and Cousin Haden here, and you, and anybody the fuck else I say."

We were so focused on each other that we both started when Stoker spoke. "What makes you think you've got me?" He had put his sunglasses back on.

Lester laughed. "Come on, man, this is destiny. I'm listening to hurricane updates, and what's the very next thing I hear? A radio ad for a personal appearance by my long-lost cousin. It's like, damn, I can take a hint."

Stoker shook his head. "There's a reason I've stayed away from you people. I don't need this."

"Oh yeah?" Lester said. He got up close to Stoker, actually poked a finger in his chest. "Got a lot of golden opportunities lined up? People anxious to give a job to the guy who committed attempted murder on live TV? What are you going to do, start a golf school with OJ? You must have burned through whatever you made a while ago. Oh, I remember watching you, fucker, wearing your goddamn suit for the draft and talking to Bob Costas. Thought your shit didn't stink. Well, where did that get you?"

"Away from here," Stoker said.

"You think so? Where are you standing now? Doesn't look very away to me. Fuck, the only reason you aren't behind bars already is because the league can't stomach the idea of players being charged for what they do on the field." He actually put both hands against Stoker's chest and shoved, with no notable effect. "I'm giving you the only shot you've got, you dumb fuck, and you should get on your knees and thank me."

Stoker stared at him. "You're saying I was always gonna end up like Daddy," he said.

"Hell, yes," Lester said. "Blood tells. Ain't no way off that road."

Stoker shot a glance at me, looked back at his cousin. "Guess you're right," he said. "But I can think of a faster way to get there." He reached out with his left hand and grabbed the front of Lester's shirt and jerked him forward, at the same time bringing his right elbow around to meet Lester's nose with a crunch I felt all the way down my spine. Lester didn't make a sound. He just dropped straight to the floor like every bone had vanished from his body.

Stoker dug into his pocket and came out with a phone. He tossed it to me. I caught it on sheer reflex. "Film this," he said. "You know how, right?"

I fumbled with the phone. For a minute I thought I was going to just drop it. The Osterman picture was in my mind, seeming more vivid than the phone I was actually looking at. I thought about the tall boy going stiff in the casino, the mirror in the dirt outside.

Finally, I managed to open the camera function and select video. I held up the phone and nodded at Stoker. He nodded back, took off his sunglasses and tossed them to the side. He looked straight at the camera. "My name is Haden Stoker," he said. "This is my cousin, Lester Trawley."

He leaned over and picked up Lester. The lower half of Lester's face was a mask of blood. His eyes were half open, but I don't think he could have possibly been conscious. I hope not, anyway. Stoker held him against the wall. Lester's feet were dangling two feet off the ground. Stoker put both hands around his cousin's throat and squeezed. What I could see of Lester's face turned purple. His arms lifted away from the wall for a second, hands contorted into claws, and then fell back.

It didn't take long. When it was clearly over Stoker let the body fall and turned back to the camera.

"Let's see how many times you replay that," he said. "Turn the fucking thing off."

I stopped the video. He held out his hand and I tossed the phone to him. He watched a couple of seconds, then started pushing other parts of the screen. After a minute he put it back in his pocket.

"I just sent that video to a dozen different TV stations," he said. "That ought to do the trick."

My mouth was dry, but I managed to talk. "What now?"

"You still got the keys to the car we drove here?"

I nodded.

"Go get in it. Drive away. Live your life."

"You want me to just leave you here?"

"You know much about digital video?" he asked. He sat down heavily on one of the chairs. "You learn a lot about this shit when people act like you're Bigfoot everywhere you go, trying to sell pictures of you just living your life. The image is tagged with a location. One of those TV stations will send it to the cops, and they'll be able to find this place from it. They'll probably be on the way within an hour."

"Some of those guys outside are armed."

"I'll lock the door behind you. Maybe they'll break in. I don't think they'll be very happy about it if they do."

I didn't move.

"Doc," he said. "What's going to happen to that brother of yours if you die or get arrested here today?"

Junebug stood up when I came out of the shed. I heard the lock click behind me. Most of Lester's other men were gathered around the boats now, looking them over, paying no attention to me. I nodded at June and walked toward the SUV, forcing myself not to run. Junebug stood on the porch, watching me, his head tilted to one side. When I got to the SUV and looked back, he had come down into the yard and was looking back and forth between me and the shed. He held his hands up, miming a question. I shrugged and got in and started the car rolling and managed to get to the edge of the yard before I punched it, fishtailing briefly until friction caught the tires and sent me hurtling down the dirt road.

I'm not proud of the fact that I left Haden Stoker in that shed, and I don't believe in fate. But I do believe that whatever he was going to meet there was something he'd been expecting to call on him for his entire life.

TALK ABOUT WEIRD

Albert Tucher

"Yuck," said Diana.

She smiled to take the sting out of the comment, but she let the opinion stand.

The new man shrugged.

"I get that a lot. Everybody so far, matter of fact."

"Well, yeah."

"In that case, you can tell me what the problem is. I thought you were in this for the money."

She turned on her side to study him on the sagging motel mattress. She liked a trim waist on a man. Too bad he didn't have one. He also seemed to need her refusal explained to him.

"You're asking for a major commitment," she said. "Stubble is quick. That I could do. But it would take me weeks to look like I've never seen a razor in my life. And as for the other thing, I couldn't work for anybody else while I was getting ripe."

"I'll make it up to you. Just tell me how much money you'd lose."

"But you couldn't pay me enough to live with myself."

"European women used to live with themselves just fine."

This time his smile took on a tinge of reminiscence. "Those were the days. I grew up in Germany. My dad was an Army officer back in the seventies. The women were the whole package—clothes, makeup, style, everything. But completely unshaved. Sophisticated and raw at the same time. Hottest thing I ever saw."

He smiled at the ceiling. "Or smelled. They'd go days without bathing. I loved riding the streetcar, especially rush hours during the summer. Sometimes I would just close my eyes and breathe. I don't think I ever went ten whole minutes without a hardon."

"You sure you weren't just an average fourteen-year-old?"

"No, this was more than that."

He looked at the sheet tenting over his groin.

"Speaking of which—"

"That's what I'm here for."

His name was Phil Handler, and he had a good reputation in the online discussion groups—gentle and considerate, always ready with his money, never canceled or no-showed. Like any man, he might have depths of the kind that a smart hooker avoided stirring up, but so far, the only thing about him was this awkward kink he kept bringing up.

She had a feeling he wouldn't call again. Sometimes the business was like that.

Diana knew the woman.

For a moment it confused her to see Bernice Stephens on the TV screen instead of face to face in a motel parking lot. It got worse when she read the crawl.

"Murder in Lakeview."

The still photo of Bernice included a teenage boy and girl with their faces digitally obscured.

Cut to the network's New Jersey reporter standing in front of a 1970s split level that the Smithsonian should preserve before a McMansion devoured it. Diana listened between the lines, but so far, Bernice was a suburban housewife. The news people didn't know what she had done to pay the bills, but sooner or later they would.

Diana turned off the TV and left by the front door of her rented Cape Cod. She started driving toward neighboring Lakeview, where she had evening dates lined up with two of her low-maintenance clients.

Their familiarity calmed her, but she couldn't cling to them indefinitely. She had used the old saying herself: "Men don't pay me for sex. They pay me to go away."

So she went. When she got home in time for the eleven o'clock news, Bernice's secret life was secret no more, and the anchorman was milking the titillation. Could it get better than a soccer-mom prostitute?

Diana changed the channel several times. No one seemed to know more, which suggested that the cops didn't either. And that told her what to expect.

The next morning, she woke early. It was tact on her part, because Detective Tillotson wouldn't want to think he had dragged her out of bed. Lakeview was his jurisdiction, and the case would bring him to pick her brain. She brewed a whole pot of coffee. He would need it.

He rang the bell just before seven. She opened the door, and, as always, she wondered what he looked like when he wasn't exhausted. His poplin summer suit was already deeply creased, and it would only get worse. She turned and headed for her kitchen. By now he didn't need an invitation to follow her, or to take his seat facing the doorway. She poured coffee and sat facing him.

"So you heard," he said.

"Just what was on the news."

"Bernice Stephens aka Jacqueline. Did you already know her real ID?"

"Sure. We don't do professional names with each other."

"Anything else you can give me?"

"How about a suspect?"

"That would help."

"Practically the only thing Bernice could talk about online was her ex. He managed to leave her with some pathetic alimony, which was why she was doing my kind of work. So he basically drove her into prostitution and then used that to get custody of the kids."

"Bryce Stephens, her ex, is a lawyer. Criminal defense is his area, but he knows how to manipulate the system."

"Sounds like he's not your favorite person. So you're looking at him?"

"We always look at the husband, or the ex. But I'm not so sure she was still hooking."

"That would be news to me. What makes you think so?"

"She was shot at home, and I'm told she always kept business and personal stuff separate."

"Most of us do."

"And there's something we've been holding back."

"Meaning I shouldn't talk about it."

Sometimes she wondered what kind of risk he was running by reporting to a civilian, and not just any civilian.

"It seems she'd been letting herself go."

"How?"

"She hadn't shaved in a while."

"I'm not sure how much that means. She was on the bush side of the big shave-or-don't-shave debate. Without her, it'll be just me versus everybody else. Locally, anyway."

"It's more than that. She hadn't been shaving at all. Legs, armpits, anything. And she smelled like she'd forgotten where the shower was. Enough to notice even over the usual crime-scene odors."

"Oh."

"What?"

"There's somebody else you need to talk to. Name of Phil Handler."

"Who's he?"

"A client. I saw him once, a few weeks ago."

She told him the rest. He absorbed it without flinching, which reminded her again that hookers weren't the only ones who had seen everything.

"I don't owe him anything," she said.

His look told her he understood. Someday she might have to choose between Tillotson and a regular client, and this relationship that helped keep her in business would suffer.

But not today.

"So Bernice might have been doing this thing for him. But wouldn't she have mentioned it online?"

"Maybe not," Diana said. "He's been getting turned down by everybody in the area. Bernice might have felt embarrassed to be the one he finally talked into it."

"Makes you wonder why she'd agree to it."

"Handler was going to pay me for not seeing anybody else. Maybe that kind of deal was looking good to her. Some girls really hate the job."

Tillotson thought about it.

"It also makes you wonder what could have gone so wrong between Bernice and Handler that she ended up dead. I mean, she was doing what he wanted, wasn't she?"

"Sounds like it."

"If I had to bet, I'd still go with the ex."

"Don't get tunnel vision," she said. "In our line of work there's always another weirdo."

He gave her another look, as if he wondered whether she meant his line of work or hers. Maybe she wasn't sure either.

"I don't suppose you'd consider taking a break from business? You know, until we get this handled."

"Can't afford it," she said.

He nodded as if he hadn't expected anything else.

"Keep me informed."

This new man's name was Lester, and he liked to touch. Tolerating it was part of the package Diana sold to every client, but even after years in the business she sometimes had to remind herself to hold off on slapping the man.

It didn't help that Lester looked like a raincoat-and-no-pants kind of creep. Not his fault, but still.

Some parts of her anatomy minded fondling more than others. A man was welcome to stroke her back, maybe because she could imagine he was someone else. But this client found her legs fascinating, and as always, the insides of her thighs wanted to flinch. She made herself stare at the ceiling. Its blankness gave her mind something to aspire to.

"You have wonderful skin," he said. "Smooth. Must take some upkeep. How do you do it?"

"My moisturizing routine is not interesting. Trust me."

"Okay, I'm really asking about the shaving."

She let her head roll toward him. What was it about body hair, all of a sudden?

"There's this guy making the rounds," he said. "He wants somebody to lose the razor for a while."

"I've met him, now that you mention it."

"You didn't go for it?"

"Good guess."

"He's promising big money."

"Why do you care?"

"Because I want to follow up. He pays you to let everything grow out, and then I pay to watch you shave." He grinned. "Every guy has his kink. That's mine."

The smile vanished.

"I know where it comes from. My mother used to make me watch her shave. And yeah, I know it's weird."

A hooker got used to too much information the way she got used to fondling.

"Oh, well," he said. "Too late to rewind now."

Diana wondered what to ask next. It would give her something to tell Tillotson. He liked to know she was keeping her eyes and ears open, even if she couldn't see how the information might help him.

"Maybe you should get together with him," she said. "The two of you could offer a package deal. Somebody might go for it."

Excitement made him climb to his knees on the bed. "Does that mean you'd do it?"

She should have seen that coming. "I'd have to crunch the numbers."

He brushed her trimmed bush with his fingers. "This would have to go, too."

"No can do."

"Why not?"

"The bush is my niche. I get the guys who are creeped out by shaved pussies."

He lowered himself onto the mattress and rolled away from her, and her hooker's radar told her she had managed to offend him. She decided it was no big deal. He had felt like another one-timer from the beginning, and this only confirmed it.

The next morning Tillotson took his customary seat at her kitchen table a little after eight. The later hour told her he was settling into a long investigation.

"We can't find either of them. Stephens or Handler. It's giving me a bad feeling."

"I do have something to tell you. I just wish I knew how it helped."

"Try me."

"I met another kink."

She told him about Lester. He grimaced.

"Don't you have anybody who just climbs on and gets off?"

That was unusually crude for him. The case must be making him crazy.

"Kinks are like baseball," she said.

"Now you've lost me."

"Streaks and slumps. Although the kinks are definitely streaking right now."

"The part about his mother—I definitely didn't need to hear that." He shook his head. "Mothers can screw up kids in so many ways."

"Where are Bernice's kids?"

"With their grandmother. Their father's mother."

"What are they like?"

"Meaning what kind of number have their parents done on them?"

"I guess."

"Bryce Junior, seventeen. Cindy, sixteen. They strike me as just kids, which means who the hell knows what goes on in their minds? They both say they hadn't seen their mother in weeks."

"You believe them?"

"For now, I don't disbelieve them."

He shook his head. "Now they'll never work out their issues with her."

Diana took steps to make sure clients never learned her last name, or where she lived, but that didn't mean they couldn't find her. They just had to stake out her natural habitat.

This motel, for instance. Named the Savoy, it sat just blocks away from her home in the declining town of Driscoll in the far north of New Jersey. She had been trying for years to wind down the Savoy. It was a relic of her early days in the business, when she hadn't done enough to keep business away from her private life. But some veteran clients still liked to see her there, and their money talked.

This client thought 101 was his lucky number, and he had been using the room for almost ten years without noticeable improvement in his fortunes. Diana refrained from pointing that out.

At the end of the hour she gave him a smile and a wave before closing the door on him. Six steps into the parking lot she bounced off a man.

That was a bad start. She didn't like men who could sneak up on her. She looked up at his face to see what he had in mind.

Whatever it was, he seemed to think he could get it without paying for it. He grasped her bicep.

"Hands off," she said. "Now."

"We need to talk."

"You'll be talking to the cops if you don't let me go."

"Relax, Bryce," said another male voice. "That's not the way to get her on our side."

This voice she knew. She tracked it to an aging Impala just a few spaces away. Her one-time client Lester was climbing out of the driver's seat.

She looked up at Bryce Stephens until he released her. Her arm throbbed, but she decided to save the rubbing for later.

"We'll pay you for your time," said Lester.

"That's better."

"Come sit in the car."

He pointed at the front passenger seat, but she didn't plan to let either man sit behind her. Trust had its limits, especially with murder suspects.

But she listened for her hooker's radar, and it wasn't warning her about Stephens or Lester. She got into the back seat and scooted to the middle, where both men would have to turn equally to see her. They climbed into the car and got settled, but then neither seemed to know what to say next. Diana decided to start with Lester.

"I expected to see you with a sidekick, but not Bryce."

"You mean Handler? I can't find him."

"So hire one of us to set it up."

"I tried that. None of the women I asked could find him either."

"So how did you two meet?"

"We were both looking for Handler," said Stephens. "We crossed paths a few times, and then we ended up comparing notes right here in this parking lot."

"Okay, I know why Lester wanted to find him, but what about you?"

"He's a suspect. At least, he should be, but the cops are obsessed with me."

"Are we sure they're wrong?"

"I finally got her out of my life. Why would I risk going to prison for her?"

He had a point. If he didn't care that it made him look like an asshole, that improved his credibility.

"Okay, but you're a criminal lawyer. You have clients you could get to handle this for you, and the cops know it."

"But I didn't."

"So what am I supposed to do for you?"

"Find him," said Stephens. "We're desperate."

"How am I supposed to do it when nobody else can?"

"I've heard about you. The hooker detective."

It made sense that a criminal lawyer had heard of her and Tillotson. She didn't know what to say, and when that happened, she usually brazened it out.

"It'll be expensive."

"We expect it to be expensive."

"And there's something you two should work out right now. What happens when we find him? I mean you want different things. You want him to be guilty. Lester wants him to be innocent."

"I'll go with the truth," said Stephens. "Whatever it is."

Lester nodded solemn agreement, but Diana still had her doubts.

An instant later none of it mattered.

"Shit," said Stephens.

Diana heard it all in his tone. Something serious was happening, and he couldn't believe he was taking it so calmly. She could have sat forward for a look, but instinct told her to duck for cover. The windshield shattered, and the noise deafened her. Stephens's head exploded like a bag of blood, but the bullet kept going and shattered the rear window.

Diana tried to make herself as small as possible in the back seat, as if that would make dying hurt less. When nothing happened, she counted to a hundred and pushed herself back up to a sitting position. Lester came into view. Gore clung to his face and made the whites of his eyes stand out as they widened in horror. His mouth worked without producing a sound.

Stephens's troubles were over, in this life anyway. Diana looked away.

Sirens were already sounding. The desk clerk of the Savoy knew what kind of commotion he could ignore and what required 911.

Diana sat in a different car, this one an unmarked Taurus.

"Can we keep the door open? I'm a little skittish about back seats right now."

Somebody must have recognized her and called Tillotson. He leaned against the rear fender, as a Driscoll detective named Rostow stood in front of her and questioned her. Rostow had wanted to put her in jail for years, but right now he knew his priorities.

"You see the shooter?"

"No, but I have an idea who it was."

"How?"

"Teenage boys and their mothers."

"What brings that up?"

She told Rostow about Bernice, Stephens, Handler, Lester, shaving and not shaving, bathing, and probably more about her business than he ever wanted to know. Tillotson listened as if he had never heard any of it, but cops endured a lot of repetition to get where they wanted to go.

"The mother-son thing can get intense, and it can get weird. Look at Lester," Diana said.

All three turned toward Lester, sitting in the back of an ambulance with a blood pressure cuff on his arm. He still had the thousand-yard stare.

"You think Bernice's son misses their shaving sessions?" Tillotson asked.

"We don't know it's that, exactly. But I'm thinking that preparing for this scenario with Phil Handler made changes in Bernice's routine. Maybe the changes led to questions, and maybe the questions led to her son finding out..."

She usually let him take the last step of any deduction. He had never let his ego get in the way of their brainstorming sessions, but he was a man and a cop, and she had her ways of dealing with both species.

He picked the story up smoothly.

"...That his mother was a..."

But there were also certain thoughts that he let her complete.

"...Whore," she said. "So he kills his mother in a rage, and then he regrets it. So killing his father is his way of making it up to her."

"It makes a weird kind of sense, I guess," said Rostow.

"Well, we're talking about weird here."

"Next question," said Tillotson. "Where's Phil Handler? Did the kid already kill him, or is he hiding out?"

"I have an idea," said Rostow. "Let's find the kid and ask him. Preferably before he shoots anybody else."

"I can think of some other people he might go after," said Diana.

"Who would that be?"

"Okay, the kid knows he has a limited amount of time. He's pissed at his mother for being a whore, and his father for making her a whore. What's the common denominator here?'

They let her say it.

"Whores."

It all depended on how much the boy knew. To Diana it seemed obvious that Bryce Junior had found his mother's passwords to the discussion groups. Then he learned why she was letting her hygiene slide. Maybe he also used his access to find Handler.

In which case Phil was dead.

"I think he's not finished," said Diana. "He wouldn't be the first guy to decide he's cleaning up the world by killing hookers."

"When really he just likes killing," said Tillotson.

"So," Diana said, "if he comes after hookers, who will be first in line? The one who reminds him of his mother. Get somebody to go online and say she's going to stop shaving. And bathing."

Rostow looked at Tillotson.

"I guess we should use a decoy. We'll have to get a woman officer from out of the area. No telling who the kid knows around here."

"You don't have time to find anybody," said Diana. "I'll do it. Bryce Junior doesn't know me."

She expected their deadpan stares. "I want this to end. It's bad for business."

Now they were staring at each other. Tillotson broke off the wordless communication and shook his head.

"We can't endanger a civilian like that."

"Since when am I a civilian?"

They weren't buying it, and it got worse. They started talking as if she weren't sitting right in front of them.

"The time factor is real," said Rostow.

"I know somebody I can borrow from Morristown," said Tillotson. "I'll clear it with her chief."

He turned to Diana.

"We're still going to need your help. You'll have to vouch for her online and set her up with a password."

"Let me rephrase that. I'll give her my passwords and change them when this is over."

He used some of his cop look to squelch her mounting resentment. Sometimes he had to remind her. In the end she was a criminal, not a colleague.

"You'll also need some plausible reasons for making her disappear again," she said. "I don't need it getting around that I let the cops into the groups."

"We'll work it out. You want to get checked out at the hospital?"

"I'm good."

"Go home and set this up."

That made her seethe even more, but she was stuck. So she went into the discussion groups and introduced Valerie, who announced that she would be doing incall at the Savoy. She would be grateful for referrals, for a cut, of course. She also mentioned her interest in kinks like the European scenario.

On the plus side, Diana could keep her two regular dates that same night. Making some money might even help sooth her jangled nerves after Bryce Stephens's murder.

Close to midnight she turned into her street. One of her security measures involved driving by her own front door for a quick look before parking some distance away. Tonight the habit paid off, because she saw someone sitting on her front steps.

She made two right turns and left the car on the next street. Diana ducked past the house that backed onto hers. Movement in the darkness to her left didn't faze her, because she was good friends with the huge mixed-breed that lived in a doghouse in the backyard. She stopped for a moment to make nice with him.

Diana spent another moment on peeking around the corner of her own home. The figure on the front steps wasn't the strapping young man she had been thinking about. The young woman had a backpack beside her on the steps. Diana stepped into view in the illumination from the streetlight.

"Cindy?"

"Yeah."

"I've been expecting your brother."

"Well, you've got me."

"Why don't you give me the gun? Just for safety's sake."

"Don't treat me like an idiot. Guns aren't safe. That's the point."

"Okay, I'm sorry. I won't talk down to you again. But if there's going to be a gun around my home, I plan to be the one holding it."

For a moment Diana thought that might be another mistake. "My house, my rules," was exactly the kind of adult bullshit the girl was complaining about. But Cindy stuck her right hand into the backpack on the steps beside her. Diana leaned forward a little, ready to lunge, but the girl's hand emerged with her index finger hooked into the trigger guard of an enormous semi-automatic pistol. Diana wondered how Cindy had held this weapon steady enough to shoot. But she must have managed it.

Diana took the gun from her. "Come inside."

She unlocked the door and led the girl to the kitchen. After a moment's hesitation, Diana stowed the gun in the silverware drawer. It looked strangely at home among the knives and forks.

"You drink coffee?"

Cindy nodded.

"I can make grilled cheese sandwiches."

"American cheese?"

"That's the only way."

The conversation paused while Diana busied herself. It was an oddly companionable silence, considering its other half was a multiple murderer. Diana delivered identical sandwiches and mugs of coffee to the table and took the seat opposite her guest. It was Tillotson's usual chair, but for now Diana was representing law and order.

Talk about weird.

"How did you find me?"

"My mother told me about you."

"Told you what?"

"If I'm in a jam, I should go to you. She said everybody in

her business does."

Diana thought back, and it was sort of true.

"She even showed me your house."

"Well, I'm not sure how much I can do for you. I can keep you from getting shot by the cops."

"Mom said they listen to you."

"Sometimes, anyway."

Diana studied the girl. Tillotson and Rostow wouldn't be happy with her for interrogating a suspect without them, but they deserved it for kicking her out of the case.

While she planned her interrogation, she got up and turned the burner on low to keep water for more coffee on a simmer.

"Where's Phil Handler?"

"Probably still running."

"So you knew him?"

"The one who turned my mother all weird. He just moved right in. Thought he was going to make her his European woman. That's what he called stinky and hairy."

"So he just helped himself to her life."

Diana listened to her own words, and her stomach lurched. She was about to learn something about Handler that she didn't want to know. "Did her life include you?"

"He said he was going to make me a real woman. No shaving. One shower a week. And then, well, take a guess."

"Your mother let him?"

"She pretended she didn't know." Now Cindy studied Diana. "This is news to you? I thought you all were sexually abused."

"Hookers? I wasn't. Sometimes it's all about the money."

"Yuck."

"Yeah, sometimes. But wait a minute. Why were you with your mother? I thought your father had custody."

"I got away from him as much as I could. All of this was his fault."

That was some consolation. Diana had been right about the motive for Bryce's murder, if not about the culprit.

"Okay, how did your mother get shot?"

"She got in the way. That's what happens when you stand by your man."

"You were trying to shoot Handler?"

"Well, yeah. So what do we do now?"

Diana stared at the girl. It kept getting worse. Okay, Cindy needed a hard shell to live her life, but how did a kid develop such a good one?

Probably with a head start from birth.

"We have to call the cops. No way around it. I'll make sure Detective Tillotson is here. We can trust him."

The logistics required thought. Diana got up and went to the gas range. She poured water into the drip pot. When the coffee was ready, she brought the pot to the table and refilled their cups. Instinct told her to stay on her feet.

"Okay, here's what happened just now. I took the gun, and I made us something to eat, but we didn't talk about anything important. And you keep saying nothing until you get a lawyer. I know some."

"I'm thinking more in terms of you giving me some cash and driving me someplace they wouldn't expect me to go. Philadelphia, maybe."

"I can't risk that, and you can't, either."

When the girl's hand came out of the backpack in her lap, it held another a gun, a revolver, almost petite in comparison to the gun Diana had taken from her. She smiled nastily and said, "You think there's only one gun in the world? My dad had lots."

Diana flipped the coffee pot, sending hot coffee into the girl's face. As Cindy clawed at her eyes, Diana set the pot down and shoved the table with both hands. It mowed the girl down. Diana elbowed her chair out of the way and stooped to grab Cindy's ankles. The girl tried to kick, but Diana held on and dragged her out from under the table. Before Cindy could remind herself that she still held the gun, Diana planted her foot on the girl's wrist.

"What if I don't need a gun?"

Talking trash felt good, and it seemed to impress the girl. Cindy's hand released the revolver, and Diana swept it into the corner of the kitchen with her foot.

"Thanks, by the way. I was feeling a little bit bad about giving you up to the cops."

"Obviously," said Tillotson, "you didn't miss anything at the Savoy. Unless you like boring."

"Boring is sounding pretty good right now. Compared to the company I've been keeping."

"I've seen it before," he said.

He was back in his usual seat at her table, and it felt right. Maybe they could get past their recent tension.

"I think there are a lot of latent psychos out there," he said. "If nothing triggers them, they might go through their whole lives without anybody noticing."

"Cindy definitely got triggered," said Diana.

"That'll be taken into account. Plus, she's a juvenile. Which means she'll get out young enough to cause a lot more trouble, if she feels like it."

"I have to wonder what her brother is like," said Diana. "Where is he?"

"He turned up at a friend's house. They had been playing video games nonstop for days. He didn't know about his father. Or seem too broken up about his mother."

"This is why I don't plan to reproduce," said Diana.

"Could you do any worse?"

SKIN AND BONES
John Bosworth

Stanley's knees hurt where the edge of his kneecaps rested on the concrete steps. He was ready to call it a night and go home.

On the other side of the street, the boy was pacing back and forth, stomping through puddles and kicking at the dented aluminum cans in the gutter. Stanley tracked his movement through the magnifying lens of his camera.

He was probably six or seven years old, Stanley guessed, but his baggy clothes made him look small, so it was hard to tell. Stanley knew some kids dressed like that on purpose, as a style, but he didn't think that was the case here.

In his own childhood, the other kids had found Stanley's clothing to be just a bit too formal, too prim and orderly to be acceptable, and they had let their opinion be known. This boy's mother had taken the opposite approach. What he wore looked more like thrift store leftovers than careful choices, but Stanley suspected the end result at school was the same.

He had loose white jeans bunched up over his hip bones and held up by a wide nylon belt. A baby blue windbreaker with a yellow logo flaking off the back caught a gust of wind and billowed out around him like a sail. His mother had probably assumed he would grow into it.

The boy was wearing the same shoes he'd had on last week. White athletic shoes with green piping on the sides and wide, flat soles. Like everything else, they were too big for him. Stanley trained his camera on their untied laces. He took a picture of the boy in profile, the shoelaces blurring loosely behind his foot as he kicked a beer can off the sidewalk.

Stanley wondered why he wouldn't cross the street and come over to his side. Maybe he wasn't allowed to cross the street alone. *Or maybe,* Stanley thought, *he knows I'm here.*

Startled by the idea, he flinched deeper into the darkness of the basement stairwell, causing his knees to radiate fresh pain. He suddenly felt trapped down there. The sun had gone down below the tops of the apartments across the street. If he didn't catch the next bus, he would be late. And if he was late again...

Well. There could be consequences.

He told himself it was certain that the boy wouldn't cross the street at this point. In truth he no longer wanted him to, and he was struck by a powerful need to flee before he could be proven wrong.

He powered down the camera, arranged it in its case with the lenses, and placed the case carefully into his backpack. When he looked up, the boy was crossing the street, heading straight for him.

Stanley was frozen by the sight of the boy's face as he passed under the streetlights. The shadow effect was arresting, and he wished he hadn't put his camera away. The boy looked sad. No, not sad, exactly. He looked deeply bored.

It's not his fault, Stanley thought, again remembering his own childhood. The boy probably didn't have any brothers or sisters. And there were no other kids around to play with that day. Stanley looked up and down the street.

There's nobody around at all.

He was again frightened by his own thoughts, and he closed his eyes against them. In the darkness, he could hear the plastic tips of the boy's shoelaces snapping against the pavement, getting louder as he came closer.

Stanley tried to refocus himself like he would a lens. *I can still go. I could just walk right past him and around the corner to the bus stop. Don't even look at him. Do it. Right now. Go.* But he didn't move, and as the boy got closer, the sound of his laces on the sidewalk became impossibly loud, shouting down the voice in his head.

The following night, a Sunday, Stanley was following a boy in Greenwood who stayed very close to his parents. Eventually they got into their car and drove away, and Stanley lost track of time as he took pictures of the traffic crawling south on Aurora Avenue. It was fully dark by the time he found a bus, and Mama was waiting at the stop when he got off. He could see her through the window, staring at the thin gold band of her watch, looking panicked.

She didn't mention the wait, but when she took his hands to kiss him on the cheek, her fingers were thin and brittle with cold.

"Did you have fun taking your pictures?" Her smile took effort, and he could see her bottom denture jogging in her shivering jaw. Water shined at the corners of her eyes and below her nose.

"Mama, I told you not to wait for me out here," he said.

He pulled her wrap tighter around her shaking shoulders and led her through the door of the diner behind her.

When they were settled into their usual table, a large booth of wine-colored vinyl in the back, she started in on him right away.

"Stanley? I really wish you'd let me see some of the pictures you've been working so hard on," she said.

"Did I get the chicken or the burger last time," he said, looking fixedly at the menu they had both long since memorized.

"The burger, I believe," she said.

There was a new waitress working that night, a girl who didn't look more than sixteen or seventeen years old. They watched her as she squinted at the unfamiliar menu, hung her order tickets on the wrong side of the kitchen window, and walked tentatively between the tables and the kitchen, looking hopelessly lost at every turn. This was a great excitement for Mama. She had been coming to the diner for years, even before they remodeled it, and she knew the layout better than anyone.

"Oh, no, not there," she whispered to Stanley as the girl put a dirty plate in the wrong bucket at the bussing station. She shook her little white afro with regret, but she was smiling. Stanley felt a strong pull toward her, looking very small and old in the large booth, wearing her favorite shawl and two heavy blooms of rouge on her cheeks. Dinner out with Stanley was her favorite activity of the week.

When the waitress finally came over to take their drink orders, Stanley noticed she was already sweating, making loose strands of her hair darken and stick to her neck. There was a coffee or gravy stain on the white apron above her name tag. Her name was Lauren.

He was surprised when Mama spoke for both of them.

"I will have decaf. And he always has iced tea," she said. Her tone implied these were obvious facts that every adult would know.

Mama watched the girl like an owl to make sure she poured the coffee from the decaffeinated carafe, her big eyes locked open and pulling her neck in an unnatural turn.

"When was this coffee made?" she said, sniffing it when it arrived.

"Oh, jeez. I'm not really sure," Lauren said. "I could go ask if you want?"

"No, don't," Stanley said. "It's okay. Really. It's not a big deal."

She smiled at him, looking relieved.

He could tell this bothered Mama to no end, because she went quiet and shook her Splenda packet with violence.

"Stanley, I wish you would order something with some

roughage in it sometime," she said when their food arrived. "Chicken breast and fried potatoes. I'd be surprised if there was one vitamin on the whole plate. And just look at you, practically swimming in that nice shirt I bought you. You're nothing but skin and bones."

"Remember when I got the Cobb salad? You insisted on sharing it, and then you sent it back because you thought the tomato was mealy."

"And it was," she said with conviction.

Then, by way of an imaginary transition, she was talking about his pictures again.

"I don't know why you are so bashful about them," she said. "I'm sure they are gorgeous. You're always out working so hard on them, and you have such a wonderful eye."

"They aren't ready yet, Mama. We don't turn anything in for a grade until the portfolio at end of the quarter."

"I don't want to *grade* them, Stanley. I just want to see them, that's all. To enjoy them."

She smiled and rested her hand on top of his on the tabletop. Stanley smiled back and squeezed hers in return.

"Soon, Mama."

"How's everything tasting?" Lauren said, startling both of them.

"It's very good, thank you," Stanley said automatically. He noticed his hand had pulled away from under Mama's, and he watched it grab blindly for something to hold, eventually gripping but not lifting his water glass.

Mama kept her smile in place through force of will.

"Why don't we do one of my puzzles this weekend?" she said brightly when Lauren had gone. "We haven't done the poppy fields in a while. Or the hot air balloons. Or, I know! We could take a nice long walk to the park. And get pastries on the way. Twenty-five isn't too old for a boy to spend time with his mama, you know."

"I know, Mama."

When their pie came, she pulled her tablet computer out of her purse and set her glasses on the tip of her nose. She used to read the headlines to him from the newspaper while they had dessert when he was a boy, and he had been surprised how readily she had adapted with the changing times. Mama could adapt to anything.

"Front Page? Or Entertainment?"

"How about local news," he said.

"Again? Pretty soon you'll be such an expert on the local news, you could run for city councilman." He watched her enjoy the thought. "All right, let's see... It's going to get cold next week, down below forty on Thursday...and they are shutting down the tunnel all weekend so they can work on it. Again. It says here the whole project is already a month behind schedule."

Stanley fidgeted impatiently with his fork. "Anything else?" he asked.

"Look here," she said. She double-tapped the zoom on her screen. "It says a little boy fell down some stairs last night outside an apartment complex in Lynwood. Broke his neck and bashed his little head in. And look what else it says." She pushed her face closer to the screen as her voice started to rise. "His shoes were untied! He tripped and fell."

She looked up at him meaningfully.

"Well, of course he did," she said. "And I'll tell you something else: I'll bet his parents were nowhere in sight. What did I tell you just last week? When we saw that boy running with his shoes untied? I had a notion something like this could happen, remember?"

"Yes, Mama. I remember."

"Of course, you do," she said.

She paid up front at the counter and gave Stanley the tip in cash to set on the table while she adjusted her wrap.

"Is this all you're leaving?" Stanley said.

"It's more than fair for the service we received," Mama said.

"But Mama. It's only her first day."

"And I don't expect she'll have many more unless she picks up the pace a little bit." She dropped her voice low. "And just between you and me, she is far too busty to be wearing that blouse. What is she thinking, walking around downtown dressed like that? At night? She's certain to be interfered with."

"Mama, please...don't."

"Oh, yes she is, Stanley. You mark my words." Her color was rising, along with the volume of her hissing whisper. "It's all fun and games to girls like her until they find themselves trussed up in some alleyway." She snapped the ends of her shawl together at her neckline with finality. "I'm certain of it. I had a notion."

"I wish you wouldn't say things like that," Stanley said. He swallowed hard. He had eaten too much of the pie, and the filling had stuck to his teeth and made him queasy.

"When you pay for dinner, you may leave as much as you like," Mama said.

She turned toward the exit with her arm out at an angle to her hip, waiting for Stanley to escort her.

They walked home in silence, but she leaned into the crook of his elbow for support, which seemed to show their spat was over. When they got to the apartment, Stanley unlocked the front door and held it open for her.

"You head on in," he said. "I need to stay out for a bit. To take some pictures. We're supposed to have some that use only moonlight."

"Oh, Stanley, tonight?" Her face fell. "I thought we were going to watch that dancing show."

"But I have to go work on my project," Stanley said, trying to sound decisive but hearing a whine instead. "For class."

"Honestly, Stanley. For a night course at the community college, they are working you around the clock." Then her big blue-gray eyes turned eager with an idea. "Where are you going? Someplace nice? Maybe I could come with you. We could spend some time together."

"No, Mama. You should stay in tonight." He pecked her on the cheek. "It's nothing nice."

Stanley waited by the rear exit, but Lauren left through the front door and he had to walk fast to make up ground. After a few blocks, she eventually stopped at a crosswalk and began scrolling through her phone.

Traffic was light and she could have crossed against the light, but she was absorbed by the screen and didn't hear the footsteps behind her.

She startled at the last possible moment, dropping her phone, but the crook of Stanley's arm was already around her, tightening fast, and she didn't have the breath for a scream.

Afterward, he fiddled with the shutter speed on his camera but wasn't having much luck. It was getting overcast, for starters, and the close walls of the alley were blocking most of the moonlight anyway. And he couldn't very well drag her out from behind the dumpster to use some of the streetlight. Then they would be in plain sight.

There was one small square of light on the ground beside her, cast from a security lamp at the rear of the alley. It was a sodium lamp, which made the light dull and yellowy-orange. And it was striated with black bars from the wire of the cage around it. Not exactly ideal.

It still could have worked as a last resort, but she lay a few inches outside of it.

He bent down to move her, and his eyes fell on the shapeless brown stain beside her nametag. He remembered it hovering in his periphery as she took his dinner order. She had been silently reading the menu over his shoulder as she wrote, trying her best to memorize its complex numbering system. He wondered how far she had gotten, then shook the thought away. It didn't matter now.

He screwed the widest aperture lens he had onto the camera, held it up briefly, then unscrewed it and dropped it aside in disgust.

His mood had curdled. What had Lauren even done to Mama, really? Tried her best to learn a new job, with nobody even bothering to help her? Stanley could never learn anything fast enough for Mama's liking, either.

Just like the previous night in the stairwell, he found himself wanting to drop everything and walk away as fast as he could.

He knelt to collect the discarded lenses.

Then he noticed something on the ground in front of him. Something just barely visible inside the box of light, casting a strange shadow along its edge. He leaned in to inspect it.

It was a dark brown curl of her hair, just an inch or two long, that had pulled free from the messy knot on top of her head. It forked into two separate strands at the end, and a leaf was caught between them, suspended in air. It was just smaller than a dime, light brown and thinner than paper.

He knelt and held the camera steady an inch from the ground. The low angle backlit the leaf and made it glow. He could see its structures illuminated, the ribs and veins. It was oddly arresting, in its own way. Beautiful, even. He centered the frame and snapped the shutter.

He reviewed the picture on the screen, pressed a button to save it, and then positioned himself to try another.

Stanley was up before sunrise the next morning. He wrote a note on the pad of paper by the front door. Then he shut and locked it silently, so Mama could sleep.

He was away all day. When he got home, right on time for dinner, he was careful to remove his mud-caked boots and leave them just outside their apartment door. The dirt and brambles in his shirt and hair he couldn't do much about. He also couldn't help the fact that he was sweaty, out of breath, and smiling to himself.

But when he opened the door to the apartment, his smile fell away. He knew instantly that something was wrong. The light in the front room was off, and he couldn't smell anything on the stove or in the oven. The sweat cooled over him all at once and he felt heavy dread.

"Stanley James Clayborne! You get in here this instant."

He walked slowly down the hallway, stalling, and looked through the doorway into his bedroom. The curtains were drawn, and the overhead bulb cast a weak light in the small room. His bed had been stripped, the pillows lying on the floor and the mattress half-slumped off the box spring. His closet doors were thrown open, a tangled mess of clothes on the floor in front of them.

And his dented metal desk had all of its drawers pulled out, with Mama hunched over them.

"What is it, Mama?"

"Just look at this. Look at all these...pictures. Just what in Heaven are these?"

She steadied herself with one shaking hand flat on the desktop. She was holding his shoebox in the other hand, seeming dazed. Stanley felt blood burning the edges of his ears and cheeks.

"My pictures, Mama. You're not supposed to see my pictures. I told you, they're not done yet," he could hear the whine in his voice. "I need my privacy."

Her face twitched, like she'd been slapped.

"Privacy? Nonsense. Who do you think has been doing your laundry? And dusting and vacuuming this room for the past twenty-five years? It wasn't you, I can promise you that."

"But the pictures were in my desk."

"So?" She sniffed. "I happened to notice them. The drawer was open."

"It was not. And it was locked, too. You were snooping."

"Well, so what if I was?" she cried. She shook the box at him.

"It's not right for a boy to be sneaking around every night, keeping...keeping *secrets* from his Mama."

She pinched a wallet-sized print from the box at random and held it up by the corner, using the tips of her thumb and forefinger like it was a stinging insect.

"But Mama. Don't you recognize him?"

That froze her for a moment. She felt her breast pocket for her reading glasses, set them on her nose, and slowly turned the picture toward herself.

Stanley said, "That's the boy from Lynwood. The one we saw running with his shoes untied."

Mama held the print up to the light and peered at it.

"Well. So it is," she said.

"You said he was going to fall and break his little neck. You had a notion. Look, Mama. You were right. Just look."

He took pictures from the shoebox and set them on the bedspread, one after another: The boy who didn't look before he crossed the street, dashed wetly against the pavement. The little girl from the Wendy's who wouldn't chew her food, her face mottled purple and her mouth flung open for breath. And Lauren, lying in the near darkness, trussed up in some alleyway, just like Mama had said would happen.

"See? Your notions, Mama. You can always tell," Stanley said. "You always know what's best for them."

"You did all this...for me?" Her voice was faint.

"I'm real sorry. Mama, am I in trouble?"

She was quiet, nodding to herself. She looked down on all the pictures he had laid out and ran her finger slowly over each child, remembering their offense. Then she looked up at him resolved, her face hardened.

"Trouble? I'd certainly say so." The firmness in her voice had returned. "Just look at this. What do you suppose this is?"

"I just told you, that's the little boy in Lynwood. The one who wouldn't tie his shoes. I hid in a staircase and—"

"I know that, Stanley. What I meant was, what's this here in the corner of the picture?"

Stanley looked.

"…blood?"

"I can plainly see that it's blood. But what's *in* the blood? Speak up boy, I can't hear you."

"A footprint?"

"A *shoe*print, I think you mean. And what would you like to bet that it matches those clunky hiking boots you insist on wearing everywhere? Honestly, Stanley. I just don't know where your head is sometimes. You might as well have left our home address and phone number. I thought I had raised you better than this."

"I'm sorry. I didn't see it. It was dark."

She scooped up some of the other prints from the shoebox and flipped through them. Stanley watched her linger on an image of Lauren, a detail shot of sheer pink fabric wound around her wrists.

"I trust you didn't enjoy that," she said, moving it to the bottom of the stack. Then she returned the pile to the box and replaced the lid. She placed the picture with the footprint into her pocket along with her glasses.

"Oh, stop that whimpering. The paper said the boy's fall was an accident, remember? Even the police can see that this fool child brought it on himself. I don't expect we'll hear from them."

"But Mama?"

"Yes?"

"You're not mad about the children? About what I had to do to them?"

"The children?" The hardness on her face broke apart in stages.

"Stanley, you're the only child I care about, don't you know that by now?" She squeezed him tight. "Besides, look at this boy. Running around at night. No scarf or hat on. Shoelaces flying everywhere, and probably raising all kinds of ruckus to boot. Why, I bet his Mama told him a million times to tie those shoes. To not play on those stairs. To come in at night. A boy needs to listen to his Mama."

Her grip had become very tight as she spoke, but she loosened it and looked into his eyes.

"I think you can tell me honestly now, Stanley. Where have you been all day?"

"I left a note by the door. I was at the park. All day. Honest."

She took his backpack from his hands, unzipped it, and scrolled briskly through the pictures on the camera's screen.

"And? Did you see anything interesting? Some boys rough-housing on the jungle gym? Or middle schoolers trying cigarettes behind the bathrooms? Or...Stanley?" Her voice rose a little. "Just what are all these pictures *of*, exactly?"

"They're leaves, Mama."

"Leaves?"

"It's a new project I started. See how pretty they are, hanging up there in the sky? And how delicate when they fall on the ground?" He was smiling again, remembering them. "I think this new project is even better, don't you? And best of all, nobody has to get hurt. It's just so peaceful all alone out there, hiking through the trees."

Mama frowned at a picture of a Maple leaf, withered and drooping from the tip of a dead branch.

"All alone?" she said.

"How much longer do you think?" Stanley asked.

"Another twenty minutes at least for the meatloaf," Mama said, looking through the glass in the oven door. "The rolls are done already. You can come and sit with me and have one if you like. And get a glass of whole milk, too. No more of this two percent business while you're wasting away to nothing. I swear you're—"

"I know, Mama, I know."

"Don't sound so glum. And will you please stop moping

around everywhere?"

"But did I really have to stop going to class?"

"Of course, you did."

"But if I don't bring my leaf pictures to my final critique, I won't pass the course. And if I don't pass, I won't be able to sign up for the two-hundred-level class next year," he said. "Mama, I have to try new things, or I'll never grow as an artist."

"Grow?" she snorted. "Tramping out in the woods all day and night, all alone, not even telling your Mama when you'll be back? Staring up at twigs like some kind of lunatic? That's what it means to grow?" She patted his hand when he didn't respond. "Stanley? Answer me."

He looked down at his roll and crossed his arms, pulling away from her.

"But I don't want to take pictures of your notions anymore," he said. "Don't you think the leaves are nice, too? And nobody has to get hurt. Don't you think it's better that way?"

She frowned. "Well, I just don't know, Stanley. I haven't been to college like you. Do you really think your leaf pictures are better?"

She rubbed his shoulder until he would look up at her.

"I know they are, Mama."

She smiled reassuringly. "Stanley? Don't worry, I know just how we can resolve this. Do you know who takes a lot of pictures like yours?" Her fingers dug into him. "The police. They're experts in the field, really."

She felt him go rigid.

"Maybe I should show them the pictures you took of the boy in Lynwood? Or the girl from Wendy's? Or, I know, how about those filthy things you did to that waitress? Is that the one you're most proud of? I'm sure they would be more than happy to offer you a *critique*."

"Oh, Mama, no..."

"Oh, yes, I think it's a fine idea. I'll ask the police if, in their expert opinion, your footprints are placed in the frame just so.

Do you think I should do that?"

"No, Mama. Please." He went limp under her hand.

He felt her hand on top of his. She left it resting there after a hard squeeze, and this time he let her.

"That's my good boy. Oh, Stanley! I'm so happy we finally have something to do together, just you and I. It's good for a boy to spend time with his Mama."

She took two dinner plates down from the cabinet and handed them to him to set on the table. When she returned to her seat, she was holding a pen and notepad.

"Okay, Stanley. You go first this time."

"Well," he said quietly, "we could go by the high school around ten tomorrow. Maybe we'll see kids cutting out on class?"

Mama wrote "High School?" on the paper.

"Well, first of all," she said, "it will be broad daylight then and anyone could see us. Second, what if the truant is some linebacker from the football team? Who's going to wrestle him into the car? You? I'd like to see it."

"Oh. Right."

"And third, we were only two blocks away from the high school last week when we got that girl who was shoplifting, remember? We don't want to go establishing any patterns, now do we?"

"You're right, Mama."

"Use your plate, please. Thank you. Now, did you get more tape and box cutters like I asked?"

"I forgot. I'm sorry."

"I thought you might. I went by the Lowe's today and got extra. I also got some cute plastic booties. Now you can wear your hiking boots without leaving any more of your little footprints."

"Thank you, Mama."

"You are quite welcome."

She took two crisp white linen napkins from a drawer by the sink.

"Oh, and Stanley? I saw a boy while I was at the hardware store today."

"A boy?"

"Yes. A little boy. And he was positively running amok in there. Sprinting around the aisles. Knocking things from their shelves. Plucking geraniums from their pots in the nursery. An absolute terror."

She was pressing the napkins in half and then in half again with force.

"And when I followed them home," she said, "I just couldn't believe our luck. A nice big house in the suburbs. A yard. Big trees on both sides, and a hedge to boot. I'll bet the neighbors won't be able to see us, even if they just stare out the window all day long."

"Oh. Good."

Stanley looked down at the crumbs on his empty plate.

"Just a few more minutes," she said.

She snapped on the oven light and peered through the glass at the meat baking inside.

"Oh, I hope that little boy is at least getting a decent dinner right now, like you are," she said. "On top of everything else, he was so scrawny he barely cast a shadow. Why, when I looked at him, I saw nothing more than just skin and bones."

JOB113

Robert Petyo

The message from Job113 appeared on Kyra's computer at two-oh-seven Friday morning, but she didn't find it until six a.m. She had just risen from another sleepless night and was checking her messages before making coffee.

"Mommy and Daddy are dead. I don't know what to do."

She had been chatting with Job113 for six days now. He acted childlike and innocent, asking awkward questions, tentatively trying to trigger a relationship with Kyra. She was using the screen name C-Lilly, and he thought she was a pre-teen girl. He was reeling her in, pretending to be a young boy, making her feel more mature, making her think that she could teach him about life and about love.

He was a predator, seeking another victim. Kyra's techs, the best in the business, had been unable to track his IP address and furnish her with a real name or a location. After a week it was time to move. She had to set up a face-to-face, which was always precarious. She couldn't appear too eager. That would trigger suspicions that would sever their connection.

But this?

She read the message again. "Mommy and Daddy are dead."

Still pretending to be a child?

"Are you all right?" she typed. She knew he would still be online. He was always online.

"I don't know what to do."

"What happened?"

"They're dead."

"How?"

"They're on the bed. There's a lot of blood."

She sucked in a breath. Had the predator killed again? And was this a twisted attempt to atone for what he had done? By pretending his own parents were dead?

She decided to call his bluff. "Did you call the police?" she typed.

"Should I?"

"Dial nine-one-one. Call the police right now and tell them what happened. Tell me where you are, and I'll come help you."

No response.

She waited and resent the message.

Still nothing.

She called Henri's cell. They would have to contact the 911 center to see if a call had come in, and if one had, they'd tag along. She was certain Job113 was local. He had once mentioned that his mommy had gone to the Cinemark off Route 81, and once both parents had gone to the Café Tuscany near the down-town square for dinner. He later told her that he loved the dessert they brought home for him. Kyra noted that he couldn't spell tiramisu.

When Henri answered she sped through an account of what happened.

"Slow down," he said. "You're always in overdrive. Don't you ever sleep?"

"There's no time."

"Kyra, I thought we decided that Job113 was just a confused kid."

"No. You decided that."

After a long pause, he said, "He's not a predator, Kyra. Face it. He's just a kid."

"Fine. I'll go myself."

"Stop looking for the man who got your brother."

After a beat, she said, "What did you say?"

"It's why you see predators everywhere. I've been trying to get you to scale back. If you don't, I'm going to take you off this detail."

She broke the connection and called her contact at the county 911 office.

"Hold on. Let me check," she said.

Kyra chewed the inside of her cheek as she waited.

"Stan just took a call about a dead couple. He dispatched a patrol car to 413 Meeker Avenue. Bristol."

She scribbled the address. "Did the call come from a kid?"

"A kid? No. Stan said an adult called it in."

She ripped the paper from her memo pad and ran to the bedroom to pull on pants and a shirt over her cotton pajamas. Meeker Avenue was in an upscale development near the golf course. Was Job113 a millionaire? He wouldn't be the first well-to-do pedophile. It was a rich one, rich enough to afford the best lawyers, who had killed her brother Mickey. That had been ten years ago last Monday.

Her brother Mickey Hirt was eleven years old when he was abducted and molested by an online predator. He survived the ordeal but was never the same. He was afraid of everyone, including his sister. A year apart in age, they had always been close, but things were never the same between them. Kyra blamed herself for being too young to understand what he had gone through. She should have been more supportive, more patient.

Mickey had hung himself in his apartment when he was twenty years old.

That was why Kyra never wanted to get married, and she pushed away interested men, including Henri. She never wanted to have children.

The morning chill made her tighten her coat around herself

as she crossed the apartment building parking lot to her gray Mazda. The engine resisted a few times before cranking to life.

After a fifteen-minute drive, she saw the strobing light of a police car as she crested the hill that overlooked the development split by Meeker Avenue. The street was wide and fringed with brick walkways. Trees and bushes sheltered the houses that were set back on sculpted lawns. The police car was in front of a wide driveway near a stone statue of a majestic lion, one paw raised. A second car, unmarked, was parked behind it.

Kyra parked fifty feet away, taking in the view as she got out. The patrolman drew himself erect as she approached. He looked nervous, as if embarrassed to be a mere civil servant amid such luxury. He held out his palm to stop her. She showed him her badge and he sighed and glanced toward the house. "Did they call you?"

"No. I heard it." She looked at the car. Someone was seated in the backseat. "Who's that?"

"We're holding him for the detectives to question."

"A witness?"

"He called it in."

Job113. A chill shook her as she crouched to get a look at him, but the windows were tinted. "May I talk to him?"

The patrolman looked from the car to the house and back. "Uhh, you better check with the detectives."

"Sure." She started up the driveway to the stone-and-brick mansion with an attached two-car garage shrouded by oak and evergreen trees. A man in a black wool coat with a blood-red tie left the house just as she approached. It was O'Reilly, newly promoted, overconfident, and totally obnoxious. She forced her gritted teeth to relax. She'd have to work with him to get at Job.

He stiffened, then smiled briefly when he saw who it was. "What brings you here?"

She jerked a thumb over her shoulder. "I think your witness is a predator I've been tracking."

His eyes widened, revealing streaks of red around his pupils.

"Oh, yeah. The predators. How many arrests does your section have?" He smiled and waited, but she said nothing. "Well, you're too late on this one. Your predator is a murderer."

"He killed them?"

"It sure as hell looks that way."

"How can you be sure?"

"I trust my instincts. No signs of forced entry. The parents are dead, and the son inherits a bundle."

"Who's the dead couple?"

"The Glimmertons."

She pursed her lips in a silent whistle as O'Reilly nodded excitedly. Glimmer of Hope was one of the most successful computer tech firms on the east coast. They did everything from web design to hardware to internet security. The husband-and-wife founders were well known on the local social circuit, attending all the charity dinners. "I didn't know they had a son." As she watched O'Reilly shrug, she realized he hadn't known it either. "Can I talk to him?"

"No way, Red," he said, jabbing a finger at her. "This is my case. You can talk to him when he's doing life in prison." He tried to move past her.

She side-stepped to block him. "At least let me sit in."

"You never could mind your own business, could you?"

"I do what it takes."

"You keep wasting your time with your kiddie unit. Homicide is my job."

"I'm not trying to steal your case. I just want to sit in."

"I know what you want to do. You're tired of playing computer games. You want to horn in on some real action. No way. Keep on the sidelines where you belong. Stay out of my way." He pushed past her and strode toward the car.

Kyra fumed and counted to three before turning to go after him, but someone caught her arm.

"Just sit tight, Kyra."

She turned.

It was Kazminski, O'Reilly's hulking, brown-eyed partner. "Give him time. For now, come on in and check the place out. You might find something."

She followed him into the house. Two crime-scene techs collecting evidence were huddled near the entrance to one of the rooms that was off an enormous den. Kazminski stepped around them and beckoned her to follow.

There was so much blood, dried black now hours after the murder, that Kyra had to be careful of each step she took. They were sprawled across the bloody mattress, the man's toes touching the floor like he had jumped for the bed and came up short, and the woman was lying face down above him like the crossing of a T.

Could Job have done this, she wondered. A predator's violence was usually aimed at the innocent and helpless. And they rarely used a gun.

"It looks like two shots for her," Kazminski said. "One in the chest, one in the head. The man took one in the head."

"Murder suicide?" she suggested.

"That was my first thought, but the gun wasn't here."

The king-sized bed was in the exact center of the room. Floor-length drapes covered a window to the back, and the walls were lined with dressers, one of which was splashed with some blood.

A predator couldn't have done this, she thought. But if Job wasn't a predator, neither was he a confused kid like Henri believed. Why did he act like a child online?

When Kazminski realized she wasn't going to ask about the gun, he said, "The gun was on the floor in the den."

"Where's his room?"

"Who?"

"Your witness. The guy O'Reilly is talking to now." She didn't really care about the homicide. O'Reilly was right about that. That was his department. But if she was wrong about Job, if he wasn't a predator pretending to be a boy, she wanted to know who he was. "He is a guy, right? Not a kid?"

"A kid? No. He's about thirty-five, I'd guess."

"His room?"

He pointed toward the door. "There's a couple bedrooms upstairs. Computer room is off the den to the other side. You're welcome to take a look."

She carefully exited the bedroom. Computer room. That's what she wanted to see. Since Job was almost always online, he probably spent his entire life with the computer.

The carpeted room she found was as big as some apartments. Three computers were against the back wall, each with a large flat screen and a comfortable leather desk chair that could swivel and rock. A gooseneck lamp hovered over each one. Against another wall was a fifty-inch flatscreen surrounded by DVD players and stereo equipment. Piled on a table like children's toys were iPads, iPods, and other hand-helds. There was a twin-size bed against each of two opposite walls, and a bathroom with a shower in the corner. A snack table and a four-chair dining-room table topped with inlaid glass sat in the center of the room. Job113 could have lived here if he'd wanted.

Perhaps he had, she thought.

She found her way upstairs where she found bedrooms that had seen little use. Guest rooms, perhaps. One of them might be Job's, but she believed he slept near his computer—if he slept at all. She tried to understand what Job's life was like, tethered to the internet.

She went back downstairs, nodding thanks to Kazminski, who was huddled with one of the techs. She almost collided with O'Reilly in the driveway as she left the house.

"I'm taking him downtown," he snapped. "I'll beat it out of him if I have to."

Kyra looked past him toward the car, which rocked slightly. The nervous patrolman struggled to ignore it. She looked at O'Reilly, who stuck his hands in his pockets.

"He keeps ramming against the door," he said. "Says he wants to get back inside the house. I swear, he's like a lost little kid."

Throwing a tantrum, she thought. "He didn't kill them."

"What?"

"I only did a quick check." She paused. "But I trust my instincts."

"What are you babbling about?"

"He's thirty-five years old and talks like a kid, right?" She paused and stroked her chin. "How about this? He's pale, isn't he?"

He nodded. "White as a ghost." His eyes suddenly widened, and he stepped back. "How did you know that?"

"Because he never leaves the house. But you dragged him out. Now he's scared and confused." She shook her head. "He'd never hurt his parents. They take care of him. Without them he's helpless." She pointed toward the rocking car. "Like he is now."

"Their money," he said weakly.

"He wouldn't know what to do with it. You don't get it, do you? The child of millionaire parents. No one even knew he existed. He lived his whole life in that house."

"That's crazy."

"He lived his life online. That's why he was always there. He probably rarely left that room."

"Why not?"

"His parents wouldn't let him. They were paranoid. Worried about kidnappers."

"Kidnappers? What makes you such an expert all of a sudden?"

Because she had been online, trying to get through to him. She had thought he was a predator, but deep down she had known he was somebody lost, lost like her brother Mickey had been lost after what happened to him. She couldn't get through to Mickey, so she was trying to get through to Job.

"Let me talk to Job. I'll get the whole story for you."

"His name is Jonathan."

She swatted an imaginary fly at that annoying detail. "Let me talk to him." She softened her voice. "A woman's touch might calm him down."

"Ahh, be my guest," he said after a quick shrug. "I'll give you fifteen minutes. If not, I'm taking him in." He held up a finger. "I'm sitting in though."

As she approached the car the patrolman stepped aside. She circled to the passenger's side and got in the front seat. O'Reilly took the patrolman's riot baton and got in the back seat.

"No need for that," Kyra said.

"I'm not taking any chances." He jabbed it toward Job as he sat.

Job reeled back against the door. "I want to go home."

"Quiet," O'Reilly snapped. "The lady wants to talk to you."

"Job, calm down."

At the mention of that name, he became still. Instead of puffing from exertion, it was as if he had shut his breathing down. He emitted not a sound. A metal grill separated the front seats from the back and Kyra twisted until she was sideways on her knees in the front seat. It was uncomfortable, but it allowed her to see him. Job was a man of about thirty-five with a drawn face but pockets of flab around his neck. He was as pale as a corpse.

"I'm C-Lilly," Kyra said.

"Lilly?" He pointed. "But you're not a girl."

"No, I'm not."

"Lilly, help me. I did what you told me, and look what happened. I called the police like you said. And they took me outside. Outside. Take me home." He shifted his hand slightly and pointed toward the house.

"Okay."

He brightened.

"No way," O'Reilly said.

"Let me take him inside."

"He stays out here."

"He wants to go home."

"It's a crime scene."

"The bedroom's a crime scene. He doesn't care about that. Come on, Job." She got out of the car and signaled for the patrolman to unlock the door.

"Don't move," O'Reilly said.

"You had your chance. And you got nowhere. Let me play it out."

After a lot of huffing and puffing, O'Reilly said, "Go. But I'm watching every move." He gripped the baton as he got out, leaving the door open, waiting for Job to slide across the seat. He came out of the car like a reluctant child, extending his hand toward Kyra.

She took it, stunned by how tightly he gripped it, like his life depended on not breaking their connection, and she guided him to the sidewalk.

O'Reilly kept rapping the baton into his palm and the patrolman who flanked Kyra kept his hand on his holster, but Job made no move to escape. The cold fear in his hand bonded him to Kyra. He had nowhere to go. Once they got into the house, they headed straight for the computer room. When they got to the door, he broke away and darted across the room. O'Reilly started to react, but she pressed her forearm to his chest. Job bolted to the computers and slipped into one of the chairs that rocked with his entry. The screen came to immediate life.

"This is home," Kyra whispered to O'Reilly.

Job cocked his head to one side as his fingers danced over the keyboard, filling the room with a clattering drumbeat.

"Who are you talking to?"

"X-man."

"Who's he?"

"He's one of my friends."

"I'm one of your friends, too. Right?"

He stiffened and swung the chair around so he faced her. "I thought you were a little girl."

"I'm sorry about that. I thought you were pretending to be a little boy."

"Why would I pretend that?"

How could she explain to this innocent man-child the evil that existed in this world? "I want to help you, Job. Is Jonathan your real name?"

"I wasn't lying. Not really. Just pretending. Mommy and Daddy told me never to use my real name online."

"They were right. Sometimes you meet dangerous people online."

He nodded. "They were scared somebody was going to try to hurt me."

"Did you ever go out, Jonathan?"

He shook his head.

"Never?"

"Mommy said someone might try to take me." Suddenly his eyes misted over and he tried to look past Kyra as if trying to see the bedroom. "Mommy and Daddy are dead."

"Someone killed them, Jonathan. A bad person. We want to find out who did that so they can be punished."

"Too late." He shook his head and tightened his cheeks as if holding his breath. "Already punished for being bad." He began to nod his head like an excited puppy.

She glanced at O'Reilly who stood motionless, his mouth open as if he were gasping for air. "Do you know who shot your parents?"

"Yes."

Kyra almost gasped. "Who?"

"Daddy shot Mommy." He fought back tears as he said it.

"Did you see it?"

"I couldn't stop him in time. They were—They were—" He started taking quick short breaths and rocking side to side in the chair.

Kyra recognized the body language, and it tore at her insides. Her brother Mickey had acted the same way. She had had no patience back then. Now she did. "I'm going to help you, Job," she said. "Try to stay calm. No one is going to hurt you. Try to answer my questions. Did you see the gun?"

"Gun?"

"When you found your parents."

"Yes."

"Were they dead when you found them?"

"Dead?" He said it like a question. "I heard shouting."

"Who was shouting?"

"Mommy and Daddy. Shouting. Fighting. I was here." He tapped his chair. "I was scared." He started to gasp for breath and Kyra came to his side. "I'm here," she said.

"Big bangs. I heard big bangs."

"So you ran to see?"

"Uh-huh." Tears seeped from his eyes. "I saw Daddy. He had the gun. He looked at me." Suddenly he squeezed his eyes shut and dug his chin into his chest. His fisted hands came up to his ears. "I took away the gun," he screamed. "Too late. Too late."

"Everything's going to be all right," Kyra said as she hugged him and patted his back. "I'll take care of you, Mickey."

THE KILLER'S DAUGHTER-IN-LAW
Scott Bradfield

"It's the holidays I dread most," Margaret told her mother during lunch at the Big Sky, sipping her first pre-dusk glass of wine since getting married. "He doesn't call or drop by for months, and then, without warning, just comes barging through the front door with his spare key like he owns the place. He doesn't bring anything or introduce himself to anybody; he just grabs a beer from the fridge and plops down in front of the television, stinking of chicken grease from that terrible Pismo diner where he works, and while everybody else is cooking and cleaning and socializing like normal people, he sits there with a tube of Pringles in his lap, monopolizes the television with the volume full blast, and watches horror movies. I mean, *seriously*. Horror movies at *Christmas*? And when he's not leering at every woman who walks past—even you, Mom, or one of the teenage girls from next door—he's laughing at people being stabbed in the face with gardening implements or being tossed in wood-chippers and so forth. And the way he *eats*; it's like some wild animal at the zoo. Gravy dripping down his face, tearing open biscuits and slabs of meat with his dirty fingers, and making these grunting noises and heavy breathing, oh God. It keeps reminding me of those horrible pornos he used to listen to in the guest room when he stayed with us after getting paroled. I'm telling you, Mom. I love Rob, and I really want our marriage to work. And I know it must sound terribly superficial, but I can't continue loving Rob if I have to spend another minute with Rob's dad. Either Rob's dad goes, or I go. I don't know how to put it more clearly than that."

Ever since turning sixty, Margaret's mother had seemed distantly bored by Margaret's life. Even when she feigned interest—leaning forward against the table, aiming her rumpled shoulders in Margaret's direction—her bird-like eyes darted distractedly around the noisy, plant-draped coffee shop, scanning for any conversation that might be more interesting than this one.

But sometimes, something would spark her interest. It was like watching fresh, cool water infuse the droopy leaves of a houseplant.

"Are you saying Rob's dad looks at *me* the same way he looks at young girls?" she asked. "An old bag like *me*?"

Margaret swirled the black sediment around the bottom of her long-stemmed wine glass. Everything tastes better in a long-stemmed wine glass, she thought. Even cheap stuff like this.

After thinking it over for a moment, she decided to say the obvious thing her mother wanted to hear.

"Yes, Mom. Of course he does. Give yourself a little credit. You're still attractive to a man like Rob's dad. Which isn't as much of a compliment as it might seem."

After every visit with her mother, Margaret thought about her father, who had moved to Oregon when she was still in preschool. He had been a huge, dominating force in her childhood—warm, bristly, flannel-shirted, roaring after her in rough games of hide-and-seek like a happy white thunderstorm—and after he went away, Margaret felt diminished in his wake. It felt as if her life had been divided into two mutually exclusive hemispheres: the vibrant, massy one with a father she could barely remember, and the slow, vaguely empty life that continued on after her father had left.

When Margaret carried her bags of organic produce into the kitchen, she found a fresh coffee ring on the oak-veneer dining-room table and a hastily scrawled note from Rob's dad.

> Hi Marge, sorry!!! I bunged up your down-
> stairs toilet again. Borrowed 40 from cash box.
> See you soon.
> Love, Dad

For the next few hours, Margaret was so upset that she couldn't concentrate on her paperback novel (a "stunning depiction of racial violence in the South"). And when Rob finally arrived home, she stood waiting for him at the front door with the note in her hand like a court summons.

"I've tried to be patient," she told him in the master bedroom while he changed into his jeans and T-shirt. "And I'm not criticizing your father; I'm really not. But by the time I got Coastside Plumbers out here, the toilet was leaking all over the new carpets, and that forty dollars he *borrowed* was for our date night on Wednesday, not to mention that the *last* time he borrowed forty dollars we never saw it again. Look, honey, I know he's having trouble adjusting to the outside world, and I'm sure he's doing the best he can. But somebody's got to talk to him about these, you know, liberties he's been taking. And I don't think that somebody should be me."

For the rest of the evening, Rob said very little, eating leftover broccoli beef out of the cardboard container and watching angry political commentators on CNN. "I don't think we should order from Madame Lo's anymore," he said eventually. And a little later: "These people are constantly shouting at one another, even though they seem to agree about virtually everything."

Margaret sat beside him on the sofa, guiltily stroking his knee as if it were a sick pet that would be euthanized the next morning. When he finished eating, she took his empty carton and soiled plastic chopsticks out to the recycle bin.

It was the clearest night she could remember: A white foamy effervescence of stars, the full moon humming with gravity. Margaret liked her neighborhood when it got like this—devoid of people, cars, and any hint of premonition. A solitary, greenly blinking satellite skimmed along the horizon of dark hills like a coyote scouting for trash.

"I know I have trouble talking about Dad," Rob said later in bed, wearing the red flannel pajamas that indicated he didn't want to make love. "When I was little, he was a huge figure in my life; everything he did seemed monumental. If he mowed the lawn, or poured concrete in the backyard, I wanted to help. Sometimes I passed him nails from a plastic case, or poured water into a pail, and these tiny gestures made me feel bigger and more important. Then, sometime after my seventh birthday—I remember he brought home a red bike with blue ribbons on the handlebars—the police showed up. I was sitting in the living room playing *Jak and Daxter* when the whole street lit up like a Christmas tree, and Mom and Dad started shouting upstairs. A voice on a bullhorn said, 'Come out with your hands over your head!' and I don't know what happened, but I felt this invincible sense of calm and well-being, as if none of it was happening to me. The voice on the bullhorn got louder and more insistent. 'Robbie!' Mom screamed from upstairs. 'Don't go outside! Can you hear me, Robbie? *Don't* go outside!' And then Dad started laughing, and his laughter grew louder and more encompassing, and the front door crashed open and all those boots stampeded past me and the men wore riot gear and rifles and helmets, just like foreign armies invading from all over the world..."

As Rob talked, Margaret stroked his damp forehead. His eyes were closed. His body generated a steady glow of warmth, like a recharging battery. After a while, Rob's weight grew heavy against her shoulder. He began to snore. And the sweetness of ownership filled Margaret like a memory of Christmas.

Everything is going to be okay, she wanted to tell him. Me and your dad will sort everything out.

The next morning, Margaret fixed scrambled eggs for breakfast, called in sick at work and drove to Rob's father's apartment on Monterey Street. It was a two story, eight-unit building with peeling white paint and heat-bubbling stucco and a pair of large, headless V-shaped pylons in the parking lot that looked like they once held the neon marquee of a budget-priced, sixties-era motel. In the ruptured, weed-sprung parking lot, an orange coyote was calmly rooting through a toppled aluminum garbage can.

"Shoo!" Margaret said, shaking her keys. The coyote looked up momentarily from an exploded In & Out bag, twitched his scabby tail, and trotted off toward town. *In my own time*, he seemed to be saying, *I didn't want to stick around anyway.*

"It's like Revelations out here," Rob's dad told her over instant coffee in two matching Styrofoam cups. "We got the coyotes coming down from the mountains, the druggies moving up from Pismo, and those real estate assholes trying to foreclose on everything that moves so they can turn this place into another fucking health food Co-Op, or something useless like that. You want something to eat, honey? I got crackers and Monterey Jack in the fridge. Or maybe coffee isn't what you need. Maybe I should run across the street to the Shell Station and pick up a couple cool ones?"

He was wearing torn gray sweatpants and a *Bermuda Rules!* T-shirt. Margaret was pretty sure it was the same ensemble he had worn the day she and Rob had picked him up outside the Men's Colony. The twisted tattoos on his gray arms were like mottled bruises. She could never tell if they represented a bundle of snakes or a skull-and-crossbones.

"I don't need anything. I just thought it would be nice to talk. We never really talk when you're at the house. Do you know what I'm trying to say?"

The living area resembled the littered foyer in one of the florescent-lit antique shops along Higuera. There was a white wicker chair bristling with broken stems, an orange osier sofa patched with strips of gray duct tape, and a large sixties-era television-stereo console being used to store clothes and torn-open boxes of breakfast cereals.

To make matters worse, the way Rob's dad looked at her over his beer bottle made clear that he didn't know what she meant. And probably never would.

"You're a good-looking woman, Margie," he said finally, after expelling a long pent-up breath of Marlboro, gazing at a torn Che Guevara poster on the wall, "but don't get me wrong. I may have been a crappy dad, but I wouldn't do nothing to hurt Rob. That being said, there are plenty of ways we could have a good time that wouldn't qualify as cheating, especially if Rob don't find out. Like, for example, if you wanna come over here and sit on my lap. I've never been much of a talker. I'll be much better at showing you what I mean."

The first time Margaret slept with Rob's dad felt like witnessing a car accident on the street. One moment she was minding her own business, pursuing minor coincidences of thought and movement—the next she was trying to understand where all the noise was coming from. Events knocked around her in unpredictable patterns, someone was falling off the couch. Eventually, a period of soft confusion took over; she pulled on her clothes, grabbed her purse, and staggered out the door. Everything was quick, sudden, unpleasant, irrefutable, over.

But eventually, she appreciated the blunt unmethodical reality of each encounter. It was like commuting on the bus, or memorizing logical principles for a multiple-choice exam.

"The place is always filthy," she told her best friend from college, Rebecca Santos, who lived in Boulder with her second husband. Every evening, after sex with Rob's dad, she would sit in the car outside the 7-11, smoking cigarettes with the windows open, and call Rebecca. "Everything, including Rob's dad, smells like sour milk. I never tell him I'm coming over, and yet whenever I show up, there he is, waiting behind the front door when I knock, like he's been standing there all day just waiting to surprise me. There's never any foreplay. He doesn't say hello or even offer me a drink. Usually, he just fucks me right there on the hall floor and it's over before I know it, and by the time I *do* know it, he's carrying me into the bedroom and fucking me again until I'm so sore I can hardly move. He's not like a person. He's like this mindless sequence of events. He's there and I'm here and suddenly we're off on separate trajectories, according to laws we can't control. The laws aren't very pleasant, either. They don't give us any pleasure. Though it's impossible to discuss things like pleasure when it comes to Rob's dad. What *pleases* that guy, and what doesn't, seem all mixed up in his head."

Way out in Colorado, Rebecca sighed audibly, and enunciated several sharp clicks of her tongue. Everything about Rebecca had always sounded slightly exasperated. Marriage hadn't changed her one bit.

"Look, Margie," Rebecca said. "Is this conversation going anywhere? I've got kids in the bath and a nice little Chardonnay chilling in the fridge."

"Of course it's not going anywhere, Becks. I just didn't know who else to call. I'm saying that I can't stop myself, and Rob's dad can't stop himself, and I've read stories about things like this, these irresistible-attraction type deals, but this *affair* doesn't have anything to do with attraction, or passion, or desire. It's more like I've unleashed something I didn't know was in me. It's like all the control I once had over my life is gone and I'm being controlled by somebody else. Not Rob's dad or even Rob, but somebody I haven't thought about in years. Like maybe my own dad, who I haven't seen since college. I know it's confusing; I don't even know what I'm trying to say. So maybe you should just go get your kids out of the bath, Becks, drink your Chardonnay, and forget I called. I don't know what I want from other people anymore. I don't even know why I called."

That night, Rob was sitting up in bed reading one of her old *Glamour* magazines and wearing the purple silk pajamas she had bought him three Christmases ago. The purple silk pajamas were the pajamas he wore when he did want to make love.

Margaret stood back from the bedroom doorway as she removed her shoes and stockings. She could smell Rob's dad's Salems on her skin.

"I'm taking a shower, hon," she said, in the sort of clipped, autonomic voice she used to tell her assistant at work that she was going on break. Rob didn't look up.

"Dad called," Rob told the magazine. "I can't figure him at all. I don't hear from him for weeks, and now I hear from him like every day. He wants the two of us to spend more time with him. He wants to do all the 'Dad' things we never did when he was in jail, like go to Beans baseball games, or superhero movies at the Cineplex. He even talked about camping up at Lopez Lake. What would you think of me going up to Lopez Lake for a few days with Dad, hon? Does that sound crazy or what?"

It was the first question anybody had asked Margaret in ages that she knew the answer to. And the funny thing was that she knew the answer even before he asked.

"I don't know, hon," she said in a voice soft enough to approach a shy squirrel with a peanut. "Maybe it's a good idea. In fact, it sounds like something that might be really good for both of you."

They spent more time together as a family, often within an hour or two after Rob's dad had fucked her at his place. They attended double-features at the Sunset Drive-In, or took long drives up the coast to Cambria and Big Sur. "I love this part of the country," Rob's dad pronounced every few minutes or so, gesturing vaguely at the latest remarkable landscape, such as Morro Rock, or the

Los Padres National Forest. "I love it so much I could shoot it in the head, chop it up in pieces and eat it. I love it so much I want to bury it in my backyard so nobody else can find it. I don't know if you guys ever noticed but love and aggression are really mixed-up forces; personally, I find it hard to tell them apart. I know that must make me real awful-sounding; but it's just the way I roll." Sometimes, he leaned forward from the back seat, rested his left elbow on the back of Rob's seat, and gave Margaret a secret reach-around with his right hand. Margaret rarely pushed him away.

"Dad's changed," Rob told her on the way home from his dad's Monterey Street apartment. "He's growing more like the dad I knew when I was little. He even laughs at my jokes. He's also less controlling. Did you notice how many times he said, 'You guys decide?' That's not even remotely like the dad I used to know. When I was young, everything had to be done his way. If he wanted to drive to the hardware store, then Mom and I had to go to the hardware store, even if we ended up sitting in the car for hours. If he ordered a medium-rare cheeseburger, then Mom and I had to order medium-rare cheeseburgers, too. He even left us in the car one night for like three hours while it turned out he was killing some Columbian guy with a plastic fork in a bowling alley. Mom and I had no idea what was going on. When he got back to the car, there were streaks of crimson blood all over his T-shirt, like he'd just come from Art class. His right hand was bleeding through a thick, lumpy bandage of brown paper napkins. "I got bit by a chipmunk," he told us. He said it totally seriously. Then he drove away using his good hand, getting more blood all over the driver's seat, the dashboard radio, and even my Social Studies textbook. The part I remember most vividly is Dad taking us through Jack-in-the-Box and ordering three Jumbo meal deals and three jumbo vanilla milkshakes, even though he must've known by then that Mom and I hated vanilla milkshakes. And, of course, we had to drink them. We were terrified of making him angry, even though he never did anything violent to us, there was always the possibility, and just the *possibility* of violence scared us more than violence itself. One way or another, that's why I still hate going to Jack-in-the-Box. I'm really sorry, hon. I should have told you that story before now. You deserved to hear it."

That night in bed, Margaret made love to Rob in all the ways that were the antithesis to making love to Rob's Dad. She kissed him on the cheeks and mouth, stroked his back gently with her nails, and squeezed the back of his neck when she came. When she said, "I love you," she closed her eyes tightly, cried for a moment, and pulled him down on top of her. She didn't know why she was crying until she stopped, and when she did stop, it all seemed totally clear. Rob wasn't his dad. He would never be his dad. He would only be Rob, forever and ever. Good old boring no-nonsense lousy-in-the-sack Rob.

"I love you, too, hon," he said after a while.

And then he grew heavier on top of her, weighing her down into the bed's inescapable deepness.

"When I met Rob," Margaret told Rebecca the next night, after fucking Rob's dad so hard that they broke his dining-room table, "he was the first man who seemed to care who I was, or how I felt, and I wasn't sure if I liked being around a man like that. He was always complimenting me about my appearance, and opening doors, and asking where I wanted to go for dinner; it really got on my nerves. Even after we married, he was always doing thoughtful little things, such as bringing fresh flowers from the store, or picking up some watch I liked at Kohl's, even when it wasn't my birthday. Even now, Rob's always asking how I feel, or stroking my back, even when he doesn't want sex; it makes me so nervous I'm afraid to go to sleep sometimes. Seriously, do you think something's wrong with me? But Rob's dad is different. I can't remember a single nice thing he ever said to me. If I got killed on the freeway after I left his apartment, he could not care less. And the weirdest part is that Rob and his dad are now getting along better than ever. They went to a ballgame last night and didn't get back until past midnight. It's grown clear to me that Rob, his dad, and I all exist on different planes of reality. We're just living our different realities together in the same family."

Later, when Margaret turned off her cell and went inside, she found a note from Rob scribbled on a paper napkin:

> Dad's in trouble.
> Will call soon.
> Rob

It was as if Margaret had been waiting to receive this note from Rob all her life.

Margaret was almost relieved to hear that Rob's dad had been charged with two counts of manslaughter, kidnaping, and extortion, and three counts of the RICO act. It made her realize how little she owed him.

"I don't want to talk about it," Rob said that night at dinner. They were still wearing their court clothes; Rob hadn't even loosened his tie. He looked like one of those tensely expectant, half-smiling contestants on *The Apprentice*. "But then again, maybe I do. After all the progress Dad was making, he turns around and blows it on some poor pedestrian who gave him the finger, and now that's it for old Dad. Mom always told me this would happen. 'Your dad will always disappoint you,' she told me, whenever I asked to visit him at the Men's Colony. 'He's a sociopath with no ability to distinguish right from wrong.' But no matter what Mom said, he was always my dad, and I loved him, and I wanted him around. Sometimes, I imagined him making daring escapes from prison just to visit me on my birthday, and I would hug him and say, 'Dad, see, you don't have to be a criminal. You have me and mom, who love you. If you can just stay out of prison, we can all live together as a happy family.'"

That night, Margaret put Rob to bed as if he were six years old.

The trial was postponed twice, and when the hearing was held in early October, Margaret agreed to stay home. "I've got to do this by myself," Rob said mysteriously, as if he were driving off to a difficult conversation with his doctor. "If you're there, my emotions might get more conflicted than they already are."

Margaret spent the day looking for part-time jobs online. Every job listing contained links to endless streams of information that didn't matter to Margaret, such as "personal qualities" and "evidence of commitment," but nothing about hours, pay or benefits. She posted two inquiries about weekend "data management" positions at CalPoly, cooked and ate an entire frozen sausage pizza, flipped through some old diet books, and called her mother, who was driving to Reno to meet friends from her book club.

"I wish they'd told me how easy it was to attach Bluetooth to my phone," her mother said. "Now I can talk to people when I drive."

For once, Margaret insisted on asking about her father, even while a cold, slow silence began to build on the other end of the line. What did he die of? What was the last thing he said before he moved out of the house? When he called Margaret, he had always started every conversation with: "I can't talk long." And why did he keep saying that, what was the big hurry? Is his second wife alive? How could I contact her? What did he do for a living before he died? Did he have any pets? Until her mother lost patience and said:

"Please, Margaret. I don't understand all this interest in your father, who never understood the basic rules of family life, and went running off with another woman just because he liked her legs. If you ask me, he isn't any different from Rob's dad, except maybe he didn't murder so many people. You want to know more about your asshole father? Go read it on his tombstone. Now, if you don't mind, I'm calling somebody who wants to talk about *me* and not your father. Then I'm driving to Harrah's, meeting the girls, and blowing twenty bucks on Keno."

Almost six months after Rob's dad returned to prison, Margaret awoke in her empty bed to the raucous sound of birds in the yard. Sunlight was streaming through her windows, sparkling with dust motes and refracted light. Everything in her house was imbued with a fresh, intangible, unfamiliar quality: her gladiolas hanging on the balcony, the clean white triangular vanity table they had purchased on sale at Target, the matching teak veneer end tables, even the high ceilings and cold, orange tile floors. It all seemed like a much nicer, brighter home than the one where Margaret had previously lived. Only someone with taste and sensitivity could appreciate a house like this. Someday, that someone might even be her.

ALL OVER BUT THE SHOUTING
Rick Ollerman

I went home with her because I had to. Tammy needed a bigger man to get something back from a smaller man and I told her yes. After obliging her, I'd been given the key to her apartment. She'd neglected to tell me there'd be only one bed and no couch.

She found me on the floor; her package, wrapped in a faded cotton tote bag, sat on the kitchen counter next to the sink. I didn't know what was in it and didn't care. I'd done what she needed and now I was out of sight and safe. Safer, anyway.

It was cold on the pressed carpet or I wouldn't have gone with her. I needed sleep and when she insisted I follow her to the single bedroom, pulling me insistently with the weight of her slender body, I again obliged. I wouldn't get onto the bed without a shower, though. The sour smell of dried sweat was rank on my body—I would have bathed earlier if I'd had a change of clothes. Now I just wanted the heat from the water and a chance to sleep. Tammy surprised me with a clean pair of men's shorts as I stepped out of the bathroom, a dark green towel around my waist; she'd removed my other things.

"I'll wash them for you in the morning," she said.

"You don't have to." I was being polite. I was happy to have her do it, but I wouldn't have asked it of her.

191

"Come on." She led the way back to the bedroom and pulled down the comforter and top sheet from a double bed that was set against a wall. I stood in the middle of the room looking around, not moving toward the bed, even though I felt an irresistible urge to lie down and close my eyes.

Tammy turned away and with a few movements was suddenly in her underwear, her slender body sleek and appealing. She was quick to slide onto the bed, and before I could figure out what I really wanted to do, she was patting the open space next to her. "Get in, Jack. I won't bite."

I decided I wasn't in a position to argue. The shower had made me soporific and my eyelids were heavy. I climbed in after her and pulled up the corner of the bedding to trap the warmth. Tammy scooted onto my side and turned, draping an arm over my chest.

"Do you want to—"

I didn't want to be mean or cruel. I needed what she could give me. "I just have to sleep, Tammy."

"Oh," she said, pulling back her arm. "I get it." But she didn't pull it back all the way. My eyes were closed, and I was one heartbeat away from not being able to feel what she did next. I kept my eyes closed as she worked her way down my body and then rolled on top. I remember she smelled sweet.

In the morning she was gone. How she got out of the corner without disturbing me was a mystery, but I was grateful.

Last night I would have slept in an abandoned car if I'd known where to find one. I had no money, and I couldn't go to my friends, or the neighborhood, or anywhere else. This woman, Tammy, who happened to be working in the bar I'd crept into with my last thirty bucks, poured me a beer and told me her troubles. "It's not supposed to work this way," I told her. She talked about ways to get out of her jam, though I think most of them involved what I could do to help her. That's how it seemed, anyway, up until we got to her bedroom.

There were two boxes of cereal next to a bowl and spoon on the small table in the kitchen. Tammy was sitting on the floor, legs crossed beneath her. The cotton bag I'd left on the counter the night before was gone.

"Good morning," she said. "I'm afraid there's not much for breakfast."

I pulled out the single chair and sat down, facing her. "Milk would be nice."

She hit her forehead with her palm and pushed to her feet. "There is milk."

She pulled a carton out of the refrigerator, and as I mixed up some Raisin Bran I felt her presence behind me.

"Last night was nice."

"You saved my life." I said it without thinking, but it may have been true—literally. My crew had scattered when the job turned to shit. We were all homies, born into this town as lifers. Each of us knew every rathole for twenty miles. I wouldn't have been able to hide on my own much longer.

Tammy put her hands on my shoulders. They were warm. "I feel the same way."

She didn't know we weren't in the same game, but it was nice hearing her say that. I liked her but she was a mystery. "Where are you from? I'd have known you already if you were from Alford."

"Not far," she said. She moved closer and I could feel the pressure of her breasts against my back. Her whole body exuded heat. "My daddy has ties here. He owns Teddy's, the bar you came into last night."

That made me think of our deal. "He have something to do with that package I left on the counter?"

"Hmm," she said. She came around to my side and got down on her knees, sliding her arms around my waist and slowly lowering her head onto my thigh, her tanned but lined face turned to the side. I lowered my spoon and stroked her hair. It was dirty blond, but natural, the dark and light strands existing in a tangle without any help from a bottle.

"You're in trouble," I said.

"Hmm," she said again.

"Me, too."

She came up and into my arms, forcing me to slide the chair away from the table as she moved onto my lap. "I could tell," she said, kissing me all the way, like it was last night. Not long after, we were back in her bed, clothes strewn across the floor.

"I want to help you," I told her. She was lying against my side, her left breast pushed into my ribs as I stared at her cracked popcorn ceiling. "If I can."

She kissed my chest. "You're sweet," she said. "But that wouldn't be smart."

I laughed before I could help myself. "Baby, I have baggage like a bundle of dynamite. You keeping me anywhere near you isn't smart."

"Do you want to leave?"

"I have nowhere to go." I thought about it some more and gave her a direct answer. "No, I don't want to leave."

She nestled her head into my arm, got smaller. "Someone's after you, aren't they?"

It didn't surprise me that she'd picked up on that. "They are."

"Are they going to hurt you?"

They'll kill me if they find me. When they find me. "They are."

I felt her fingers trace a pattern along the ridges of my abdomen. "Maybe I should help you."

"You already are," I said. "What do you think you've been doing?" I squeezed her as best I could with her weight on my arm. We didn't speak for so long I thought she'd fallen asleep.

"Do you know what you did for me last night?"

I wasn't sure how to respond to that. "I hope I do."

"I'm talking about the package."

"Yeah," I said. "That. I haven't thought about it. I just did what you asked."

"Was it hard?"

I shrugged. "Not really. It's not very noble but I hit him as I walked up to him and he dropped. I found the bag and took it. He was unconscious when I left."

A wave of tension moved down her body. "Could you have killed him?"

The answer was yes, but it hadn't happened. "No," I said.

She relaxed but the closeness we shared earlier was gone. She said, "That's good," but more to herself, it seemed, than to me. We stayed like that for a time. Peaceful.

Finally, she asked, "Why are people after you?"

I looked down and found her staring at me. She ran a bar in the blue-collar area of town, a joint that probably stayed in business because there wasn't a strip club within thirty miles. If she didn't know about me in particular, she certainly knew all about me in general. "We pulled a job, my friends and I. It didn't go well." I moved her hair behind her ear. It was soft. "Actually, it went perfect, until the law showed up."

"Someone called the cops?"

"No. I figure they must have been moving on the same deal we were." I didn't really want to give her any details, but I was so screwed I knew it didn't really matter. It would be good to tell her, to talk about it. Because it was *her*.

"We knew some guys that were taking a truck, hijacking it. We also knew who was buying."

"So you stepped in."

I shrugged. "There was a lot of cash. We needed a score."

"What happened when the police came?"

"What you think. We got the hell out of there, the four of us. I even had the money."

195

She sat up, pressing against my chest with one hand. Her naked figure was beautiful, the tanned skin uniformly covering her body. I wondered how often she used a tanning bed. "How much?" she asked.

"It doesn't matter. Not enough." I didn't like how intent she'd become. Gently I moved her hand off my chest, taking her weight with my arm and forcing her to return to her previous position. She snuggled in but kept her eyes on my face.

"Where is it?"

"We had a spot where we'd meet if things went wrong. I took it there."

"With your friends?"

"No one was there. I left the money and kept running."

"You left the money? Why?"

"It was light. Way light. The buyer must have been shorting their end of the deal. There were dollar bills where there should have been fifties or hundreds."

"Oh," she said, a lot of the tension leaving her. "But that's not your fault."

"No," I said. "But my guys are going to look at the take and think I fucked with it. They're going to think I took the real money and left the dollar bills. The problem is I'm the one who had the money when the cops showed." I twirled some of her hair between my fingers. "Thing is, we were all screwed, just none of us knew it."

"You can't tell them? You don't think they'd listen?"

I shook my head. "When the doors came down in the front of the warehouse we didn't know what was happening. I said it was cops. Powell, the asshole, looked at me and said how'd I know? Was I the one who called them? The rest of them looked at me a little funny, but I had the case and I turned and ran. Powell started in my direction but there was an explosion, not a gunshot, and he fell. I kept moving, and I heard him yell something at me as I ran."

"That doesn't mean—"

"Powell's a dick," I said. "He'd screw his mother for a cigarette."

She hit my chest. "So why not keep all the money?"

I shook my head. "Then I really would be guilty of screwing my guys."

"You think Powell called the cops?"

"Not really, but you never know. But my crew's going to come after me now. They're going to think I ripped them off. Doesn't matter what I did or didn't do."

"But the real crook—"

I laughed again. "Honey, we're all real crooks," I said.

She didn't argue.

"You working tonight? At the bar?"

It was late in the afternoon. We'd stayed in bed another hour after I'd confessed my sins, and we'd shared each other's bodies with a lessening urgency but a deeper sense of purpose. At the end we'd managed to become Jackson and Tammy, something beyond just two bodies rutting for comfort in hard and desperate times. I was feeling an intensity I hadn't experienced in a long time.

"I have to," she said but I could see the muscles in her face tighten.

The thought of the package from the night before made me ask, "Is it safe?"

She went to the bathroom and returned with a large plastic comb and started to work on her hair. "I don't know. Maybe."

"Look, I know what goes on with bars. Behind the scenes, I mean."

She didn't say anything, just kept on with her hair.

"Your father. He runs cash through there, doesn't he?"

Bars are still a cash business and, as such, convenient for people who need to launder bills from less convenient ventures. Declare it as bar revenue, pay taxes on it, and you make clean money from bad. Uncle Sam even gets a taste.

Tammy nodded.

"You skimming?"

Her eyes jerked to mine, then she relaxed and resumed combing.

"And he caught you."

The teeth caught in a snarl and she pulled at it, making it worse. Finally she pulled the comb out and threw it on the bed near my feet.

"No. It was my brother."

She told me that her father owned a string of bars across the state and that they served one real function for him. Her brothers oversaw the rest of the joints while Tammy had her own thing. "Taking a little bit is expected," she said.

"But you took more than a little."

She nodded. "One time."

"Why?"

She turned her head. "It doesn't matter."

I left it. "Your father know?"

Her widened eyes and stiffened posture answered that question.

"But your brother..."

"He wanted the skim. Plus the rest of it. But that was already gone. Daddy might have been okay with what I took, but when you add what Marcel..."

"Why not just let Marcel tell him? Would it be so bad?"

"It's my father. He's always been very specific in his expectations. I went too far. But it was only supposed to be temporary."

I thought about it while she stood there, close to crying. The urge to take her in my arms was strong but I wanted to figure this out.

"Who'd I slug? Marcel?"

She nodded. "You got back the money I gave him, the extra that was supposed to keep him from calling Daddy now, before Daddy gets back from Europe. Marcel knew he could take that money from me and there was nothing I could do about it. Daddy would believe I took it all and Marcel would deny he knew anything about it."

I gave in to my instincts, got up from the bed, and crossed over to her. She came easily into my arms. All I wanted to do was hold her and forget about the outside. "So you're still screwed."

"Just like you," she said.

She understood I didn't want to leave her. It wasn't just the sanctuary her little apartment provided. She gave me a warm kiss and then went out to the market, returning after ninety minutes with a collection of bagels and other convenience foods. We didn't speak much as we spent the afternoon together. I provided support for her, and the way she leaned into me, relaxed when we were touching, I knew that she felt it all, too.

"How did you find me?" she asked, once again lying against my side.

"You mean the bar?"

She nodded.

"Dumb luck." I thought about it. "When we left the warehouse I didn't know where to go. I dropped the money at our spot and took off."

"What would have happened if those other guys had caught you there?"

I kissed the side of her head.

"And then you found me." She said it in a way that made it sound like good news.

"Yours was the only bar on this side of town. What else would be open? I had to get off the street and there you were."

"What would you have done if I hadn't been there?"

I shrugged. "I don't know. I had a thought about breaking into a store, something like that, but I didn't want to risk any alarms." Her body gave off a noticeable amount of heat, more so than most people, I thought. Like it was imperfectly stored energy, trapped in her skin, that was slowly oozing out. The warmth carried her smell, a combination of lotion and oils, up to my nostrils and I breathed her in deeply. "It's just good you were there."

She moved away from me, turned to face me. "Is it?" she asked. "Really?"

I knew she was talking about the consequences of her family problems. "We'll figure it out," I said. I got up to use the bathroom, told her I'd be right back. That was when Marcel came in.

I heard the door open with a bang and jumped to my feet. My hand was on the bathroom doorknob when I heard Tammy yell her brother's name.

That stopped me. I tried to make out what they were saying but I couldn't get all the words. It was clear he was after more money, but Tammy seemed to give as good as she got. She didn't sound fearful, at least not at that point, so I stayed where I was. I knew if I went out there Marcel might recognize me, and everything could change in an instant. If Marcel had a gun, I wouldn't have been able to do anything anyway. So I waited.

The front door slammed again, and I rushed out to find Tammy, tears tumbling down her cheeks. She looked up and ran to me.

"I hate that bastard!" she said, snarling.

"I couldn't get it all. What did he say?"

She used part of my shirt to dry her eyes. The intimate gesture made me want to protect her even more. "He accused me of sending someone to rob him last night. I told him he was crazy. I don't think he even cares. He just wants the money back. And more. Now he wants more."

I led her back to the bed and we settled down and faced each other. "Can you get it?"

She blinked. "You want me to give it to him? My father..."

"No, no." I shook my head. "If there's more, we could take it. We could run, go somewhere…"

Her laugh was unexpected. "There's no running," she said. "Not for me. You don't know my father. He's everywhere." Tammy wiped her eyes and looked into mine. "But I'll do it. With you. It's just…it's just…"

"What?"

"It won't work."

We sat there together in her living room, her two hands in mine, until she found her resolve. "I'll have to give him the money."

"But—"

"There's a second safe. In the bar. It's separate from the main one, the one we use for normal business. The second one is where Daddy's money goes."

"Two safes?"

She nodded, lines creasing her forehead as she considered. "If someone robs the place, anything like that, the first safe is there, in the office. But Daddy says no one thinks of a second safe. So that's the important one."

That made sense. I'd been part of a few things where we took out a safe; I'd never thought there could be more than one. "Pay Marcel," I said. "We'll take the rest and run. Unless you think your father will understand. Stick up for you over your brother."

She shook her head. "He'll never understand." Tammy brushed her hair back from her face with her fingers. "You know what will happen if they find us? Because they probably will."

I nodded. "I know. Maybe we'll get lucky, make a new start."

"What about—what about the guys that are after you?"

"They're not as bad as your father, they don't have the reach. If we can get a jump, I won't worry about them."

* * *

Dark was falling as we made our way to the bar, my arm around her shoulders, hers around my waist. I wore a baseball cap Tammy'd had in her closet and kept my head down during the six-block walk. Everything seemed fine when she unlocked the door and we went inside. She'd called Marcel and told him she could pay him tonight. Everything was happening so fast, but that was the only way it could. I was exhausted as I sat at the empty bar while Tammy went down to the basement. When she came back it was with a gym bag full of money.

"How much is there?" I asked.

"Daddy would know. He always knows."

She poured me a beer without my asking, counted out the amount Marcel was after, and put the bills in a series of plastic grocery bags. The gym bag still looked to be about half full.

The door of the bar opened and a short man walked in, brown hair, scruffy haircut, round glasses, dirty olive-green jacket. He stopped when he saw me, then came on slowly.

"'Evening," he said.

I nodded and turned back to my beer as Tammy whisked the money below the bar.

"Mind if I join you?"

"Bar's open," I said.

He sat two stools away and told Tammy he'd take a bourbon, rocks, any brand.

"Early, isn't it?"

I didn't take his point. I didn't care what he wanted, and I didn't want to talk about it anyway. For an answer I jerked my head and didn't look at him. Maybe he'd take the hint.

Tammy set a glass in front of him and he slid a ten-dollar bill toward her. He took a sip from his glass and made a sound like he was about to say something. Then he quickly brought his hand to his jacket pocket. I tensed and started to turn but he pulled out a cell phone with one hand, holding the other toward me, telling me it was okay, it was just his phone.

I felt like an idiot, but I saw that Tammy had been just as

jumpy. The little man moved down to the other end of the bar, then back toward the door, as he said, "Hey, Mom," into the phone.

Tammy's hand came over the bar and gripped mine. "We're like to explode. I'm going to have a drink." She took out a glass and poured herself some whiskey. "You want one of these?"

I said, "Sure," as the little guy finished his call. He was holding the phone almost at arm's length, as though his vision were poor, and he was trying to make out the screen. He held out his other hand, too, index finger extended, waiting to kill the call. He brought a finger down upon the hang-up button but coughed as he pushed it, then made a show of wiping his mouth with his sleeve.

The phone disappeared back into his pocket and he returned to his seat and his half-finished drink. "Bad throat," he said, tilting the glass back. "I need this."

I said nothing. Tammy kept her eyes on him as he told her he'd see her later, rapped the bar with his knuckles, and left.

"You know that guy?" I asked.

"No," she said. "I don't think so."

"You should call your brother."

There were a dozen or so people in the place when Marcel arrived. He wasn't alone. The guy he'd brought with him was huge and had a nose that had been flattened more times than a bishop's collar. Tammy whispered his name as the two of them stopped just inside the door and looked around.

Tammy didn't move. I got the feeling Marcel wanted her to come to him but she didn't move. He walked to the bar while his bodyguard stayed where he was.

"Give it up," Marcel said to his sister.

Tammy hesitated, glanced at me. I tensed. As Marcel followed her gaze she looked past me at the booths in the corner and let her eyes linger.

"What is it?"

"Nothing," she said.

"Well?"

Her hand was under the counter as the door opened again. My gut turned over.

It was Powell. From my crew.

Powell.

I don't know whether Tammy saw me blanch or she'd been planning on going for the gun all along, but she came up with a pistol-grip sawed-off and put a ragged hole through her brother before he had a chance to blink. Marcel's man brought out his own handgun when there was another explosion. The big man went down, suddenly limp, the back of his skull blown away.

Powell.

My old crew was coming at me and all I could think of was protecting Tammy. I reached for the shotgun but she pushed me away, hard. I didn't understand. I turned from the bar and Powell shot me in the stomach. I went down where I was, the room spinning red.

Tammy dropped down next to me. Maybe she'd come over the bar. She thrust the shotgun at me and backed away.

Powell.

I pumped a shell into the action as I felt my hands go numb. I pulled the trigger with Powell standing over me.

Nothing happened.

Powell laughed and kicked me hard in the leg. Then he held his hand out toward Tammy, who took it as she rose.

I saw the duffel slung over her shoulder. She gave me a sad look as she walked away. It was everything we'd shared the past twenty-four hours: her tanned skin, the lines about her forehead and face, and I could swear the scent of her skin and lotion floated down to where I lay. She pursed her lips into a pout as she walked into the black-dotted mist at the edge of my vision.

Tammy had known I'd be her answer. Her father would find the second safe open and the money gone, one of his sons killed, possibly by me. Tammy had disappeared with Powell, knowing that the hint of a deeper conspiracy just might buy her some time to escape, get out of her situation.

Later, in the hospital, I wondered where she had gone, though I knew I'd never be with her again. That little man with the phone, he hadn't been talking to anyone, he'd been setting up so he could take my picture, coughing to cover the sound of the electronic shutter. He'd have sent it to Powell who would have been waiting. For me, for the money, for the girl.

Powell and Tammy had set me up.

They hadn't told me yet if I'd live. I don't think they had any idea, but I knew. It was confirmed when I heard the door open and a nurse tell someone that visiting hours would be over very soon.

Not soon enough, I thought.

MOTEL AT THE END OF THE WORLD: TUESDAY AFTERNOON

Trey R. Barker

I can remember her face.

Sweat tickles my face.

His, too.

This room, the "security" office, sweats me like my prison cell did. Ten feet to a side, walls painted institutional white but faded to gray with stains and streaks of nicotine-yellow. It houses the motel's low-end surveillance cameras that, sure as shit, somehow fell off the back of a delivery truck. There's a cheap computer and extra hard drives stacked up like the motel's whores in the wee hours, waiting on a room or a dark corner of the hallway.

Small, tight, claustrophobic.

Just like the cell. The walls are exactly the same, except that the nicotine stains have been traded for dried piss in the corners, the stink of men's shit slathered to the underside of the metal toilet seat and the edge of the metal mirror, and probably on the lip of the faucet.

The video skips across the monitor, herky-jerky, people

moving in and out. "The hell am I watching for?" I call to the front desk.

The day manager, Magpie, chuckles. "A fight or something. Two nights ago, maybe?"

"Anybody dead?"

A snort. "Maybe Consuela's girls can check the rooms and hallways?"

"And the roof."

"Found Dylan up there again this morning," Magpie says. "Gonna fall off, Dude. Can you fix that door or something?"

Dylan is a good kid, maybe ten years old, but saddled with the weight of a junkie daddy who regularly goes hands-on. They've lived at the motel for just about a month. "Maybe the fight is someone tuning Daddy up again?"

"We could be so lucky. Let *that* fucker fall off the roof."

"Found him jerking off in the hallway yesterday. All tweaked up, yelling at Dylan...who was at school, by the way. Wasn't even there."

With the video on fast-forward, everyone moves quickly; in and out of the lobby, up and down the stairs. The door opens, slow even in fast time, and various members of our geriatric community teeter in and out. One of them yells at Dylan's daddy. He flips them off.

I'm janitorial, a shirt that says *Arnie* over one tit and *Janitor* over the other. Arnie was the previous janitor, knifed in the basement. They washed the blood out, mostly, and hung the shirt on a doorknob until I came along.

In another life I was a copper. That was before I was called out in the middle of a night off that was resplendent with three women, booze, pills, and rough sex that, when the women were later threatened with jail, suddenly became unlawful restraint and sexual assault.

The itch is at me again, blazing through my left eye. Thought I had it beat for today. Thought last night's stomping was good and hard. No skin-pop bruises on my arms, though. It had been a stomping by the bird—a fifth of Old Crow. So much Old Crow that I couldn't even remember what time it was when someone knocked on my door. I hadn't answered, being both drunk and off duty.

Trying to stomp not just the itch, but the memory.

I can remember her face. His, too. Siblings holding hands.

I push stop on the playback and go into the main office. The lobby opens up from the front desk and right now it's full. The walking dead. The walking dying. The dispossessed and hopeless. Those for whom our joint with holes in the walls and curled and stained linoleum that I can't fix fast enough is a step up. Half the lights in the lobby are dark but the sun limps in.

Magpie stares at me. "Itching?"

"You can tell?"

"Eyes are red," he says. "Left one is scrunched up. Like a cheap-ass Clint Eastwood."

Sighing, I plop on his desk, shove the real-time monitor of every door, the roof, and three angles in the parking lot outta the way with my ass. "I *am* a cheap-ass Clint Eastwood, you can believe that."

Laughing, Magpie points at the real-time monitor. "Believe that, chump."

Someone is at my wreck of a car. They move from the right rear tire to the left, then go for the street. A tall guy, beard, a limp slowing him down.

I dash to the rear parking lot, then to the empty street. Guy is gone and all I have is a car on four flat tires.

"Son of a *bitch*." I bang a fist against the car's roof.

The lot and street, shimmering beneath the heat's oppression, are empty except for the industrial smoke. The motel is trapped by industry; chemical and light manufacturing. Smoke and chemical tang, amplified by the heat, are part of my life now. I wipe my forehead with Arnie's shirt, leave a wet smudge across his faded blood. The air is toast-dry, like my face is desiccating.

I head indoors, the itch is in both eyes now, like a third-world shithole disease.

When the elevator door groans open, I ride up a floor. Just a quick stop in my room, spend a few minutes cooling the itch, then back to reviewing video for whatever Magpie thinks happened.

Just a quick stop.

A quick pop.

I'm clean.

Mostly.

A quick pop.

Warm, fuzzy edges.

So another quick pop; what can it hurt?

Second pop puts me back in that hallway.

Gammy dead on the floor, most of her in the hallway. Grampy dead mostly in the kitchen. Sonny Boy and his two kids in the basement bedroom below us.

Two doors into the basement, one window out. All three covered by the Special Response Team cops, huddled over their rifles and scopes, hats backward, gloves fingerless.

Command post is a block away, but I don't do my Talk-Talk from there. Too far away and out of touch. So I'm in the kitchen. Basement bedroom below me but offset. Didn't want to be directly above in case he shoots.

We've been talking for three hours, his eight-year-old daughter and seven-year-old son absolutely silent in the background, and finally, he's getting tired.

Expressing no remorse for killing his ex-wife.

Expressing some remorse for killing his parents.

Expressing extreme love for his children.

Worries about them getting through life without too many psychic scars. Worries about them getting an education, a good job, a good spouse. Wants them to live their fullest lives.

Says he wants to be done with all this.

I breathe easy. His words are future continuous tense, which means he wants to stay alive.

I stumble into the office. Magpie watches afternoon soaps. "What am I looking for?"

Concern is tattooed on his face. "You didn't find it?" He speaks in abstract terms, demons writ large, rather than specific to the video I'd been reviewing. "You were three hours fighting those two demons, dude."

Yet I still see their faces.

I punch up the video. The picture, always small and scratchy, totters to life. I hit fast-forward to try to lose the demons in my job.

The barricaded subject was seven years ago, the trial six. Then my thirty-seven months in stir. Upon release, I climbed into a bottle and eventually spilled out here, and every hour of every day, I see their faces.

His and hers…matching grimaces.

On screen, people move in and out of the lobby, up and down the hallways. I move, too, in and out of rooms, constantly to the payment drop box. People frequently sign their Social Security checks over to the hotel so they can exist here uninterrupted.

People in…people out.

This is visual proof of how my then-wife said I'd end up. Served me divorce papers as the bailiff hooked me up after the verdict and said I'd die lonely in some flophouse.

Well, I'm in a flophouse, I'm probably dying, but I'm sure as shit not lonely.

'Cause I can see their faces. And I hear them at night.

I cry and my eyes itch and my whole life is just people in and people out.

But then, in the video, there's a tall man. He limps into the lobby and talks to Magpie. After they talk, he looks toward the elevator, holds up two fingers. Magpie nods, then shakes his head and waves his hands. He's not there, Magpie's body language says.

I know that limp.

"Who's this guy?" I freeze the image.

Magpie hauls himself out of the chair and into the office. Hits play, then watches it again. "Said he was a friend of yours. Wanted to see you. I told him you weren't in."

"You told him my apartment?"

"Said he was your friend. Used to work with you. Showed me a badge and everything." Magpie looks pained. "Did I fuck up? Who is it?"

I clap him on the shoulder. "Nah. We're good."

When he leaves, I heave painfully. Everything inside me is suddenly unmoored.

Officer Timothy Roberts.

As Magpie shouts at me, "I'm'a go grab a sammich," I squeeze my fingers so hard I'm afraid they'll break. I sweat. My vision narrows and I can't hear anything.

Unlike my ex-wife, Officer Timmy sat through my whole trial.

Last row of the gallery, crutches at his side. I turned my chair half around so I could keep him in my peripheral vision...in case he jumped the gallery rail to get to me.

I punch in a date and time and the computer gives me the video from last night. I don't know when I'd heard the knock on my door, so I hit play and start from midnight.

At 2:47 a.m. by the computer clock, I see him.

He comes through the lobby and goes straight to the elevator. The elevator camera and elevator landing camera don't work so the next time I see him is when he limps down the hallway. Steps over two near-death junkies and avoids a pool of piss two doors down from mine.

He knocks hard. When he gets no answer, he limps away.

Just like I watched him limp away from my car.

Just like I watched him limp away from my trial.

* * *

Franny Trevino is forty-two, unemployed, not particularly successful. Exactly who you'd think would kill family members and take his children hostage, demanding a muddied list of random things.

Because this wasn't about getting something for his children. This wasn't transactional.

This was emotional.

I gingerly talk him through the surrender process. I don't call it that. Surrender is a loaded word for some men. Triggers their need to have the swingingest dicks. So I stay away from that, talk generally about "when it's over," "when we're done here." It's all the right words and at the right time but none of it feels right in my mouth. Too many words, or too complicated, or something.

Says he wants to be done but I'm stepping on him, not letting him talk.

Says again he wants to be done.

My head hurts and I'm sweating and maybe I'm not hearing clearly. I always worry about negotiations and people dying. Wearing a badge is tough, low-grade PTSD 24/7, but these calls are everything we do amped up times ten; jazzed with three-phase high voltage electricity.

But this isn't just negotiation-worry. This is also women and pills, freaky sex, and booze worry.

Franny is a control fiend. Wants to be large and in charge all the time, and fuck him I got time for this? I was enjoying my night and he decided to psycho-Rambo all over his parents and ex-wife and kids?

When did he start yelling at me and what the fuck dude and we go back and forth about letting the kids go and I ask him what the fuck he's doing is he going to kill them like he did everyone else and he screams that I don't understand he's agitated all to be damned and I yell back that I understand perfectly well this is just another bullshit argument that probably started over goddamned fucking pancakes or some shit and he's wasting everybody's time and it's goddamned good and well time to

fucking surrender like a man and—
  It's a screwup. I know it instantly.
  I try to walk it back but can't. Done is done.
  He's suddenly at one of the doors. Standing behind his children, human shields, popping rounds at the cops. One officer goes down quick, his head a thick, chunky red mist. SRT boys hesitate, unsure. Can't shoot because of the kids.
  A second copper—Officer Tim Roberts—goes down, bullet in the spine and I watch the carnage unfold.
  I fucked up.

Officer Timmy had promised me.

After the bench trial was over—manslaughter pleaded down to unlawful restraint, sexual assault, and possession of meth-amphetamine by a DA eager to keep the police department out of the news and three whores eager to stay out of jail—and after my then-wife had served me and after my attorneys had me sign my pension over to pay my legal bills and after the bailiff had shackled, chained, and cuffed me, Officer Timothy Roberts put himself less than two feet from me.

"Guess it's different now. Guess you're rethinking coming to that call stoned outta your fucking head, aren't you?"

"I am so sorry, Tim. I'll carry this for the rest of my life."

"Shove your sorries up your ass. I'm always going to have a bullet next to my spine. Always going to limp. I'm always—" He grabbed my collar and yanked me close while the bailiff looked elsewhere. "*Always* going to be rocked out of law enforcement on medical disability. You son of a bitch. I promise you: when you get out, I will kill you."

I break away from work and race to my apartment. Slam the door, shove a chair beneath the knob, and check my Glock. Full magazine and one in the chamber.

I hide between the bed and the wall, and point the gun at the door.

The itch takes over. Slides across my eyes like skin across bones. I see their faces. Not the bloody, dead faces from after it was over, but the clean faces of life.

Christ, I want to fix, but when I go to the toilet and see the H, I flush it. I've managed to stay off the horse for six days, I'm not going back now. It's a process: beat the heroin, then beat the whiskey, then save a few pennies and a few more. That's when life will be on the right track. That will be the beginning of me getting out of here and getting right with the World.

I grab the Old Crow and down it hard. The bird pecks my throat and I listen at my door. Is he there? Maybe he's standing on the other side of the door, waiting to kill me.

Pressing the gun against the door, I say, "Wanna kill me? Stupid fuck, I died with those kids."

I hadn't been able to do anything about Trevino's ex and his parents, Trevino had killed them before I even knew he existed. But after I got the call? An innocent cop, Trevino himself, his children?

Those dead are at my feet.

Moving to my closed curtains, I down another blast of Old Crow. The bird goes down harder this time. A ragged skeleton of dirty sunlight dances into my room. Another shot of Crow and this one goes down hardest of all.

I open the curtains about halfway. I need to see the sun. I need to look for God. Maybe I can see if he's paying attention, or if I've forsaken him completely.

Instead, I see Officer Timothy Roberts.

Sitting on the hood of my car. Calm AF. When he sees me, his face slips into a predator's mask. He stands and slowly, like some shitty reality show, pulls a gun and shoots my car. The windshield explodes and tinkles of safety glass rise almost in slow motion. They catch the light of the sun, glint and wink at me.

Laughing, he shoots the quarter panels. He puts rounds into the dashboard before going to the trunk. I hear the gunshots and stupidly expect to hear the metal tearing beneath the bullet.

I shoot out the window in my room and lay down the entire magazine. "Lemme put a few more in your back, asshole."

He ducks behind the car and I shoot and shoot and shoot until the magazine clicks empty and the slide locks back. There's nothing left and I laugh at the metaphor. The gun is me...clicked empty and slide-locked back.

He knows I'm empty. Face stone-set, Timmy steps from behind the car, limps to the street and disappears with a wave.

I stand at my window, breath fast and hot, heart pounding so hard my chest is screaming, my finger gone bloodless white it's wrapped so tight on the trigger.

Magpie bangs on the door. "What the fuck is going on? You dead?"

I've been at this motel for a while now, and I've seen everything this nasty cesspool can vomit up. I've seen tweakers and junkies, heard every moan of the beaten and abused, the pleadings of the victims and the laughter of their tormentors. By the time the customers get here, they're dead, even if they don't realize it. Even Dylan.

I was dead the moment I took a room, the moment I put on Arnie's shirt.

A guy here when I first moved in said this place was for the expiation of sins. I thought he was full of shit. Staring at my car now, remembering their faces, I think maybe he was right.

I've many sins. But my greatest sin, resultant from my smaller sins, is the death of two children, murdered by their father just before he was gunned down by angry and horrified cops.

Time to pay for those sins.

Finally.

The itch is back. Hardcore, hard-assed.

Why is it in my eyes? Because I saw them die, because I see their faces. Physical manifestation of guilt, as simple and cheap as that is.

When Timmy finally kicks in the door, he stands tall, packing a semi-auto and already firing. Bullets pinpoint around the room. Wall board shatters and dust fills the room. Timmy does a tactical reload, drops his mag, shoves in a full one.

I rush him. I crash him. His gun goes flying as he falls out of my room and hits the hallway wall opposite my door. He recovers quick and blocks the way to the elevator.

I fly up the stairs, taking two and sometimes three in a single step. I barely see the motel around me. The holes in the walls, some patched and painted, some barely patched. The carpet is loose beneath my feet, where it still exists, and I slip a little.

As I run, I listen for his steps. I gotta be losing him, I run...he limps. He has to be falling behind.

The halls are mostly dark, lights burned out and doors closed. Windows at the end of the hallway have tattered curtains that blot out most of the sun. At the third-floor landing Marguerite blows a john. I shove them out of the way and keep moving. The fourth floor and I know Timmy is miles behind me now. Maybe he's not even coming. Maybe he's given up.

I go to the roof. I can take the fire escape down, get to the office where the shotgun is, circle back around and stop this bullshit dead in its limping tracks.

I bust open the roof door and am two, maybe three, steps onto it before I see him.

Dylan's father.

Lurching around the roof, screaming for Dylan, bottle in one hand...

...gun in the other.

The sun is high and burns us with something like yellow or maybe even greenish-yellow out of Dylan's Crayon box.

"The fuck're you?" He drinks as he swivels the gun lazily toward me.

"Whoa."

"You're that shit-worthless janitor. Used to be a cop."

Scared words dribble over my lips. "Don't know about shit-worthless but yeah, I was a copper once. Long time ago. It didn't work out."

He grabs a vent pipe to steady himself. "Here to arrest me?"

Rumor says he'd popped two people last year at a homeless shelter when some residents had tried to snatch Dylan to get him to Family Protective Services. No one had seen those residents since then.

"Just working on the AC."

"Ain't no idiot." A long pull of vodka. This guy is so blown my nerves ratchet up. "There ain't no AC in this rathole."

I see Dylan then.

On the far side of the roof, hidden between a storage bin and the parapet. All I see is a small foot, clad in a sock.

I move slow. To my right but also toward Daddy. I move my arms out rather than up. I want to fill his vision to keep him from seeing Dylan.

"You know," I say, "I don't even know your name. I've been trying to learn all the residents' names, and I know Dylan, but I don't know you."

"Don't cuddle up to me, Bitch, we ain't buddies." The bottle jams up at his lips and the gun plays near his waist. "Fucking kid. You know that retard ain't even mine?"

Fear is a boulder on my chest, Niagara Falls in my blood, panic that sounded like the air-shattering fusillade of bullets from the SRT boys when they cut Trevino to ribbons.

"His mama, that stupid bitch, managed to kill herself two...no...three months ago. Maybe four." His eyes flatten and look backward into the alcohol-haze of memory to dredge up some accuracy. "She bought some shitty skag. Blew her brains out right there on the bathroom floor."

"That's tough, man." I keep moving and start praying for Officer Timmy, too. He's armed, he's angry, but he's also a decent man and a former cop. He'll either grab this fuck or whack him straight out.

"I don't even want no kids but...that bitch can suck. Took the skin right off'a my dick. Best mouth fuck I ever had, man." His eyes are sharp now. "Where you goin'?"

"Trying to get the sun outta my eyes."

He looks over his shoulder and tries to find the sun, then back at me. "Quit moving, Mister Pig Cop. Trying to do your cop voodoo on me." His chest puffs. "I'm immune."

"Yeah? Not many people are immune. When I was copping, I could hypnotize damn near anybody. Just like that." I snap my fingers loud enough to draw his eyes to my outstretched hands.

"That ain't being me."

"Well, I ain't trying to be no cop anyway." I keep stepping toward him, waving my fingers while I talk. Keep your attention on me, asshole, I think. "Like I said. Fixing the AC. I been up here all damn day, working for the man, you know."

He laughs and waves the bottle as some sort of liquid high five. "Right? '*Working for the Man, every night and day.*'"

Maybe twenty feet away now. He backs up and doesn't even know he's doing it. Moving farther from Dylan. "You got it. '*Never lost one minute of sleeping*—'"

Over his right shoulder, deep behind his peripheral vision, I see Officer Tim Roberts, pistol clamped in his hand, eyes searching for me. When he sees us, he stops.

And keeps staying stopped.

I'm confused. Can't he see what's going on? Why's he not doing anything?

Dylan's dad's head goes back in a triumphant howl. "'*Worrying about the way things might have been.*' That's fucking right, asshole. I am who I am, and I didn't need no fucking woman with no fucking kid."

Maybe eight feet now between us. He's still backing up, lost in the song and whatever yawp of freedom the Creedence song was for him.

I am three feet away when he sees me. That boulder of fear

explodes like a mine shaft collapsing. I know what will happen from here: he will raise the gun and—

His eyes go wide. "There you are, you fucking punk bitch. I told you to clean that fucking bathroom." He drops the bottle and tries to push me back. At the same time, he tries to get a bead on Dylan with his gun.

"Run, Dylan." I hope he can hear me.

Daddy stumbles to my left and I counter, trying to trip him. "Tim, let's go. I need some help."

Timmy just watches.

Daddy howls at Dylan. "Come on, boy, time to pay the daddy."

Fuck you, I owe that debt. Do your worst.

He lurches the opposite direction and I counter again.

I see his gun come up, see him yank back the hammer, see him squeeze the trigger.

Timmy finally raises his gun. Finally fires at Drunk Daddy.

But Drunk Daddy gets his shot off.

I hear the hammer grind against the frame. I hear the hammer hit the firing pin, hear the firing pin strike the primer in the round. I hear the powder explode to life, push the bullet down the rifled barrel and out toward me.

I hear it and am amazed. Had never thought I'd hear my own death.

Timmy fires. Twice. Thrice. Four times as I also hear Drunk Daddy's .380 round tear into my guts, into my liver and stomach, my colon and intestines. Probably the round is going to fragment and damage my kidneys and bladder. Probably I'll piss myself and then lay here and bleed out 'cause this motel is at the end of the world and ain't nobody coming for me.

Drunk Daddy is dead, four rose blooms on his chest puddling on the roof.

Officer Timmy stands over me. "That son of a bitch fucked up my play."

"Dylan's dad. Well, dead mom's boyfriend."

"I wanted to shoot you."

"I know."

His face is cold empty. "In the back."

"I know."

Curiously, there is no pain. Not yet or did the round sever my spine so I feel nothing?

"I wanted you shitting in a bag."

"Sorry to disappoint."

"You think that absolves you? Some self-sacrifice that makes the world whole again?" Officer Timothy Roberts spits on me.

"Hey, man, you're the hero now." Something is coming at me in the distance. Sounds like a freight train but feels like someone stomping on my feet with steel-toed boots. "You get to walk Dylan downstairs and call the cops and tell them how you saved him from his drunk daddy and a useless old junkie cop who's already killed kids."

"Maybe, but I'm still taking what's mine."

I open my mouth, but the stomping works up through my guts and catches fire.

He wrenches me over, belly down, and shoots me twice.

The growing pain hammers to a stop and it's a relief. It's almost the soft haze of my dear old friend heroin.

I watch Dylan go with Officer Timmy while I bleed. The former cop talks softly and moves as slowly as Dylan needs. Dylan never looks back as they walk through the door and down the stairs.

Officer Timothy Roberts does. Once. Quick and final; a facial fuck-off.

THE RUNDOWN
Gabe Morran

Derek

Panicked, the old man looked over his shoulder as the headlights lit up his back and the road around him. He ran at little more than a hobble, his long, scraggly hair drifting back and forth across a tattered green jacket. I pushed harder on the accelerator and started to close the distance. Beside me, Arlo wiggled his finger around in a can of chewing tobacco and turned around to Clint in the backseat.

"When we get him down, you're the one doing this," Arlo said as he put a dip in his mouth.

"Okay," Clint said.

As our truck drew closer, the man turned off the road and lumbered into a cornfield. The stalks were brown and only about knee high, stunted by the summer floods earlier in the year. I whipped around and continued chase. I glanced over at Arlo. His eyes fixed on Clint.

"You know if it was anyone else, they would be fucking dead right now. If any one of us did something half as stupid, your brother would have shot us himself."

"Yeah," Clint said.

The old man looked back at us again. I didn't say anything because it didn't matter, but Bob Ramley wasn't a bad guy. As a kid I remembered him working at the school and around town as a handyman. By the time I was a teenager, he was the go-to guy for anyone underage who wanted beer from the mini-mart. One pack for you and one pack for him, and no hard liquor. No hard liquor because he always said he didn't want to be a bad influence. I don't know when he added meth to it all, but it also didn't matter. I looked over and saw the silhouette of a large grain silo in the distance.

"We're coming up on a canal soon," I said.

Arlo turned around. "I was hoping he would wear himself out. Well, go ahead and tag him, just make sure you don't run him over."

I pushed the accelerator to the floorboard and lined my edge of the bumper with Bob's right leg. He screamed as the lights got closer. I barely felt a bump as the truck hit him, but the impact sent Bob face first onto the ground. I backed the truck up and parked so the lights shined on him. Bob struggled to get to his feet. I saw a long streak of blood running down his jeans and a broken bone jutting out above the knee.

Clint, Arlo, and I climbed from the truck and walked toward him. Bob tried to get up again and I saw the bone stick out farther. He yelled and rolled onto his back, his breath lit by the beams of the truck.

Arlo turned to Clint. "Forget something?" he said. Clint put his head down and walked back to the truck. As Arlo and I approached, Bob fumbled through his coat pockets and pulled out a small wad of cash. "Here," he said shaking the money at us. "Just take what's left and I will make it up to you." Arlo and I stood over him. I heard the gate of the truck open and shut and Clint coming toward us. Bob reached back into his pockets and pulled out a bag of meth. "Take this too, there's about a hundred left."

Arlo put the heel of his boot against the exposed bone and

pressed down. Bob screamed and clawed at Arlo's boot. "The blue trailer at the back of the lot, where's the computer?" Arlo said. Clint joined us, carrying a large piece of lumber. Bob laid his head back and started to cry. Arlo pressed down harder, and Bob yelled again. Clint shifted from side to side, head down, and hands shaking. As soon as I saw the cash I knew where he had taken the laptop, but it wasn't my place to tell Arlo or Clint what to do. The only place that could pay a damn for anything second hand around here was Alleycats Pawn Shop in Sutton about ten miles up Highway 44. I picked up the money and meth and handed it to Arlo.

"Alleycats Pawn Shop," Bob said. "The door was wide open, I had to get something."

Arlo let his foot off Bob and looked at Clint. Clint shook his head and trembled. Arlo spit out a thick glob and looked at me. "You let some junkie walk into your house and take your shit today?" he said.

"No," I said and turned to Clint.

"Neither did I, so I guess that leaves you," Arlo said.

Clint held one end of the lumber with both hands and slowly walked to Bob. Bob raised a hand toward Clint and tried to push himself off the ground with the other. "I didn't know it meant that much. I'm sorry, I swear I won't tell anyone, and I'll never take from you again," Bob said.

The board shook so hard in Clint's hands I expected him to drop it the moment he tried to swing. Arlo told Clint to hurry and looked over at me. "That pawn shop open all night?"

"No," I said.

"How far is that quarry from here?"

"It's a pretty good haul, two counties over."

Clint raised the board and slammed it down on Bob's head. Bob lay still and moaned. Clint hesitated for a moment, then raised the board and hit Bob again. Bob quit moaning. Clint hit him again and split his head open. "There," he said and came back over to us. "Let's get to Alleycats and get this over with."

"No," Arlo said.

Clint suddenly looked even more nervous than before. He stared at the ground for a moment and cleared his throat several times. "Why not? We know where it is. Let's just go get it."

Arlo spit again and shook his head. "Pawn shop is long closed. Pawn shops can have security out the ass, I mean like small bank, fucking-level, alarm systems and bars over the doors and windows."

"Fuck," Clint said and put his hands on the back of his head. "So, what's the fucking plan then?"

"We wait until tomorrow, there's not much other choice. You didn't use the actual chemical names in there or anything did you?"

"No."

"Good, then they shouldn't know what the hell any of it means anyway. Besides, it's not like the pawn shop is going to go looking for trouble." Clint shook his head and smiled, but his lip quivered, and tears started to well in his eyes.

Arlo and I dragged Bob over to the truck and hauled him onto the bed. Clint carried the blood-and-bone-soiled lumber and tossed it onto the bed beside him. I pulled a folded tarp out of the backseat and covered the bed of the truck. "We're dropping him off at home first, and then you and me are ditching the body," Arlo said as we got into the truck. Clint sat in the middle of the back seat and stared forward. I nodded and drove to Clint's trailer. We dropped Clint off and drove back out toward the quarry.

"Longer he's with us more chance he'll fuck us up," Arlo said.

I grinned but kept my eyes on the road. Even though Clint was a pussy, there was something about having someone else with us that helped keep my mind at ease. Alone, with Arlo, it felt like there was another presence in the truck, something quietly threatening about the man. I came to complete stops and drove the speed limit, hoping he would think it was because of the corpse in the back. I felt like any little mistake would be the excuse he needed though. I had been around enough like him in prison to know the type, the type that could tap into a reservoir of anger and violence whenever the slightest reason presented itself. Clint did the cooking, and I did the deliveries and dealing; we never needed anyone like Arlo until now.

I turned off the highway and onto a gravel road that led to the quarry. The old limestone pit hadn't been used since before I was born, and other than the occasional scrap-metal scrounger, rarely had any visitors. We passed through a missing section of rusted chain-link fence and onto the scrub grass. The edge of the quarry came into view and I rounded the truck and backed up to the edge. Arlo and I exited the truck and walked to the back. Arlo picked up the piece of lumber. "Got something to burn this with?" he said. I pulled a can of gasoline out of the truck toolbox and soaked the wood. Then I sat it on the ground, pulled a lighter out of my pocket and lit the soiled board. The small fire glowed as we pulled Bob out of the back and dragged him to the edge of the quarry. It was too dark to see very far into the pit, but I knew it was a long way down. Everyone knew who Bob was, and they probably wouldn't question how he fell in and died.

Bob disappeared into the dark. I turned back toward the truck and saw the dying light of the fire. Arlo's phone rang.

"Yeah," Arlo said. I walked to the back of the truck and leaned against the bed. I saw Arlo shake his head and look at the ground. "You're fucking kidding me," he said. The fire dwindled down to a faint glow and Arlo hung up the phone.

"Dumbass just got himself arrested," Arlo said and pulled his can of dip out.

"What?"

"Clint, he just got arrested trying to break into that damn pawn shop."

* * *

227

Jamie

I felt the front tires rest against the parking stop and quickly set the car in park. Sometimes, if I got lucky, the old thing wouldn't roll if I did it fast enough, but more often than not I counted on the parking stop to keep it in place. I got out and winced as my weight shifted onto my left boot. After people started asking me about the bruises on my arm I switched to shooting between my toes. The narrow curve of my boots made the pain worse for a moment, but the feeling always eased after a few steps. I saw a pile of glass on the ground below the rear window of the shop. I walked over and saw the security bars were slightly bowed out with dry blood smudged on them. This guy didn't try very hard, at least not compared to the others over the years. Most of the time there would be three or four windows busted or the door gate would be dented and half kicked in. Wayne had his tweaker defense system down to a science. Keep everything strong, but simple, because most tweakers are high effort and low ingenuity. I walked around the side of the building toward the front door.

How long until I might be on the other side of a set of bars with someone like that? Low ingenuity, high ingenuity, I doubt a judge cares which way when you get caught buying. Cheap heroin is easy to get delivered, even out here in God's country, when you know the right dark website. None of it matters when someone talks though, a final post warning you to stay away, but should be warning you that you're fucked.

I walked through the front door and saw Wayne and Tom talking to a pair of guys at the counter. A stack of computers sat between them. Aside from tired eyes, the customers looked like complete opposites. The blond one I had seen before, usually driving a big truck up and down the highway with stacks of lumber in the back. The other man I didn't know and didn't want to. I walked by and, as I rounded the counter, I glanced at him again. He was bald on top with brown hair that crowned from ear to ear, and he had a patchy goatee with chewing tobacco stains along the bottom. There was nothing particularly physically imposing about him, but there was something about the way he stood and the way he glared, calculating and on the verge of hostile at the same time. Wayne and Tom were usually chatterboxes, leaning against the counter and leading the conversation, but now the two stood a few steps behind the counter.

"There aren't any more in the back?" the blond one asked.

"No, this is it. It's what we have for sale today," Wayne said.

"Fuck," the blond one said and turned to the other. Another customer walked in and the man with the goatee smiled and nodded. "We'll check in another time."

The two walked out of the store and Wayne sighed. I patted him on the back, and he leaned forward onto the counter. "I swear this place is going to kill me one day. Police called me at four this morning to tell me someone had tried to break in again, and then those two were sitting in the parking lot waiting for me to open up. Fucking A people! Can't you at least wait until nine to get your damn meth money."

I smiled. "On the bright side there's still plenty of day left for things to turn around. Now, you have a computer that needs looked at?"

"Yeah, it's the black and red laptop in the back. Sorry for calling you so early, but Tom bought this one just before closing last night and we can't get into it."

"Did you try opening it and hitting the power button? You know, the big round thing with the blinking light?"

Wayne looked at Tom and shook his head. "She is funny, isn't she?"

Tom grinned. "If I'd have known they were teaching comedy over at Community South, I'd have gone back to school years ago."

"You haven't learned to ask for a login or password on a computer after four years, only school you need to go back to is elementary," Wayne said.

Tom picked up the stack of laptops and looked at us. "This

stuff sells faster than anything else in here so excuse me for making some quick money, it's not like we have the pick of the litter when it comes to customers around here."

"I'm open to suggestions," Wayne said.

"Easy, owner gets a prettier face," Tom said and walked toward the back room.

Wayne chuckled and shook his head. "Yeah, well, fuck you, too."

I followed Tom to the back storage area and he pointed to the laptop on the inventory station. The computer didn't look like the typical dated models I was used to seeing at the shop. Usually, the operating systems were a couple years out of date, half the time the screen was cracked, and the batteries on the laptops were always shot. This unit looked sleek and modern, with a lot of features that only come from custom builds. I pulled a chair over and opened it.

I recognized the operating system and quickly accessed the command prompts. I sifted through the lines of code until I was able to get into the keyboard log and wrote down the last entered username and password. I restarted the computer and logged in.

Wayne walked in and put a hundred dollars down next to me. With all his backwoods and good old boy candor, I knew Wayne thought the money was going to something decent. I couldn't look him in the eyes when he paid me. "Before I forget, I better give you this," he said and looked at the computer screen. "That was fast."

Normally I was content to just get into the computers for them and not pry, but I couldn't resist playing around with something as high end as this. "Who brought this in?" I asked.

"Some old guy," Tom said.

"Did he say where he got it? It is a really nice custom build."

"No, someone dropped him off and left. When he took off, he started walking the same way he came, looked like he was trying to thumb it back down Highway 44."

I kept browsing and came to a folder called housekeeping. I

clicked on it. I saw dozens of icons labeled *expiration dates* and kept scrolling. Then, more labeled grocery lists, and kept scrolling. I kept scrolling until I saw a group of unlabeled jpeg icons. I clicked on the first one. A young girl looked at the camera, confused, scared, crying, and naked. An older man stood behind her, smiling, one hand full of her red hair and the other on her shoulder. A blue, quarter-machine ring on his pinky finger stuck out against the pale skin canvas. I covered my mouth with my hand.

"What the hell," Wayne said and looked at me. "Is that real?"

I pulled the screen down and scooted away. "Yeah, I think so."

I stared at the wall while Wayne and Tom went back and forth about who brought it in. The girl's face had looked eerily similar to mine from my third-grade yearbook. The picture wasn't. of me, but that expression was in frames all over my mom's house. About nine years old. She couldn't have been much over that, if anything she could have been younger. I started to cry. Wayne rubbed his eyes and looked away. I turned around and saw Tom pacing with his hands clasped behind his head.

The chime from the front door went off in the other room. "Tom, can you go up front and keep an eye," Wayne said. Tom nodded and walked to the main room.

"Jamie, I had no idea," Wayne said.

"I know, just wasn't expecting anything like that."

"Me either," he said, and pulled his cell phone out of his pocket. "You have class today?"

"No."

"Usually takes about an hour to sort out when we accidentally buy something stolen. But this, I have no idea."

"It's okay, I have time."

Wayne dialed 911. "They are just going to love dealing with me again already," he said and pushed the call button.

I got my phone out and saw I had a calendar notice. Class today at ten. The reminder had not been useful in some time.

Wayne had started calling me in about three years ago, after I helped him get into a simple number-locked tablet. I had come in looking for a cheap computer before classes started and had been coming back ever since. Wayne didn't have any stake in the matter, but I had been lying to him about going to school for the last six months, anyway. I knew he didn't usually practice safe business or follow the law to the letter, but he was always the decent sort who hid behind giving people a hard time. If I told him the truth, I knew he would ask why I quit. Or worse, offer to help.

Wayne and I waited in the back room and listened as Tom helped customers in the front. When he talked to someone he sounded like his usual self, but I could imagine how hard it was for him to put on an inviting face. The door chime went off again and I heard Tom telling someone to walk around to the back. The back door opened, and a tall man walked in wearing a brown County Sheriff Department uniform. He walked toward us and pulled a pen and pad from his shirt pocket.

"Of course, it's the same guy from this morning. I bet he just loves me," Wayne whispered.

"Hello again, Mister Russo?" he said.

"Probably didn't expect to see me again this soon, but I have something I think you ought to see," Wayne said.

The officer looked at me. "Can I have your full name please, ma'am?"

"Jamie Anderson Grace."

The pen moved back and forth in an awkward motion, like he could barely hold onto it. I looked closer at the officer's hands. His right middle finger looked broken near the second knuckle, and both hands were covered in scrapes and small cuts. "Are you okay?"

"Yeah," the officer said and finished writing. "This is from when I was here earlier. Good thing I gave up trying to be a hand model years ago." I saw Wayne bite his lip and chuckle. Even with everything going on I knew he was fighting back a masturbation joke. "I assume you work here," the officer said and looked at me.

"Yeah, she's my on-call tech help," Wayne said.

"Is this the computer you called about?" the officer asked, pointing at the computer. "I need to have a look." I pulled the laptop screen up and turned the other way. "Who brought this thing in?"

"Tom bought it last night," Wayne said. "He might be able to help you more, but basically the guy sounded like an old junkie. Then, Jamie came across the picture while she was going through the computer this morning."

"Is there anything else on there?"

Wayne looked over at me and I shrugged. "I don't know. I quit looking when I saw it. Everything seemed fine, just like normal, at-home PC stuff until I came across that picture."

"Nothing else caught your attention?"

"No."

The officer closed the computer screen and sighed. "I need you both to stay here for a bit until I can get some help this way," he said. I saw his face drop and skin start to flush. "If you don't mind, Mister Russo, could you please close up for a bit?" he said, and moved toward the door. I saw his legs trembling and hands shaking as he walked.

"Yeah," Wayne said, and followed him out.

I walked out behind Wayne. The officer pulled his phone out of his pocket as he walked outside, and then looked back in through the glass storefront. The officer looked at Wayne, then Tom, then me, and then turned away from the building. Wayne flipped the open sign over to closed and Tom rang up the remaining customer. The three of us pulled up stools and sat behind the counter.

"Guess I'll be the first to say it, I'll be glad when this day is fucking over," Tom said.

The officer stayed outside and kept a customer from coming in. Wayne grunted and looked at his watch. Tom stared at his phone. I ran my hand through my hair and bit my lip. The ring worn by the girl in the picture was the kind of ring I got on the cheap at every gas station and won as an easy prize at every fair when I was a little. The kind of ring that could turn a poor girl into a princess for an afternoon. The kind of ring that a sick old man uses as bait, apparently. I took a deep breath and looked back to the storefront. The officer ushered another person away and looked back at me. I forced a smile and he turned away.

Tom stood up.

"If he needs me, I'm going to the bathroom."

"Hey, if you short-dick that urinal again I'm going to make you sit to pee," Wayne said. Tom shook his head. "I mean it, I'm tired of stepping in piss every time I go to take a piss."

Tom looked at me. "I can't help you one way or the other on this one," I said.

Tom laughed and looked outside. "Oh, c'mon, not these two again already," he said.

I looked outside and saw the officer talking to the blond man and the intimidating man from earlier. The officer let them pass. Wayne and Tom walked toward the door. Wayne pointed to the *Closed* sign while Tom tried to wave them off. The men outside reached the door first and opened it. The chime went off, then two gunshots. A spray of pink mist splattered across the storefront and the nearby wall. Wayne and Tom fell to the floor.

Derek

The woman dove before Arlo could squeeze off another round. I stepped over the dead store owner and walked toward the counter. The door behind the counter opened and then slammed shut as I reached the desk. I tried the knob, but it was locked in place. I heard a deadbolt lock on the other side and banged my fist against the door. The wood didn't have any give to it. I prodded around the frame and it felt solid, too. I turned around and saw Arlo staring at me from the other side of the counter.

"It's locked and the door is solid. I need something to get in," I said.

Arlo walked over to a cluttered hardware aisle and started searching. I threw my shoulder against the door, but it would not give. Pain reverberated down my arm and up my neck. I winced and leaned my forehead against the door as the adrenaline began to subside.

Things had gone bad before and people had gotten roughed up, but nothing like this. Arlo was a different man after we left the store this morning, after the phone call with Clint's brother. When Arlo told him we couldn't buy the computer back, I could hear the cracking and hesitation in his voice. Afterward, instead of giving me calm instruction, he talked with an obvious edge of desperation. I knew then that things were never going to be back to normal, unless normal changed. When would Arlo decide to kill me? After the girl? Never? Right now? I turned around and saw him pick up a sledgehammer and walk toward me.

Arlo handed the sledgehammer to me and I hit the door above the knob. Splinters shot through the air, the deadbolt fell to the floor, and the door flung open. I walked in with Arlo close behind me. I saw the woman holding a laptop with the screen flipped open.

Arlo was a fucking liar. I saw the look on the little girl's face and felt short of breath. I saw the smile on the man's face and squeezed the sledgehammer tighter. Arlo looked over at me, then to the screen and back at me.

I felt my heart start to race and my mouth went dry. Clint killed me the moment he got arrested.

I swung the sledgehammer around and hit Arlo in the stomach. Arlo buckled to his knees and dropped the gun. I picked the gun up and held it to his head. "You said they found the meth," I said. Arlo tried to speak, but only mustered a few grunts and gurgles. I pulled the trigger and Arlo collapsed to the floor.

I tossed the sledgehammer aside and turned to the woman. "What's your name?"

"Jamie," she said.

"You're the one that got into the computer, right?"

"Yeah."

I took a deep breath and wiped the blood from the gun onto my jeans. "Jamie, I wish I could tell you I had some kind of plan, but I don't. I wish I could tell you that I am sorry about your friends up front, but I'm not. I swear I didn't know about that though," I said and pointed at the computer. "I just feel like I should tell you that, don't know why."

Jamie closed the computer.

I sat on a stool nearby and looked at Arlo. I had lived longer than I was supposed to. Clint's brother would send someone like Arlo for me, and it was just a matter of time.

"Is there anyone you can get that to? Anyone outside of the surrounding area? I don't know, maybe state police?" I asked.

Jamie ran her hand through her hair and took a deep breath. "I'm pretty sure if I can just get home with it, I can make something happen."

"Make something happen?"

Jamie crossed her arms and looked at the laptop. "I get heroin off the dark web, at least I did, and I am pretty sure my IP address at home is being watched. I don't know why, but I just feel like I should tell you that."

I nodded, walked over, and looked out into the store. The deputy outside looked in and I nodded to him. The officer looked around the area, and then got into his car and drove off.

"He's leaving because he thinks Arlo and I just killed you. Probably doesn't want to be around for when Arlo was supposed to kill me. Sheriff's department is going to call it an armed robbery and arrest the first meth-head they find. Just about anyone with a badge in that office is dirty." I checked the bullets in the gun. "I don't know if the right thing to do is still the right thing to do when there isn't much other choice, but I know I can't run from this."

"I don't think I can run much more than I already have," she said, and picked up the laptop.

We walked out of the store. Jamie looked at the pair of dead men in the entryway and glared at me. I looked away and walked to my truck. Jamie went to a junk car near the back of the lot and put the laptop on the passenger seat. I looked back at the road to make sure no one was watching.

"Do you know who the girl is?" Jamie said.

"No," I said.

"Do you know who the man is?"

"No."

Jamie

The unspoken gift of addiction is being able to spot a liar. Being an addict makes you so good at lying that spotting it in others is as simple as a passing glance. He wasn't lying and I felt a small degree of comfort knowing that. I turned right down Highway 44 toward home and he turned left toward town. The pain in my feet came back for a moment and quickly passed. I took a deep breath. There was going to be pain to come, but that pain, the physical hurt, somehow seemed less important than before. The image of the girl burned in my thoughts, but also felt like Lidocaine to my body, numbing the feeling of withdrawal. Maybe it's just been a while since I've done anything to feel good about, but I was determined to upload the drive from the laptop as soon as I got home.

Derek

Clint walked out of the jail service entrance and headed toward the parking lot. I always figured a junkie would kill me, or a rival dealer, maybe the police, another inmate if I had been arrested again. I never expected it to be Clint, though. A porn-monger, maybe even a pedophile, I'd known my whole life. Make the assumption that the bad things you see your friends do are the worst things that they're doing and pay the price. But I never thought he could be into something like that. I also never thought I would be able to kill, but an innocent smile and an evil face are apparently enough to change a man under the right circumstances.

Clint crossed into the parking lot. I got out of the truck and slammed the door. Clint turned to me and froze. I closed the distance. An officer came out of the building and yelled something I couldn't hear. I raised the gun to Clint's head and pulled the trigger. He fell to the pavement and I felt a sharp pain in my chest. I saw the officer coming toward me with his gun drawn. My knees buckled and I fell to the pavement next to Clint. I struggled to breathe as a crowd of officers gathered around me. I looked at their faces, one at a time, and smiled at the panicked look in their eyes, not because I had been shot and was about to die, but because they all knew what was coming for them next.

THE LAW OF LUCY'S LUCK
J.D. Graves

In the kitchen, the pot boiled. Lucy twisted the dried pasta. It crackled between her hands. Both halves dropped in. Steam rose from the bubbling cauldron. Lucy barely noticed the wilting sticks of spaghetti, her mind far off. Her day—one full of dumb luck, one for the history books. It made her feel bulletproof.

She knew he'd call. If not now, then later. He always did.

From the other room, Jimmy shouted over the TV's constant gunfire, "Mom, someone's calling you...*again!*"

Lucy rolled her eyes, "Well since I'm making you dinner, d'ya think you could pause your game long enough to answer?"

The spaghetti sank farther into the pot as Jimmy rounded the corner, "Yeah, Aunt Jackie—I'm fine. I made the honor roll, so Mom got me the new *Battle Royale* game. Oh yeah—lots of 'em! Can't ya hear the machineguns?" Then to Lucy, "When are people gonna stop calling to congratulate you?"

"Go tell your sister dinner's almost done," Lucy said to her eight-year-old son and took the phone. "Hey, Sis..."

Jackie squealed, "Lucky Lucy's made the *front page!*"

"More like dumb luck...I didn't think there'd be a good pic of me in the uniform. Believe it or not, I'm always afraid I come across butch. It's the gun belt. It sits too high on my waist."

"Oh my gosh, hon," Jackie said, "you look good enough to eat. I bet Robert's gonna lose his mind when he sees how stunning you are these days."

"I don't give a flip about him," Lucy stirred the pot.

"You know he comes into the restaurant from time to time, asking about you."

Lucy laughed, "Well, even fools gotta eat."

Jackie cackled, "Anyways, did ya know about the drugs when you pulled 'em over?"

Lucy laughed quietly. She tucked the phone into the crook of her neck and bent to check the oven, "Well, he had one of those big *I've got more weed than good sense* signs wrapped around his truck."

"I'm serious," Jackie said unamused, "Just spill it."

"I wish I could, but I can't...ongoing investigation...with a haul as big as that, Sheriff White thinks it's part of something bigger." Lucy opened the oven door. The heat dried the sweat on her face. The open-face hotdog buns covered in butter and garlic salt had browned evenly. "All I can say is the guy had a taillight out and that's why I pulled him over."

Jimmy called out from the other room, "*Mom!*"

Lucy shut the oven, "I'll be honest with you—I felt sorry for the guy. He didn't speak any English."

"Don't tell me you're getting soft on these crooks?"

Jimmy called again, "Mom I think someone's pulled up outside!"

Lucy ignored her son and continued, "Of course not—he genuinely seemed unaware of the cargo. It's not uncommon for the cartels to employ rubes. They think it helps them if they're stopped. What those morons don't know—our justice system is black and white—a crime's a crime."

"What was it stuffed inside again?" Jackie asked, "The paper was vague about the details—some kind of child's toy?"

"Like I said...ongoing investigation...but don't worry, I caught it all on the body cam."

Jimmy hollered again from the front room, "*Mom!*"

Lucy pressed the receiver to her chest, "*I'm on the phone!*"

"There's somebody parked outside the house...*in our front yard!*"

Lucy stuck her head through the doorway between the kitchen and front room and saw her son on the couch. "What do you mean front yard?"

Jimmy pointed, "Look, you can see headlights through the window!"

Lucy looked. Headlights peeked through the closed shutters. She stepped absently toward the large window and pinched open the blinds. She immediately squinted. The headlights' glare made it impossible to see anything. Lucy heard a car door slam. It happened so fast: Random flashes of light as the windowpane spider-webbed. The shutters jumped. Shards of broken wood splintered. Lucy instinctively dove for the floor. The carpet burned her arms as she slid and finally heard the gunshots ripping through her house.

Time slowed. Lucy screamed only vowels at Jimmy. No matter how fast she crawled, it felt like moving through tar. The drywall behind Jimmy's head became an avalanche of powdered snow. Lucy watched her oldest child freeze with fear. She reached and caught his ankle and yanked. The boy collapsed like dead weight. Lucy wrapped her arms around Jimmy's head. Her hands slid through his wet hair. She pressed herself on top— desperate to cover his small body with her own. The deafening gunfire shredded the television. Sparks and plastic rained down as bullets whirred overhead.

Then it stopped.

Reloading, Lucy thought quickly. Her gun belt hung from the coat rack near the door. "Stay down, Jim," Lucy said and hustled across the smoky room. She half-expected the gunmen to kick in the door and attempt to finish the job.

Lucy drew her Glock from the holster and crouched. She aimed the piece at the front door, now pocked with holes. The gun felt unusually heavy—it shook with her adrenaline. Her breath became a rusty bicycle pump.

Somewhere in the house, the oven's timer screamed. Jackie's tinny voice, muted on the floor, hollered for her sister. Her daughter, Daphne, cried from the other side of the house. Outside, two doors slammed. The lights threw moving shadows across the walls.

Lucy thought, *The cowards are fleeing!*

She raced forward—gave the lock a hard twist—just in time to see the red glow of brake lights. She leapt from the front porch and dropped to one knee. The car's wheels gouged the front lawn as Lucy returned fire.

Pop! Pop! Pop! Pop!

The car turned onto the two-lane blacktop. Lucy's legs pumped underneath—pushing her forward. Tires squealed. She smelled the burning rubber, close enough now that she could make the car as some old boat of a sedan. It offered Lucy its broadside—she unloaded the clip.

Pop! Pop! Pop! Pop! Pop!

A headlight went dark, but other than that, the sedan sped away, disappearing into the good country night.

Lucy stood alone. Crickets chirped among the pines, unaware that anything had happened.

Her heart thundered throughout her thin frame. She still held the gun with both hands. The grip felt slick. As if another good squeeze would cause it to slip from her fingers. Her first thought, *Sweat*. Her second…

…*Jimmy!*

She raced back inside.

Sheriff John White offered his deputy the Styrofoam cup of coffee. Lucy didn't look up. She knew he was there but couldn't stop staring at Jimmy's blood on her hands, sweatshirt, and yoga pants. Her face felt hot from crying in the ambulance, but other than that, she felt nothing. A big bad wolf had knocked at her door and blown down her heart.

Now, her heart lay fighting for its life in an operating room.

Sheriff White spoke. Whatever he said didn't register with Lucy. She sat in the waiting room—a thousand miles away. Then her chin tilted. The sheriff held Lucy's face to meet his, "I know what you're thinking, Little Sister," he said. "These doctors are doing everything they can… Jesus is in that room with your little boy now. Heaven's full of angels and he ain't taking Jimmy today."

Lucy's face wrinkled in agony. Fresh tears leaked from her clenched eyes. The sheriff pulled her toward him. His strong arms wrapped around her. For a split second, Lucy lost herself in his squeeze. "We're gonna get those bastards who done this—mark my words."

The sheriff dissolved into her sister Jackie. Again, arms wrapped lovingly around her. Two hearts beating out of time, unsyncopated. This strange rhythm filled Lucy's emptiness with fleeting thoughts. Silly things, like how everyone's just waiting for the other person to stop talking so they can babble on uninterrupted. How grief must be shared to be tolerated. Lucy wished she knew who deserved such a high honor. If the shadows behind the wheel ever grew faces, she'd freely spread her new-found wealth around.

Jackie dissolved into Robert. The red-faced man shared the sheriff's sentiment, "They're gonna fry for this." More sweet lies from the father of her children. The more she heard it, the harder it became for Lucy to believe. Clutched in the unpleasant arms of her ex-husband, Lucy knew the real truth. Each passing second drove the gunmen further from her grasp.

Robert mercifully dissolved into their youngest child, Daphne, whose tiny arms could not wrap themselves around her mother. Lucy held her so tightly the child cried, "Mommy I can't breathe."

After seven hours, the doctor finally appeared. The old man

spoke no hope.

They held Jimmy's funeral on Saturday.

The sweltering East Texas sky threatened to rain, but never did.

Sheriff White ordered Lucy thirty days' paid leave.

Jackie refused to let her sister go home—back to the massacre—stating there's no reason to sleep at the scene of a crime. Without resistance, she packed Lucy and Daphne's things and moved them into the open duplex right next door—a safe and quiet neighborhood full of middle-class families and their ordinary problems.

Could they even fathom Lucy's?

Daphne clung to her mother. Said she liked her new room but insisted on sleeping with her mom. Which came easy for Daphne. The snores came soon after. Despite everything that had happened, Lucy needed to be alone. She felt bad about leaving her daughter, but reasoned, "My sister's right on the other side of the wall." Lucy casually slipped out of bed, into her sneakers, quickly passed the living room window, and out the door.

Her new neighborhood appeared calmer than the hurricane's eye.

Lucy ran the block. She didn't bring headphones. She didn't keep track of her steps. Her footfalls echoed. The streetlights glowed. Her breath stung her lungs like a needle through a stitch. She ran until her feet ached—until her knees burned—until she could no longer stand, and she collapsed in the middle of the road, too exhausted to shriek at the eye in the sky that allowed her son to die.

As she lay panting on the asphalt, she heard it. Somewhere close, an engine turned over. She looked up and saw a big late-model sedan. This rust bucket suddenly high-beamed her with one headlight. Tires squealed. It roared forward. Lucy twisted sideways. A cacophony of trashcans rattled and skittered, emptying garbage bags all over her. Lucy felt the swoosh of hot air. With pure dumb luck the car missed her by inches. The car peeled out of the neighborhood. Her heart galloped after them in her chest. Lucy's legs jellied underneath, unable to stand, let alone to follow.

No doubt it had been the same car...the same driver. They'd come back to finish the job.

She crawled home, unable to close her eyes, robbed of sleep. Her mind raced and painted faces on their shadows. The next morning, after Daphne's school bus drove away—Lucy tucked her beige shirt into her matching slacks—polished her boots and badge. *To hell with paid leave.*

"It's admirable, Lucy," Sheriff White grimaced, "but you need to be home recovering...mourning, even."

"Whoever killed Jimmy tried to kill me again last night."

His brow wrinkled, "Did you call it in?"

She shook her head.

He eyed her suspiciously, "Why wouldn't you?"

Lucy bit her lip. *Did he think she made it up?* "I think it's the cartels."

The sheriff grunted incredulously, "That's a big finger to point."

"Well, who else could it be?"

Sheriff tapped his desk, "We're working on it. I'll send a deputy over to watch your new place. Give you some peace of mind."

Lucy gritted her teeth. She came out with it, "I want on the CID team."

Sheriff White steepled his fingers. His eyes narrowed to points. He spoke slowly. "I will not jeopardize the mental health of any of my deputies. Now go home and get some rest."

"I appreciate your concern, but my mental health is already—"

"It's too soon, Deputy Law," said the Sheriff. "You're a

witness in the case...I will dispatch a detail to your house and that's the best I can do...for now."

Lucy raged, "We both know I can do more than just be a *witness!*"

The sheriff paused.

Lucy felt hot all over, realizing she'd just yelled at her superior.

He sniffed, "Lucinda Law, you just can't. Not for this. And I don't wanna hear any more about it. I'll see you again in twenty-seven days. Unless you think you need more. No need for you to feel rushed."

Lucy couldn't believe it: *The first-twenty-four-hour rule of law enforcement...rush, rush, rush!*

This is no way to live, Lucy thought as she dropped Daphne off at Jackie's that evening. Every thirty minutes a squad car had cruised past the duplex, yet no one had followed her to Jackie's. It didn't make her feel any better. Especially after she arrived at an empty parking lot. At nine o'clock on a Tuesday, Top Shot 24-hour Shooting Range was emptier than a bachelor's pantry. The scruffy clerk sold Lucy a box of shells and gave her the lane closest to his register. Even dressed down in grey sweats, she could feel the wall-eyed clerk roaming her acreage. She ignored him by slipping on headphones and zeroed in on the target's dark shape. Its shadowy hands gripped the wheel, its cowardly foot stomped the accelerator. She emptied the clip at its faceless head.

She called the target home and the clerk laughed, "Looks like you're all over the place tonight, Miss Lucy."

Lucy sneered—reloaded then unloaded and brought the new target back. Lucy showed it off, "Is this better?"

The clerk swallowed hard at the target's gored groin. He spoke nervously, "That's...um...more like it."

The front door chimed and the clerk happily escaped Lucy's withering glare—the same glare she'd give her son's triggerman if ever given the chance. If only looks could kill. Lucy knew they couldn't—but her bullets could and would. Now somewhat alone, she dumped the box of shells onto the little bench divider in front of her. One rolled off. Lucy bent to grab it. A shiny ostrich boot caught it on the first bounce.

A deep voice crooned, "Thought I'd find ya here."

The familiar square jaw greeted her warmly. Lucy gritted her teeth, "They won't let me work my son's case, Red."

"Can't blame 'em, can ya?" Red Whitaker removed his hat, revealing his high and tight stubble of auburn hair. He brought the hat chest level, covering his Texas Ranger badge. "No telling what you'll do once you catch the suspect."

She bit her lip, "I'm his mother."

Red Whitaker's smile dipped, and he said, "Sorry I couldn't make the funeral."

Lucy looked away, reloading the two clips. "It's okay," she said flippantly. "The Rangers keeping you busy?"

"Like ya wouldn't believe," Red smiled and stroked her cheek, "Darlin'."

Lucy noticed his bandaged hand, "How did you get that? Did you cut yourself shaving?"

Red shook his head, "House call. Followed a person of interest home and just as soon as I knocked—they started shooting. Can ya believe some people ain't got good manners?"

"Lucky you didn't get hit anywhere else," Lucy inserted the full clip. "Or did you?"

"Buy me breakfast and ya can find out."

Lucy rolled her eyes and fired into the far target. She didn't aim as much as point. With Red present, she found it tough to focus her anger on the faceless shape.

"Speaking of luck," Red unplugged his ears. "Guess whose lap my Captain dropped your boy's file in?"

Lucy brightened, "You've got Jimmy's case?"

"Before ya even ask—yes, I'm gonna let ya in on the investigation at every step."

Lucy smiled for the first time in days.

Red pleaded wolfishly, "C'mon, Pretty Lady, let's get out of here. I'll buy the breakfast."

Despite Red's charming good looks and broad shoulders, and the fact that they hadn't seen each other for months, their time spent together didn't fill her void. In the dark, she hated him...hated his facelessness...his hands clutching her steering wheels. She hated her struggle to do more than just lie there while his tires vigorously spun. Maybe he felt it too as he peeled off and dressed. Red promised to call soon. Lucy painfully watched *her man's* brake lights fade into the night. She rubbed her chin with the back of her hand, feeling Red's beard-burn on her lips. *Distance makes the heart grow fonder*, she thought, thankful that she wasn't expected to go through these motions more frequently.

The new neighborhood's security lights spilled orange horizontal stripes through her windows, across the new carpet and onto her bare feet. She ran a bath. Steam rose from the white tub. Lucy stripped and dipped herself completely below the surface. Air bubbles rushed from her mouth as she finally purged herself of all noise. She screamed until stars popped behind her clinched eyes. She came up gasping for air and noticed the bathroom. Just like her, it still had that freshly scoured look. Together, their clean surfaces hid their business.

Red called two days later. There'd been some development.

Outside Dallas, a veterinarian had been found murdered at his office. Human blood discovered on an operating table didn't match the vet's. Two bloodied slugs had been found in a wastebasket.

"Nine-millimeter. Must've pulled 'em from the guy who killed him. Gonna request ya gun for a ballistics test."

"Are you coming yourself to collect it?"

"No ma'am," Red sighed. "But I'll be back through in a

couple of weeks. Got some loose ends I'm tying together. We can talk details over coffee...and I can buy ya that breakfast."

"Or you can stay here, and I'll make the breakfast," Lucy said, holding back the feels.

"Sounds great," Red said flatly. "Call ya soon."

They hung up.

The next few weeks flew by, but their days expired slowly. If Red called back, Lucy never noticed because her phone never rang. The blistering Texas summer had decided to stick around for October. Lucy wanted to call Red, wanted answers, but she thought better of it. After all, *her man* was on the case. If there'd been anything new...she'd already know. During this long silence she wondered how she'd gotten lucky enough to have her boyfriend leading the investigation? Maybe Sheriff White had done it as a favor to her. After all, her relationship with Red was a poorly kept secret down at the station. Surely it wasn't just dumb luck, like everything else. Then another thought gnawed at her. Maybe it *was* done on purpose...to shut her up. Keep her from investigating personally.

When Lucy's paid leave ended, she found a crop of Academy graduates greeting her at the station. These new faces gave her seniority. It wasn't a promotion, but she got first dibs on any extra duty and she took it. She wanted everyone to see that she couldn't be intimidated. Unlike Jimmy's killers, she wanted her face seen. If there was gonna be another hit on her, she wanted everyone to see her smile before hitting back. Newspapers could print her photogenic revenge all day, every day.

At Smith City's Friday-night football game, she stood between the home stands and concessions. Sweat leaked onto the flak jacket under her uniform. Her eyes tracked these good country folks with suspicion. *Maybe one of you was behind the wheel. Maybe one of you pulled the trigger. You want me...here I am, come and get me.*

Her nerves edged closer to her days on patrol in Iraq, where every smiling face hid a bomb, every prayer call demanded death. Hunting for early morning speeders while parked under school-zone signs began to feel the same as waving traffic through checkpoints. Eyes peeled for any late-model rust buckets. She pulled them *all* over, regardless of speed, missing bullet holes, or her own knowledge of probable cause. She tossed their cars and reasoned that whoever had killed Jimmy was probably hiding in plain sight, thinking she was too dumb to find them. She'd find them and when she did...

It got to the point where people complained. Lucy found herself sitting across from the captain this time, not the sheriff. She hadn't seen him or Red in weeks.

The captain wagged his finger—offered platitudes—threatened unpaid leave. "This department has zero room for vigilantes. Leave the investigation up to the detectives and go do your real job."

Get back in the kitchen, Lucy heard, *make us sandwiches. Kick off your shoes while you're at it, and let the men handle everything.*

Lucy apologized for overstepping her bounds but didn't mean a word she said. She donned her Stetson and headed out for the lonely twelve-hour shift on Highway 269.

Lucy cringed when static broke over the radio and interrupted her daydream.

She'd just pulled over a lady in a tricked-out jeep—LED light bars, big chrome wheels, black running boards, the whole *East Texas Truck Accessories* catalog. The lady had *Hottie* bedazzled across her pink tank top; with a face like hers, Lucy knew why she needed to advertise. She'd been going ten over the posted limit. Sold Lucy a sob story a mile long. Something about a sick kid, *blah, blah, blah.* Lucy smiled as she printed the ticket, which the woman promptly merged with a wallet full of credit cards. Lucy wanted this *Hottie* to get nasty for the body cam, give Lucy's nightstick an excuse to bust a tooth loose, but nothing happened.

Some gals have all the luck.

"—shots fired across Highway 269 near Ray's Automotive—"

"Roger that," Lucy said into the radio. She knew the place, on the hill next to a junkyard as you enter Smith City, less than a mile from where she sat. "On my way."

A minute later she drove her patrol car up the ramped driveway and parked beside a wrecked Chevrolet S-10. Lucy heard a shot the moment she opened the car door. She pulled her new sidearm, a nickel-plated revolver, and hit the radio for back-up. Lucy said a prayer, took a breath, and approached the modest red-brick home overlooking the highway.

Ka-cow! Ka-cow!

Back-to-back shots echoed from the carport. A puff of smoke rose over the cab of a busted Dodge only ten yards away. Lucy crouched and called, "Sheriff's Department! Cease fire!"

A head, balder than a baby's bottom, popped into view, its pink face wrinkled, "Huh?"

She repeated, "Put down your weapon!"

More of the man emerged. At his ears, the head sloped onto a pair of immense, blistered shoulders. A hand pushed a pair of gold-rimmed glasses onto his nose, "Can I help you, ma'am?"

Lucy aimed her piece over the hood of a crinkled Toyota.

The man stood like a white-trash Mr. Universe way past his prime. Sweat poured from every pore, making each of his defined muscles glisten. At least, she prayed it was only sweat. The man moved around the front of the truck toward her, "Don't tell me someone called the cops."

The sight of it gave Lucy a shock.

At first, she didn't even notice that he hadn't dropped the weapon. Her eyes busied themselves on his naked and hairless torso. She caught sight of his shriveled and sad package and immediately averted her eyes. A multitude of valid questions ran through her confused mind.

Still the man approached, rifle in hand.

"Stay where you are!" Lucy yelled.

The gravel ceased crunching under his flip-flops. "Is this about me shooting hogs?"

Lucy kept her eyes just above his bald dome, "Drop your weapon, or so help me!"

"No need, ma'am, I'm setting it down."

She commanded him to turn around and put his hands above his head. The man obliged. Lucy saw that the man's sunburn extended from his neck to his ankles—no natural tan lines; this wasn't his first rodeo outside in the buff. She quickly handcuffed him.

"There's no need for all this," cried the man. "I didn't shoot nobody!"

"You can't fire a gun across a highway," Lucy said.

"I was shooting at hogs!" the man explained. "Over yonder— see them bastards!"

Lucy looked and saw the dark carcass of something large on the side of the road. "What if you'd missed and accidentally shot someone?" Lucy then added, "And you can't be nude in public."

"I ain't in public—I'm on my own private property."

The man went on and on, but at least he didn't fight Lucy as she put him in her cruiser. She radioed in and paused before describing the situation in full.

"Can I at least put some pants on before ya haul me down-town?"

"Why weren't you wearing them in the first place?"

The man scoffed, "That ain't none of your concern!"

When the other deputies arrived, Lucy swore their laughter could be heard all the way into Dallas. Despite everything, Lucy blushed. She knew she'd be the butt of jokes for the next year. One of the deputies gallantly offered to help her save face and bring the man in himself. But Lucy's pride refused. After all, it was her arrest. "No thanks, Spud, I've already cuffed him."

This drew even lewder calls from the deputies.

"C'mon boys," the naked man cried, "persuade her to let me get some pants on."

More laughter.

One of the deputies crowed, "I think Deputy Law's got you right where she wants you."

"I swear I was just taking a shower," the man cried, "when I saw them ole hogs across yonder, I grabbed my rifle and came out. I ain't no pervert!"

Lucy opened the door and commanded the male deputies to take him inside and dress him. They complied, laughing the entire way.

Lucy didn't watch him go, choosing to look out over the field of junked cars. She wondered how many of these accidents had been fatal. How many souls were still trapped inside these wrecked vehicles? She stopped wondering as one soulless car stood out. The gravel crushed under her boots as she neared the dented frontend. Her breath hitched.

Dumb luck, she thought. *But what's it doing here?*

Lucy touched each of the bullet holes along the Buick's driver side. Behind her she heard the screen door slam and the cackling deputies. She returned quickly to her cruiser as if nothing had happened.

"Put him back in," Lucy commanded.

One of the deputies started a "That's what she said," but Lucy wasn't having it. She scolded them and they obeyed before driving off with their tails tucked. As soon as they were alone again, Lucy grabbed the man by the ear and dragged him out. Her fist pounded his jaw and he squealed, "Police brutality!"

"You have no idea how brutal it'll get, pal!" She pointed at the Buick. "What's that junker doing here?"

Of course, the man denied all knowledge. Lucy's right boot jogged his memory. He gurgled and whimpered, "A fella dropped it off a couple of weeks ago."

"Why didn't you report the bullet holes?"

"He said it was part of a shootin' range. Asked me to sell it for parts."

"What's your cut?" Lucy grated.

"I get fifteen percent commission."

The idea hit her with such force that she struck the man once more for good measure and led him indignantly inside the house. Once in the man's kitchen, she held her gun at his temple. Told him what to say as he dialed the phone.

"Yes, sir...this is Ray down in Smith City. Just wanted to let you know I sold your car...well, since it was still running, I was able to get fifteen hundred...that's right. I got the cash if'n you wanna come collect."

The man nodded as if the voice could see him, then hung up.

Her mind raced, "How long will it take to get him here? Days?"

"No," the man swallowed, "he's here in Smith City now. Be about fifteen minutes."

Her trap baited, Lucy strode outside to prime the spring.

Time ticked slowly. In the man's living room, Lucy waited at the window, excited for her sudden good fortune. She chewed her lip as a car slowed at the driveway but kept going. She wondered if they could see her cruiser from where she'd hidden it in the junk yard. Another car passed by. Then another. Then a shiny new truck turned onto the gravel and drove up the drive.

It parked.

When the door opened, the driver got out. All of Lucy's good senses fled. Her legs propelled her forward. She didn't hear the screen door slam behind her. She didn't hear the man screaming for help from the kitchen. She didn't hear her own boots click on the carport.

Her heart and chin ached as she recognized the driver.

Red's square jaw lifted a reflexive smile. An instant later it vanished. Lucy's gun leveled. Her lips quivered. Red's brow arched. A thousand valid questions ran tripping across his face. A puzzled Red showed her his palms. His words helped her connect the dots.

"Let me explain," Red said. "Darlin'."

Lucy had long ago realized that people don't listen to one another, they just wait until the other person stops talking before taking their turn. Red's words had as much impact on her as Texas wind rattling through pine needles.

Red pleaded his case. He'd gotten in over his head on his last investigation. He hadn't meant to harm anyone. Not her. Not Jim.

He finally stopped pleading. Stopped talking. Stopped making any sound at all.

Lucy didn't respond. Her gun did.

She watched her man's face when realization hit him at the same time as the bullet. Lucy thought, *Our justice system is black and white—a crime's a crime.*

She stood over the dying man and apologized for every-thing...for nothing.

When she realized what she had done, she clutched her chest in raw panic. Lucy saw the headlines. She saw herself pictured on the front page of every newspaper in the country, except she wasn't smiling anymore. Everyone would know what had just happened. Everyone would know the awful truth. Intense guilt shuddered her with self-loathing. How could she have been so damn lucky?

To suddenly see everything, and still be blinded by revenge.

Lucy's bottom lip trembled. Her fingers crawled up her shoulder. She felt the cold and heartless glass of a lens. The small connected box condemned her fingertips. This moment of dumb luck had been recorded for eternity by the eye of her body camera. The same one she'd forgotten to turn off.

The System doesn't care a lick about luck...it's black and white...a crime's a crime.

She fell to her knees, wilting under an eye in the sky. The

same one that allowed her man to kill her son and doesn't care about the history books.

SALVATION
Michael Bracken

Stealing the Salvation Army Red Kettle outside the upscale department store at the mall was a crime of opportunity. The elderly bell-ringer was warming her hands inside the store, watching the kettle through the glass door, when Zig-Zag stopped his second-hand black SUV at the curb. I hopped out and grabbed the kettle, almost dropping it because it was far heavier than expected. I was back inside the SUV before the bell-ringer realized what was happening. As we sped away, she could do nothing more than express her displeasure with an unseasonal one-finger salute.

Later we dumped the kettle's contents onto Zig-Zag's kitchen table and found ourselves with too many coins and not enough green. We also discovered a folded piece of lined notebook paper buried among the change. While Zig-Zag separated the coins into stacks by denomination, I unfolded the paper.

Send help someone had written in a waxy brown script that reminded me of the notes my ex-fiancée used to write me with her eyeliner pencil when she couldn't find a pen. Beneath that, the same hand had written an address. I showed the note to Zig-Zag.

"That ain't our problem." He took the note from me, crumpled it into a ball, and threw it toward the overflowing trashcan. It bounced off an empty soda bottle and fell to the floor. "So, quit messing around, and count."

I did, and when we finished, we had two-hundred-and-sixty-two dollars and seventy-three cents, a significant portion of it in pennies and nickels.

Zig-Zag looked at the stacks of change. "That ain't near enough."

Later, after Zig-Zag smoked a fattie and fell asleep on the couch, I retrieved the note, flattened it on the table, and reread it.

Send help

Only a woman would write something with an eyeliner pencil. I memorized the address, stuck the note into my wallet, and grabbed my jacket.

As soon as I opened the apartment door to leave, Zig-Zag opened his eyes. "Where are you going, Wilson?"

I poked at the note. "To this address."

"Why?"

"It's Christmas."

"What are you going to do when you get there?"

I shrugged.

Irritated, he said, "I'm not letting you go alone. Let me get my coat."

After he pulled on his coat, Zig-Zag scooped up a handful of change and dumped it into his pocket. He jingled all the way to his SUV.

An hour later, following directions from my phone's Google Maps app, we were lost in a neighborhood of McMansions, twisting streets, and cul-de-sacs on the north side of the city, only a few miles from the biker bar where my ex-fiancée waitressed.

"If we don't get the hell out of here soon, somebody's going to call the cops."

"We're not leaving until we—" Google Maps indicated that we had arrived at our destination. I pointed toward a two-story faux Tudor and said, "That's the place."

Zig-Zag drove past the house and we found ourselves caught in another dead end. He circled until we were pointed out of the cul-de-sac, and we rolled past the house a second time. While many of the surrounding homes were festooned with Christmas lights, the only light at the Tudor came from a second-story window where, as we passed, someone pulled back the drape and looked out. The man silhouetted in the light had the build of a refrigerator, but I couldn't tell much more about him. He let the drape fall back into place.

"You've seen the house," Zig-Zag said. "We're leaving."

As he accelerated away, we passed an approaching Lincoln Continental, as black as Zig-Zag's SUV. I twisted in my seat to watch it turn into the Tudor's circular drive and slow to a stop in front of the porch. The driver's door opened, but I saw only the silhouette of the driver when he stepped out just before Zig-Zag swung a right at the corner.

As we exited the neighborhood a few minutes later, Zig-Zag said, "Did you see those houses? Can you imagine what's in them?"

"There's a woman who needs help," I said.

"You still on that?"

"Something's wrong with that house," I said. "How come it doesn't have Christmas lights?"

"Maybe the owner don't celebrate."

"Who doesn't celebrate Christmas?"

Zig-Zag named three different religions that didn't.

I thought about that awhile. "I want to go back."

"And do what?"

"I want to see what's inside. I want to know why it's so dark. I want to see if there's really a woman in there who needs help."

"So what are you now?" Zig-Zag asked. "Santa Claus checking to see who's naughty and who's nice?"

"Beats nickel-and-diming the Salvation Army."

"We did all right."

"As if," I protested. "I damn near broke my arm when I grabbed the kettle."

Zig-Zag stopped at a convenience store near his apartment. After arguing about our culinary desires, we carried a two-liter bottle of soda, a large bag of barbecue-flavored potato chips, and a box of powdered-sugar doughnuts to the counter, pushing aside a stack of flyers promoting Santa's Workshop, a Christmas decorating service, to make room for our selections.

After the pimple-faced cashier rang up our purchase, Zig-Zag stacked change on the counter.

The cashier stared at us. "You guys rob somebody's piggy bank?"

"Yeah," Zig-Zag told him. "Your mama's."

We took our purchases and left the cashier to deal with the change.

As we exited the convenience store parking lot, Zig-Zag fired up a fattie and offered me a toke. I declined, but the second-hand smoke filling the SUV made me hungry, so I opened the doughnut box.

I didn't sleep well that night, and it wasn't just because I'd downed most of the soda before Zig-Zag even realized I'd opened the bottle. I didn't sleep because I kept thinking about the note.

I woke early, showered, and shaved for the first time in three days. Most of my clothes were still in the cardboard boxes my ex-fiancée had left on the front stoop of her house when she kicked me out, so I dug through them until I found the black oxfords, black chinos, and button-front white shirt from my last job. After dressing, I added a Christmas tie my grandmother had given me when I was fourteen—a red one with *Rudolph the Red-Nosed Reindeer* printed on it—and pulled on my jacket.

After I left Zig-Zag's apartment, I stopped at the convenience store for a large soda and I grabbed several of the Christmas decorating service's flyers from the counter on my way out.

The bus ride to the neighborhood with the faux Tudor involved two transfers and took an hour longer than the drive in Zig-Zag's SUV, so I had time to examine the price list and blank form printed on the back of each flyer before I exited the bus at the subdivision entrance. I walked another twenty minutes before I reached the house.

I rang the bell and knocked on the door. I repeated the process several times until the door opened and I found myself facing the man who had peered out the upstairs window the previous evening. He wore a tight-fitting blue Polo shirt over jeans and black cowboy boots. His graying flattop had been Butch-waxed straight up and the scar on his left cheek indicated that someone had once attempted to shave him with deadly intent. "Yeah?"

I thrust a flyer at him and said, "I noticed you haven't decorated for the season. We can put up your lights, add some blow-up features, and—"

"We ain't interested."

He tried to push the door closed, so I stuck my foot in it. "Look, Mister, I don't get paid unless someone hires—"

"The fuck I care?"

"I'm just saying," I said. "Your house draws a lot of attention because you haven't put up any Christmas decorations."

He glared at me.

I added, "Especially at night."

His eyes narrowed to slits. "How would you know?"

"We were out here the other day working on a house over on Mesquite Drive," I said, naming one of the many cul-de-sacs Zig-Zag had blundered into the previous evening. "We didn't finish until well past sunset, so we looked around and made note of the houses without decorations. Yours is the only one on this block that isn't lit up at night. We thought the place might be deserted, but since you answered the door, it clearly isn't."

"You can put up Christmas lights?"

"Yes, sir," I insisted. "Best service in the city."

He released his hold on the door, snatched the flyer from my hand, and examined it carefully. Without anyone holding it, the door slowly swung open and I saw the unfurnished foyer behind him. A stairway on the right curved up and to the left. Open archways on the left and right led into other rooms, but I could not see into them.

When the man finally looked up, he asked, "How much?"

"Depends on what you need," I said, "and whether you supply the decorations, or we need to supply them." I flipped the flyer over to show him the price list and the form I would have to fill out. "This covers all the basic services, but if you want something special, we'll prepare a custom quote."

"Only house on the block, huh?"

"Yes, sir."

"Can you do the porch and the front windows?" he said. "Upstairs, too?"

"Yes, sir. Of course, sir."

"You'll have to supply the lights."

"Of course." I dug in my pockets until I found a pen and used it to calculate the price. There was no way we could do the work and accept payment by check or credit card. I lowered my voice and leaned forward as if I were about to share a secret. "We give a twenty percent discount if you pay cash."

"You can do this tomorrow?"

"Yes, sir."

"I'll have your cash when you finish."

"You have a name?"

"A name?"

"For my boss," I said. "He'll want to know who approved the work."

"Smith," he said. "Mister Smith."

"Okay, Mister Smith," I said. "We'll be back in the morning."
I walked away, uncertain what I'd gotten myself into.

Later, after I exited the bus near the convenience store closest to Zig-Zag's apartment, Zig-Zag drove past, and I realized that the rear bumper, filled with political stickers from elections long-past, made his SUV easily recognizable. He must have seen me in his rearview mirror because he pulled to the curb, rolled down the passenger window, and leaned across so he could talk to me when I reached him. "Where the hell have you been all day?"

I didn't answer directly. Instead, as I climbed into the passenger seat, I said, "We need to buy some Christmas lights."

"Why?"

I explained what I had done and interrupted his protests by telling him how much we would be paid.

"Just to hang some lights?"

"First thing in the morning," I told him, "so we'd better get the things we need."

We returned to his apartment, put much of the stolen change into a canvas shopping bag, and carried it to the grocery store. There, we fed it into the change machine and turned it into spendable greenery. We purchased a dozen strings of outdoor lights and several packages of hooks with which to hang them. As we drove out of the grocery store's parking lot, we stopped long enough to steal an extension ladder from the bed of a painter's pick-up truck.

Later, we carried the ladder into Zig-Zag's apartment so it wouldn't be stolen from his SUV overnight and, while Zig-Zag lit up a fattie, I returned to his SUV for the lights and hooks. I had just loaded up with all the bags when I heard, "How big is your tree?"

I recognized the accusing tone and turned to see my ex standing on the sidewalk, arms folded beneath her breasts. Though I would have if I had been paying attention, I had not recognized her car, which was parked only three spaces away from Zig-Zag's SUV.

"We have a job," I said, "putting up Christmas decorations."

She snorted with disbelief.

"What do you want, Charlene?"

"I want the pawn ticket."

"I told you I would get the ring back."

"You've had a week, Wilson," she said. "I'm not waiting a month."

"Fine."

I put all the bags on the sidewalk and dug into my pocket for my wallet. I didn't have it.

"Well?"

I stopped patting my pockets and looked up at her. "I lost my wallet."

"How convenient."

"No, seriously," I protested. I didn't carry much in my wallet—driver's license, rolling papers, condom, a couple of singles, the note I found with the Salvation Army money, and the pawn ticket Charlene wanted. I had no idea why she wanted the ring back—after all, she'd called off the engagement—but before she threw me out I had promised to get it out of hock for her.

"Find that pawn ticket," she said. "Get me the ring or the pawn ticket before dinner tomorrow or I'll send my brother to collect it."

Charlene's brother Mick worked security at the Iron Horse, the biker bar north of the city along the old state highway where she waitressed, and he made the man who answered the door at the Tudor appear malnourished. I had no desire to be crossways with Mick, so I promised my ex-fiancée I'd have something to her the next afternoon.

"You'd better." She glared at me. "If you don't, I'll tell my brother and he'll get it for me."

When I returned to Zig-Zag's apartment with the lights and hooks, I realized he'd been watching through the window. He asked, "What'd your old lady want?"

After I told him and told him why I couldn't give it to her, he said, "Where'd you lose your wallet?"

I didn't know, so I shrugged.

The next morning, I showered, dressed, and drank a large bottle of soda before I woke Zig-Zag.

"Why are you bothering me?" he groaned. "The sun isn't even up."

"We have a job."

"We really going to put up Christmas lights?"

"I'll do it by myself if you won't help, but I'll need your keys."

"You ain't driving my car, not after what you did to your girlfriend's."

I'd drained my bank account and hocked Charlene's engagement ring to pay for the repairs. Wrecking her car had not been the straw that broke the camel's back of our relationship, but hocking her engagement ring certainly had been. I kicked the couch and said, "Then get your ass up."

After Zig-Zag had pulled on clean clothes, we loaded his SUV with all the things we'd removed from it the previous evening, grabbed the toolbox he kept under the kitchen sink, and drove to the faux Tudor. By then, the sun had risen far enough above the horizon that we had light to work by. I tore open the boxes containing the Christmas lights and unraveled the strands. After that, I climbed the stolen ladder and began affixing the lights around the second-story windows, trying as I worked to sneak peeks through gaps in the heavy curtains. Four of the five upstairs windows belonged to bedrooms while the center window, the one directly over the porch and the one I could most clearly see through, was for the upstairs landing. The bedrooms were nothing special and could have just as easily been hotel rooms for all the personality they displayed.

While I worked the upstairs windows, Zig-Zag worked the

downstairs. When I finished and climbed down from the ladder for the last time, I asked, "Anything?"

He shook his head. "There's no woman here needs help," he said. "I think we did all this for nothing."

"Not for nothing," I said. "At least we'll get paid."

"Go collect," Zig-Zag said. "I'll clean up the trash."

Mr. Smith must have been waiting for me. When I knocked on the door, he jerked it open and shoved the flyer in my face. "You ain't from Santa's Workshop. Who the fuck are you?"

"Just a couple of guys trying to earn some extra cash."

He grabbed my shirt collar, choking me with the wadded-up cloth as he dragged me into the house.

Zig-Zag saw what was happening. He ran from the yard and followed us inside. Before he could reach us, a second man I hadn't noticed before grabbed him from behind.

Mr. Smith pulled my lost wallet from his pocket, opened it up, and withdrew the note I'd found in the Salvation Army Red Kettle. As he dropped my wallet to the floor, he shoved the note in my face. "Where did you get this?"

I shook my head, but after some physical persuasion that left my lips swollen and at least two teeth loose, I told them about stealing the Salvation Army Red Kettle.

"Son of a bitch!" He spun around and told the other man, "Bring Jessica down here."

"What about—?"

Mr. Smith pushed me to the floor and drew a revolver from the small of his back. I grabbed my wallet and stuck it in my pocket as he told the other man, "They won't be a problem, Tony."

Tony pushed Zig-Zag to the floor with me and climbed the stairs two-at-a-time. He returned, dragging a slender brunette behind him. She wore a hot pink tube top, matching hot pants, and platform shoes that caused her to stumble down the stairs.

Mr. Smith shoved the note in her face. "You write this?"

"No, I—"

He backhanded her with the butt of the revolver, sending a spray of blood across the marble floor.

"Hey!" I pushed myself up.

Zig-Zag grabbed my arm and held me back. "This ain't none of your concern."

I tore away from him and charged the man who was hitting Jessica. I plowed into his midsection, knocking him backward as he squeezed the revolver's trigger. Zig-Zag dropped to the floor.

Mr. Smith pressed the hot muzzle against my forehead, burning a circle into my skin. "You want to be a dead hero?"

I swallowed hard.

"Your friend over there didn't have a choice."

I side-eyed Zig-Zag. Half his face was missing, and he wasn't moving. My knees grew weak and I started to shake.

Mr. Smith lowered his revolver. "Take them downstairs, Tony, and then come back and help me clean up this mess."

Tony had his own revolver and, with it prodding my kidney, I followed Jessica across the foyer to a door beneath the grand staircase that opened to stairs leading into the basement. Tony's gun continued prodding me until Jessica and I were forced into a windowless room not much bigger than the bathroom in Zig-Zag's apartment. He locked the door behind us, leaving only a sliver of light along the bottom of the door.

Then the light went out.

After a moment of silence, Jessica asked, "You are police?"

When I told her I wasn't, the hopeful sound disappeared from her voice.

"Then we are dead like your friend."

"No," I told her. "There's a way out of this."

"You should not have come—"

She hesitated so I told her my name.

"You should not have come, Wilson. You do not know these people. They bring the girls down here who do not cooperate. One day. Two days. Who knows? But when they return, they do whatever the boss tells them. Or they do not return."

"Why did you put that note in the Salvation Army kettle?" I asked. "What did you expect to happen?"

"I—I do not know, but I hoped someone would come, someone who would—" She stopped herself. "Now the other girls—without me, they—they—"

Jessica began to cry. I located her in the dark, gathered her into my arms, and let her tears soak my chest until her tear ducts ran dry.

Later—how much later I had no idea—she told me about the half-dozen girls that were kept in bedrooms upstairs. "I am the—how do you say it?—the den mother. They take me to the mall to buy the makeup and the clothing and the things women need that men do not understand. They tell me if I try to leave or I make a mistake when I am out, they will hurt the others. And now I have done that—but I had to try—I think the Salvation Army, they will save us. They will save us." Jessica stopped to consider what she had just said and then asked, "You are with the Salvation Army?"

I didn't want to, but I told her how Zig-Zag and I had stolen the Salvation Army Red Kettle and found her note among all the change.

"You stole from the poor?" Jessica asked as she pulled away. "You are no better than they are."

We sat in silence, and I felt myself crashing from the perpetual caffeine high that usually sustained me throughout the day. I must have fallen asleep because I did not hear the door open several hours later.

My first realization that we had company was the toe of a cowboy boot, prodding my ribcage. I opened my eyes and looked up at the silhouette of a fridge-sized man.

"Get up," Mr. Smith said. "It's time to go."

"Go where?"

He zip-tied my wrists together and did the same to Jessica. Then he marched us up the stairs and out the back door, where dusk had covered the neighborhood. Zig-Zag's SUV waited in the driveway and, as we approached, Tony loaded into the back a tarp-wrapped bundle that was the size and shape of Zig-Zag.

Mr. Smith put us in the rear seat, Jessica on the driver's side and me beside her on the passenger side. He climbed behind the wheel, and Tony settled into the passenger seat in front of me. As the car eased around the house to the street, I realized that someone had turned on the Christmas lights Zig-Zag and I had installed that morning, and the Tudor looked just as festive as the other decorated homes in the cul-de-sac.

I did not know where they were taking us, and I certainly didn't want to ask, but I realized we weren't headed into the city when Mr. Smith exited the subdivision and drove north. We traveled along the old state highway, a two-lane road that had long ago been replaced by the multilane interstate highway eight miles east, and far ahead of us I could see the neon sign advertising the biker bar where my ex and her brother worked.

Charlene had just arrived to start her shift and was getting out of her car—the car I had pawned her engagement ring to repair—when Zig-Zag's SUV passed the Iron Horse. Our gazes locked for a moment and then she started screaming. I couldn't hear what she was saying, but I recognized the look of anger on her face, and I twisted around to watch her running toward the bar.

Soon, half a dozen motorcycles roared out of the Iron Horse's parking lot and were strung out along the highway behind us. Mr. Smith glanced in the rearview mirror. As the bikers closed the gap between us, Mr. Smith accelerated. I watched the speedometer needle climb well above the posted speed limit.

The bikers dropped back when a state highway patrol cruiser roared onto the highway behind us, lights flashing and siren blaring. Mr. Smith swore as he slowed the SUV and eased it onto the side of the road.

"One word and Tony blows your head off."

Two highway patrol officers exited the cruiser. One approached on the driver's side, his hand resting on the butt of his sidearm, while the second approached on the passenger side.

"Sir," said the first officer, "please put your hands on the steering wheel. We have reports that your vehicle was involved in a robbery—"

"He has a gun!" I shouted from the rear seat.

Before the officer could react, Mr. Smith shot him twice.

The officer on the passenger side couldn't draw his weapon fast enough, and Mr. Smith shifted into drive and stomped on the accelerator. The second officer fired at us, his shots shattering the rear window as I pushed Jessica to the floor and covered her with my body. Tony twisted around and began firing through the broken rear window.

After four shots, he said, "He's down."

"You think they called it in?"

Mr. Smith hazarded a glance over his shoulder and saw me on top of Jessica. "This car is hot. We need to dump it and these bodies right away!"

Because I was still on the floor, covering Jessica, I couldn't see what was happening outside the car, but I heard the distinctive *potato-potato-potato* sounds of Harley-Davidsons rapidly approaching. Then something smashed the rear driver's-side window, showering Jessica and me with safety glass, and the SUV swung wildly left and then right.

Tony fired his revolver twice before the hammer snapped down on spent shells. Mr. Smith tried to hand Tony his revolver, but something smashed the windshield and Tony's head erupted, spraying me with his last thoughts. Mr. Smith lost his grip on his revolver as he lost control of the SUV. I grabbed the gun as the SUV swung left again, bounced over a curb, crashed through something, and came to an abrupt halt when it hit something solid. The airbags exploded, but they didn't do us any good on the floor.

I climbed off of Jessica, opened the door, and fell out of the SUV onto a plastic baby Jesus. It didn't register right away that the SUV had plowed through the nativity scene in front of a church and pinned two of the three plastic Wise Men against the church wall.

I helped Jessica out of the car and pointed the revolver at Mr. Smith. He wasn't moving. Neither was Tony.

"Charlene wants her ring, Wilson," my ex's brother shouted over the sound of the motorcycles.

Before I could respond, approaching police sirens interrupted us and Mick led the other bikers away from the church. Three patrol cars slid to a halt and Jessica and I found ourselves surrounded by armed cops with itchy trigger fingers, who shouted confusing instructions at us.

I dropped the revolver and thrust my still zip-tied hands into the air. So did Jessica.

That was a few days ago. Since then, Jessica and the six other women held in the faux Tudor have been freed; my best friend has been buried by his family; my ex is pissed because the pawn ticket is still in my wallet, which is being held as evidence; I didn't get paid for putting up the Christmas lights; I have a circle burned into my forehead; and I'm sitting in a cell on Christmas Eve with two drunken Santas and an elf who exposed his candy cane to some elderly shoppers—all because I can't make bail while I'm awaiting trial for stealing one of the Salvation Army's Red Kettles.

I can't wait to see what fresh hell Christmas Day brings.

CONFESSIONS ON A TRAIN FROM KYIV

Hugh Lessig

The compartments are spacious, almost the size of my son's old dorm room. Passengers can walk up front and get a rolled-up mattress that includes bedding. Then they can make up a berth and go to sleep. The train sways and doesn't go very fast. Strangers get thrown together in the same compartments, but you can walk around and see what others are doing. That's how I found Myron, sleeping alone in an upper berth, and smothered him with a thin Ukrainian pillow that was still crusty with bleach.

It can take minutes for someone to die because they have no air, according to YouTube. He'd fallen asleep with an empty bottle of vodka, so it didn't take much to get the upper hand. But I kept up the pressure once he went limp, fearing he'd wake up with permanent brain damage and smile blissfully for the rest of his life, not caring that he had killed my son.

"Myron, Myron," I whisper. "It's a shame you didn't know it was me."

The compartment has four padded benches. I'm calling them benches, but each one is couch-size. Two lower and two upper, so four can sleep comfortably. An unending snowscape passes by the single window. Clapboard houses lean into the wind, plastic flapping around the windows. Back home, the office drones in IT are no doubt complaining about the Christmas party. They'll have to rub shoulders with the senior partners and pretend to enjoy their jokes.

Their jokes...

My body begins to tremble with laughter. This train can't be moving faster than forty miles an hour and I don't know exactly where I'm going, but it doesn't matter. All the things that once gave me heartburn—getting sub-tweeted by Gloria in HR, getting dragged into an email chain with corporate—it all seems sad and pathetic. I gaze into Myron's half-lidded eyes. Neither of us is worrying about the small things.

Then someone jiggles the door.

"You still in there, Myron?"

Myron's mouth hangs half-open, as if ready to answer the question. I flip him toward the wall and bundle blankets around his chin. Something is mushy down there. I think he wet the bed. Jumping down from the upper berth, I unlock the door. A bear of a man looks down at me, his smile big enough to swallow my head.

"Ola, comrade." He claps me hard on the shoulder. "Don't mind me. You a Ukrainian? Because I know like two words of your fucking language."

I recognize Myron's boss from the news release. Donny or Denny or something. He looks at the upper berth and shakes his head. "My buddy is out like a light, huh? Christ, he stinks, too. We gotta get showers later. My compartment is four doors down, but no one's there and I need some company. Thought I heard him talking. He's probably dreaming about girls again."

He shuts the door and sits below his dead friend, swiping at his phone with thick fingers. "I had a signal at the Holiday Inn in Kyiv and now it's kaput. But I got this golf game. My people think I'm always busy, but half the time I'm fucking around on my phone and don't know what I'm doing."

My son knew what you were doing.

"I'm not a world traveler," Donny or Denny says. "I like sleeping in my own bed at night, but this trip is mandatory. I got relatives in—what's the name of their shit town?—Putvyl. It's to the north. I got other relatives even farther north, this border village. The kids play soccer and if they kick the ball too far, it rolls into Russia. You know what they do? They get another fucking ball."

He laughs and waves a hand. "What am I saying? You don't understand a word of English. You're a stupid piss-ant. You probably ain't got no dick. You dress up in baby clothes every night and let your wife spank you and watch while the neighbor nails her six ways to Sunday."

I nod politely.

"That's what I thought." He looks me over again. "Christ, I could have used a dozen of you back home. You got a trusting face. When you're in a business like mine, you learn how to read faces. It helps with chicks, too. Myron up there, he's got a schlong halfway to his knees. Girls can't get enough of it. That's where his brains are, too. He knows two words of Ukrainian: *da* means yes and *dobre* means good or okay or very well. Something like that."

I had flown from Newport News in Virginia to Atlanta, then to Frankfurt, then to Kyiv. I got to the train station and watched for Myron, my son's voice echoing in my head. "It won't go sideways, dad, but if it ever does, we're all heading to Ukraine, where the organizers are. We go to Kyiv and take this train north to some bumfuck town. Stop begging me to come home. I've got this."

The guy at the ticket booth spoke broken English and said this train goes around the country. He drew a circle in the air. I got the most expensive ticket he had, so maybe I'll end up at that soccer field near Russia or somewhere in the Carpathian Mountains. Donny or Denny shuffles his feet. I hadn't been looking for him. Only Myron.

"My Myron is a decent guy, a little rough around the edges. But who isn't? At some point, everyone does something they regret. My Myron. I call him that because he's like a son. Misbehaving, sure, but his heart's in a good place."

The police had found my son in a fetal position under a bridge. He'd been shot in the stomach and left to die in the cold. Twenty-five years old. Nothing I said could separate him from a life of quick, dirty money. You work in an IT department and solve problems that Ivy League-trained lawyers are helpless to understand. You throw around so many five-dollar words it sounds like a different language, and you silently rejoice in their confusion. But you can't persuade your own son to see what's ahead. I pray he understood in the end. The patrolman who found his body noticed two tear tracks on his face, dried to salt. Maybe he was thinking of me.

"In some ways, Myron just needs boundaries. He has—what do you call it—a hair-trigger temper. One minute he's laughing, then he's busting on someone. You can't predict it." He frowns at his phone. "I wish I could get online here. Curious about what's happening back home."

What's happening back home is my son's funeral, you piece of shit. He's being buried in the hard, cold ground at a veteran's cemetery in Hampton with no one to say words over him. I missed my son's funeral to find Myron and now I'm listening to you.

"You okay, buddy?"

I had brought an ice pick just in case. Found it in a kitchen drawer next to the meat thermometer and turkey baster and other stuff I no longer use since my wife died. I bend forward as if stretching my lower back and pull the ice pick from my boot. I stand up and smile, making him recoil.

"You want to suck my dick? Because I'm not like that."

The door slides open and a young woman steps inside, cradling a baby. Our eyes connect. She is big-boned with straw-colored hair and a heavy face that some men would call handsome in a back-handed way. But her soft blue eyes speak to an inner beauty. That sounds stupid coming from a guy with an ice pick up his sleeve, but her gaze hits me hard and fast. I gather my bedding and vault to the upper berth, as if to say, you take the lower. I can kill this guy later.

"Thank you," she says. "That was very nice."

"Hey, you speak English," says Donny or Denny. "That's great."

I'm sure she speaks Ukrainian, too. And she'll want to talk to me, her fellow countryman.

I lay down and face the wall. As the train sways around a curve, the smell of fried food fills the cabin. Great, she brought dinner. Maybe that will mask the scent of dead Myron. I feel a tap on my shoulder and turn toward her. She offers what appears to be a slice of pizza crust. I smile and roll my eyes to mimic being tired. The baby makes a few noises, and I'm hoping it doesn't scream. I don't want everyone figuring why Myron isn't waking up. Donny or Denny asks what the woman does for a living.

"Well, I'm a mother," she says. "This is my son. But I work as an assistant in the Euro-Ukraine Fellowship Enterprise. We promote understanding with the European Union and have exchanges. Speakers and the like. We don't do politics. It's more of a cultural effort."

"So you're like a secretary?"

She makes a dismissive noise. "More like a, uh, administrator assistant."

"Like an office manager. Making copies and shit."

"Sure. You want coffee? It's so cold in here."

The smell of coffee fills the cabin. I wonder when a body starts to stink of decomposition. Maybe I'll get out at this Putvyl place and follow Donny or Denny. I could slip the ice pick into the base of his neck and let him die in the snow like my son. Wait, what am I thinking? He'll try to wake up Myron before getting off the train. I have to kill him in here.

"Nothing wrong with being an office manager," he says. "Me, I'm a private investigator. I look into cases for people."

Are you kidding me?

"Like in the movies," she says. "What sorts of things do you work on? Do you find lost children and the like?"

Papers rustle. "You can read it right here. I'm tracking these guys. You can read English, right?"

"I read it better than I can speak it. I'm German, so that's my first language. I learned English as a child because we grew up near an American military base. Then I moved here and learned Ukrainian in my later years." She whispers words while reading. "This says the police are looking for fugitives who recruited homeless men. The fugitives made the homeless men cash counterfeit checks, but one man died. These men have made a ruse."

"More like a scam."

"Yes, thank you. Not a ruse. A scam."

It sounds like she's reading the news release issued by the Department of Justice after they found my son and pegged Myron for the shooting and Donny or Denny for ordering it.

"As I understand it," he says helpfully, "the fugitives stole mail from local business parks to get information, company logos and the like. Then they forged checks. They recruited homeless people from shelters and offered them day-labor jobs, driving them miles away. But once the homeless people got to the work site, they were told to cash the fake checks that looked like the business checks. That way, the homeless people appeared on bank footage but not the masterminds. Pretty slick, huh?"

"It says they killed one man."

"He had a problem with using homeless men, so I'm told. Some men are cowards. They want to wear the uniform but they don't want to play the game. What's your name, honey?"

"Marina."

"My name is Don Meredith."

Don Meredith was a quarterback for the Dallas Cowboys and Jesus fucking Christ if I'm not thinking about Monday Night Football and Dandy Don singing "the party's over." But now I remember. His name is Donald Morrison. If that news release was online, it would link to his photo, but it's just a goddamn piece of paper. So there he sits with clueless Marina who dedicates herself to international relations and asks why can't people just get along, and now she's talking to the baby in the universal language of gibberish. Years ago, I would come home from work and my son would yell, "Hey Poppo, Moppo, Choppo." I guess I was his version of pop or poppa. Then it became, "Don't call me again, fuckface." Tears sting my eyes. Don't cry here. Don't be a coward.

Dandy Don shifts in his seat and makes a restless noise. Then comes a series of electronic beeps, which sounds out of place on a train that probably hasn't changed since the days of the Iron Curtain. This compartment needs a clacking typewriter or a telegraph chittering out the Morse code. It needs the smell of wet flannel and the crackle of a transistor radio. It doesn't need the future. It needs the past, and Christ, so do I, but now it's slipping away.

"What do you have there?" he asks.

"My phone." She sounds amused. "You've never seen a phone before?"

"Yeah, I've seen phones. We had wi-fi back at the hotel, but mine is useless now. Feels weird to be disconnected. You can get online here? We're in the middle of fucking nowhere. Excuse my French."

"This is a satellite phone. We have them at the institute."

"Who are you calling?"

"No one. I'm looking up this case."

He laughs nervously. "There's not much online."

More beeps. "Bear with me. I'm sure I can find something. This paper has the names of the criminals. A man named Stetson is the prosecutor. Like the hat, yes? I know my American movies."

"It's not...it's not like the movies."

I want to scream for this lady to stop. She and the baby should just get out.

"I see your picture," she says slowly.

Stop talking.

"Your picture... It says you're one of the men involved in this ruse. Excuse me, this scam. Donald John Morrison. That is your face. A little younger, but that is your face. You and an accomplice. Myron Ward. It says both men are being sought by authorities."

Donald John Morrison begins huffing and puffing like a Brahman bull. His feet stomp on the floor and something rattles. "Myron, get the hell up. We got a problem here. Myron? Be useful for once in your life."

I roll out of the bed and hit the floor as the baby starts to cry. The ice pick slides from my sleeve into my hand. Donald John Morrison turns and laughs. He still thinks I'm a passenger on a train in the middle of a snowy Ukraine who doesn't know shit. He shakes dead Myron with one hand and fumbles in his pockets with the other.

"Don't bother with Myron," I say. "He's not waking up."

"Who the hell are you supposed to be?"

"My son was gut-shot and left in the freezing cold."

His eyes turn hard as the dots connect. "You're the father? Shit, you followed us?"

"Da, motherfucker."

He tries shoving Myron once more, then gives up. "I'll make it right. I've got money. Your son was going to turn us in."

The ice pick feels like an extension of my hand. I jam it into his throat, angling upward. He stiffens and gasps. My other hand covers his mouth. The ice pick sinks to the hilt. Blood flows down the wooden handle and onto my wrist like a warm blanket and I almost cry with joy. My son was going to turn them in. My good son. The baby gurgles and coos as I ease Dandy Don onto the lower berth. I turn back to see Marina pointing her phone at me.

"Let me explain," I say.

The train slows as we near the next stop. Other people might want to use this compartment and hang out with two dead bodies and the mother and her baby and the satellite phone that connects to the world. Jesus.

"I only tracked Myron. The guy in the upper berth. He killed my son. I didn't think this other guy would be here. They must have come on separate flights and hooked up at the train station. I was just looking for Myron and didn't see this guy come onboard. Understand? I won't hurt you. I didn't plan this part."

She smiles coldly. "We always stumble into war."

"Are you going to turn me in?"

She sighs and settles herself. Even the baby seems to be thinking it over. "This man would have killed me and my son. So I must weigh that. Are you some kind of hit man?"

"Like in the movies," I say.

"Really?"

"Hell no. I work in IT for a law firm. I have a cubicle next to a window. I worked there five years before I got a view, and it looks out onto a parking lot. Up until now, that was my life."

The train lurches as it slows and comes alive with the thud of luggage hitting the floor, zippers zipped, the laughter and movement of people.

"My son left college his junior year, strung out on drugs. I couldn't talk to him. I wish I had a good excuse, but I don't. I wrapped myself in a soul-crushing job and pretended I didn't have the time. That's the truth. I told myself it was his fault, that all he had to do was accept my help. But I didn't try hard enough. I didn't work to understand what he was going through." I hold back tears and wonder if anyone is crying at my son's funeral.

Marina looks past me. I follow her gaze to the window. The

train crawls past buildings, then a platform filled with people, then it stops. She cradles her baby in one arm and grabs the handle of the compartment door. People are muttering just beyond the door.

She turns a deadbolt and locks it.

"You're in big trouble," she says.

"I'm aware."

"I don't mean from the police. You're in trouble...in trouble with yourself. Get off this train with me. Right now. I have friends who know English. My husband will come. He likes the American football. The Patriots. Tom Brady. You'll feel at home."

"This can't be your stop. You just got on."

"It doesn't matter. You saved the life of my child, and that means something, yes? My organization helps others, people who are seeking a safe harbor, who need time to think things through. They are dissenters. Dissidents." She cradles the baby, but she's no longer a mother. Her eyes are sharp and commanding. "You need to come with me before it's too late. You're sick."

"Marina, I've never felt better."

She swipes at her phone and shows me the video of Donald Morrison's murder. The ice pick goes in just above his Adam's apple and he falls onto the lower berth.

"So I go with you or you'll post the video?"

"Look at yourself."

I replay it. My eyes squint with effort as the ice pick slides in, and my face twists into a smile. As he shudders for the last time, I am a portrait of joy. I watch it again and freeze it at the moment of death. I pinch the screen and zoom in on my face. I'm smiling so wide that I barely recognize myself.

"According to that piece of paper, these two dead men are part of a larger group," Marina says. "You will want to hunt down the others. You are headed toward them now. You won't be able to let it go. This will be your life, tracking them to different places."

The train comes to a full stop. She stands near the sliding door.

"What's wrong with tracking the others?" I ask.

"Because you're not a hit man. You're a man with a cubicle near a window. If you try and do this again, you might make a mistake. Maybe next time the mother and the baby will die. It happens with countries—they kill two of our soldiers, we kill five of theirs, pretty soon we're killing hundreds on both sides."

Donald John Morrison has shit himself and the stench fills the compartment. I open the single window and cold air rushes in. The sticky blood on my hands begins to dry.

"You're smiling again," she says.

"Random thoughts, Marina. I'm thinking of when my son enrolled in Virginia Methodist and I came to visit on Parents' Day. His dorm room smelled of potato chips and sweat. I opened all the windows and turned on the ceiling fan. That's the last time I remember him laughing. Later that semester, they kicked him out of school for drugs, and I told myself that young men needed to make their own mistakes and learn from them."

"Like father, like son." Marina slides the door open a few inches. I can't tell if she wants to stay or go.

"What is the name of your baby?"

"His first name is Bogdan. He will grow up to be a crusader." She steps into the hallway. "What was your son's name?"

"Thomas."

"And yours?"

"It doesn't matter."

The door closes as she leaves. The train lurches forward and begins to pick up speed. I sit with my head near the window, the lights of the town beginning to recede like embers of a forgotten fire, my face hurting from the cold air and the expression of joy that will never fade.

ABOUT THE EDITOR

MICHAEL BRACKEN has edited several previous crime fiction anthologies, including the Anthony Award-nominated *The Eyes of Texas: Private Eyes from the Panhandle to the Piney Woods* and the three-volume *Fedora* series. He co-edits (with Trey R. Barker) the serial novella anthology series *Guns + Tacos*. Stories from his anthologies have been short-listed for Anthony, Derringer, Edgar, Macavity, and Shamus awards, and have been named among the year's best by the editors of *The Best American Mystery Stories* and the editors of *The World's Finest Mystery and Crime Stories*.

Bracken is the author of eleven books and more than thirteen hundred short stories, including crime fiction published in *Alfred Hitchcock's Mystery Magazine, Black Cat Mystery Magazine, Black Mask, Down & Out: The Magazine, Ellery Queen's Mystery Magazine, Espionage Magazine, Mike Shayne Mystery Magazine,* and *The Best American Mystery Stories.* In 2016 he received the Edward D. Hoch Memorial Golden Derringer Award for Lifetime Achievement in short mystery fiction. He lives, writes, and edits in Texas.

ABOUT THE CONTRIBUTORS

TREY R. BARKER, cop by day and crime writer by night, is the author of more than three hundred short stories and a handful of novels. His most recent is *The Unknowing*, published by Down & Out Books. He is also the author of the Jace Salome novels and the Barefield Trilogy.

JOHN BOSWORTH's short fiction has appeared in *Mystery Weekly, Switchblade*, and the Akashic Noir Series, "Mondays are Murder." He lives in Seattle and can be found on Twitter @John_Bosworth_.

SCOTT BRADFIELD is a novelist, short story writer and critic, and former Professor of American Literature and Creative Writing at the University of Connecticut. Works include *The History of Luminous Motion, Dazzle Resplendent: Adventures of a Misanthropic Dog*, and *The People Who Watched Her Pass By*. Stories and reviews have appeared in *Triquarterly, The Magazine of Fantasy & Science Fiction, The New York Times Book Review, The Los Angeles Times Book Review, The Baffler*, and numerous "best of" anthologies. He lives in California and London.

S.M. FEDOR has previously appeared in *Burning Love & Bleeding Hearts* (Things in the Well) and *In Filth It Shall Be*

Found (Outcast Press). He has also had multiple stories in *Punk Noir Magazine.* Scott splits his time between writing neo-noir and new-weird-influenced stories and creating award-winning VFX for film and television. He currently resides in Montreal beneath a mountain of cat fur. Visit his website at smfedor.com or follow him on Twitter @s_m_fedor.

NILS GILBERTSON is a crime and mystery fiction writer, UC-Berkeley graduate, and practicing attorney. His short stories have appeared in *Mystery Weekly, Pulp Modern, Close to the Bone, Serial Magazine,* and others. Nils lives in Washington, D.C., with his wife. You can reach him at nilspgilbertson@gmail.com.

J.D. GRAVES is an author and playwright whose work has been produced at the 2016 New York International Fringe Festival. His short fiction can be found, or is forthcoming in, *Black Mask, Mystery Weekly, Tough,* and other publications. He currently serves as the Editor-in-Chief of *EconoClash Review.*

JAMES A. HEARN is an attorney and author who writes in a variety of genres, including crime, science fiction, fantasy, and horror. His fiction has appeared or is forthcoming in *Alfred Hitchcock's Mystery Magazine, Black Cat Mystery Magazine, The Eyes of Texas, Guns + Tacos, Mickey Finn: 21st Century Noir,* and *Monsters, Movies & Mayhem.*

JANICE LAW is the Edgar-nominated and Lambda award-winning creator of the Anna Peters and Francis Bacon mystery novels. A Derringer finalist, she regularly publishes short fiction in *Alfred Hitchcock's Mystery Magazine, Ellery Queen's Mystery Magazine, Sherlock,* and *Black Cat Mystery Magazine,* as well as various anthologies. Learn more at JaniceLaw.com.

HUGH LESSIG is a former journalist and Derringer Award

finalist whose short fiction has appeared in *Thuglit, Shotgun Honey, Crime Factory, Needle: A Magazine of Noir,* and *Mickey Finn: 21st Century Noir.* "Confessions on a Train From Kyiv" was based on a two-week stay in Ukraine as part of a journalist exchange.

GABE MORRAN is a career firefighter and part-time paramedic in Indiana. He received his B.A. in English from Indiana University in 2008, and this anthology will mark his first publication.

RICK OLLERMAN is the author of four novels and a non-fiction collection. He also writes short stories, non-fiction and has edited several anthologies, including the 2019 Bouchercon book *Denim, Diamonds & Death.*

JOSH PACHTER's crime fiction has been appearing in *Ellery Queen's Mystery Magazine, Alfred Hitchcock's Mystery Magazine, Black Cat Mystery Magazine,* and many other publications since 1968. In 2020, he received the Short Mystery Fiction Society's Edward D. Hoch Golden Derringer Award for Lifetime Achievement. He also translates Dutch to English and is the editor of numerous anthologies.

ROBERT PETYO is a Derringer award nominee whose stories have appeared in small press magazines and anthologies, most recently in *Hardboiled, Classics Remixed, COLP: Big, Mysterical-e, Gypsum Ground Tales, Flash Bang Mysteries, Amongst Friends,* and *The Black Beacon Book of Mystery.*

STEPHEN D. ROGERS is the author of *Shot To Death* and more than eight hundred shorter works, earning, among other honors, two Derringers (with seven additional finalists), a Shamus Award nomination, and mention in *The Best American Mystery Stories.* His website, StephenDRogers.com, includes a list of new and upcoming titles as well as other timely information.

ALBERT TUCHER is the creator of prostitute Diana Andrews, who has appeared in one hundred hardboiled stories and the novella *The Same Mistake Twice*. He recently launched a second series set on the Big Island of Hawaii, in which *The Honorary Jersey Girl* and *Pele's Domain* are the most recent entries.

JOSEPH S. WALKER lives in Indiana. In 2019 his stories won both the Al Blanchard Award and the Bill Crider Prize for Short Fiction. His stories have appeared in a number of magazines and anthologies, including the first volume of *Mickey Finn: 21st Century Noir*. Visit his website at https://jsw47408.wixsite.com/website.

SAM WIEBE is the author of *Hell and Gone, Cut You Down, Invisible Dead, Never Going Back*, and *Last of the Independents,* and the editor of *Vancouver Noir*. Wiebe's work has won an Arthur Ellis award and the Kobo Emerging Writers Prize, and been shortlisted for the Hammett, Edgar, Shamus, and City of Vancouver Book Award. Visit SamWiebe.com or follow at @sam_wiebe.

STACY WOODSON made her crime fiction debut in *Ellery Queen's Mystery Magazine's* Department of First Stories and won the 2018 Readers Award. Since her debut, she has placed a number of stories in *Mickey Finn, Mystery Weekly, Woman's World*, and *EQMM* among other anthologies and publications. You can visit her at StacyWoodson.com.

BOOKS

On the following pages are a few
more great titles from the
Down & Out Books publishing family.

For a complete list of books and to
sign up for our newsletter,
go to DownAndOutBooks.com.

Trouble No More
Crime Fiction Inspired by Southern Rock and the Blues
Mark Westmoreland, editor

Down & Out Books
October 2021
978-1-64396-230-6

The authors bring the rough living of the Southern Rock genre to the page, and communicate the ache of the blues.

Edited by Mark Westmoreland with stories by Bill Baber, C.W. Blackwell, Jerry Bloomfield, S.A. Cosby, Nikki Dolson, Michel Lee Garrett, James D.F. Hannah, Curtis Ippolito, Jessica Laine, Brodie Lowe, Bobby Mathews, Brian Panowich, Rob Pierce, Joey R. Poole, Raquel V. Reyes, Michael Farris Smith, J.B. Stevens, Chris Swann, Art Taylor, N.B. Turner and Joseph S. Walker.

Velvet Elvis
Greg F. Gifune

Down & Out Books
October 2021
978-1-64396-231-3

Sonny Cantone is having a really bad day. He's broke. His girl-friend left him. He drinks more than he should and smokes a lot of pot. And now some lunatic stole his car.

So when Sonny's partner in crime and stoner buddy Crash of-fers to bring him in on a caper that promises to yield some quick money, he has to listen. But nothing has prepared Sonny for the vortex of mayhem and madness he's about to fall into.

Sonny Cantone is having a really bad day. Wait until he sees the next twenty-four hours.

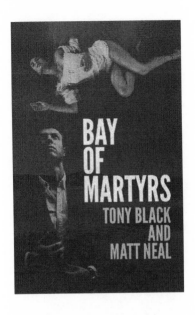

Bay of Martyrs
Tony Black and Matt Neal

Down & Out Books
November 2021
978-1-64396-235-1

A young woman washes up at the Bay of Martyrs in Australia. The police say it's a case of misadventure, but cynical reporter Clay Moloney suspects there's something more to it.

Can he achieve justice for the student, or will those in power stop him?

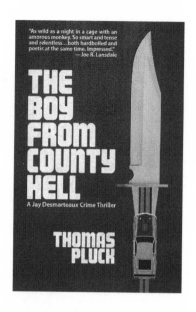

The Boy from County Hell
A Jay Desmarteaux Crime Thriller
Thomas Pluck

Down & Out Books
November 2021
978-1-64396-234-4

Jay Desmarteaux raised a whole lot of hell after he was released from prison after 25 years for the murder of a rapist bully at his school.

Now he's on the run in his home state of Louisiana, and traces his roots to an evil family tree that's grown large and lush, watered with the blood of the innocent.

A tree that needs chopping down.

Made in the USA
Middletown, DE
22 June 2023

33248280R00182